The Ital

CW00558020

Victoria Springfield inherited a love of Italy from her father. She first visited the charming seaside town of Minori, which inspired *The Italian Holiday*, in 2015. Two years later she 'eloped' there to get married. Victoria grew up in Upminster, Essex. After many years in London, she now lives in Kent with her husband in a house by the river. She likes to write in the garden with a neighbour's cat by her feet or whilst drinking cappuccino in her favourite café. Then she types up her scribblings in silence whilst her mind drifts away to Italy.

THE ITALIAN HOLIDAY

Victoria Springfield

This edition first published in Great Britain in 2021 by Orion Dash,
an imprint of The Orion Publishing Group Ltd.,
Carmelite House, 50 Victoria Embankment
London EC4Y 0DZ

An Hachette UK Company

A CIP catalogue record for this book is
available from the British Library.

ISBN (Paperback) 978 1 398 70809 9
ISBN (eBook) 978 1 398 70369 8

Printed in the UK

www.orionbooks.co.uk

For Robert Geoffrey Wasey

Chapter One

Sun, sea and . . . spaghetti. What more could she want? Most people would jump at the chance of a free holiday, especially if they were twenty-eight, recently single and a little bit broke like she was. Italy was Bluebell's dream destination, but this trip was most definitely not what she had in mind.

'Not going? Whatever do you mean? Opportunities like this don't come along very often.' It wasn't even seven in the morning and Granny Blue was on the phone already. 'I can't believe you're thinking of turning this down,' she tutted.

'It's your prize, Gran. You won the competition, not me. It's not fair that you're going to have to miss out now they've rearranged the date of your op. Are you sure you can't just go another time?' Bluebell leant against the kitchen counter, her elbow resting on a pile of takeaway leaflets.

'There's no chance of that, love. The people at *Loving and Knitting* magazine can't change the arrangements to suit one person. Anyway, it could take me weeks to get fully mobile once this hip replacement finally happens. And you said yourself you haven't got any holiday plans now you're not seeing that Jamie.'

Jamie was taking Carrie to Cornwall this year. Beautiful, blonde, slim Carrie – the girl who was supposed to be marrying his best friend. Bluebell still could not quite believe it.

'You're so lucky,' Granny Blue chatted on. 'I've always wanted to go to the Amalfi Coast. It's going to be such a wonderful trip. It says here you'll be staying at a luxury hotel in the quaint seaside town of Minori and visiting all sorts of places like Sorrento and Capri. Ooh, and you'll get to see Pompeii, that old buried city. There was a programme about it on the telly last week.'

'The trip sounds great, but everyone on this holiday is going to be so . . .'

'Were you going to say so old? What's wrong with old?' Gran's voice rose in indignation. 'Shame on you, Bluebell, you know us old folk are just young folk whose packaging has got a bit bent and bashed about. And there's no reason to think everyone who reads *Loving and Knitting* is a certain age. And even if they are, there's no age limit on loving. Or knitting, come to that.'

'But . . .' Bluebell was running out of excuses.

'I've been looking at the weather forecast. It's raining in London next week. Not as bad as the South West though. They're going to get drenched in Cornwall whilst you're off sunning yourself.' Gran chuckled.

The venetian blind over the sink was still closed. Bluebell tugged on the plastic toggle at the end of the greying cord. Raindrops were clinging to the smeared glass and the path leading to the wheelie-bin shed was darkened by overnight rain. For a moment she imagined stepping off a white boat in a bustling harbour then walking along the seafront licking the drips from a triple-scoop ice-cream cone. But she wouldn't go. The idea was ridiculous.

'I'll have to ring you back, Bluebell, love. I need to go. That nice lady from down the road's at the door. She's come round to walk Trixie.'

Bluebell replaced the receiver, flicked the switch on the kettle and reached into a cupboard for a packet of cereal. There was no point going back to bed now. As she walked over to the fridge, she was aware of a knocking sound coming from the hall. The early morning light streaming through the wavy glass panels of the front door was creating a strange optical illusion. It looked as though the man standing on the doorstep was dwarfed by a giant package twice his size. Cursing her missing dressing-gown cord, she clutched the flimsy material together in one hand and opened the door.

'Ordered a wardrobe, have you?' the man quipped, heaving a massive parcel into the corner of the hallway, with a grunt. As soon as the door slammed behind him, Bluebell grabbed a pair of scissors from the kitchen drawer and sliced open the packaging. There was no note enclosed, but there was only one person who could be responsible for today's delivery.

She washed her face and scraped her long dark hair back into a ponytail. Then she put on her favourite stripy T-shirt and yanked an old pair of jeans over her hips. Perhaps she ought to try cutting down on the biscuits – again. She peered at her face in the mirror. She didn't look too bad considering she had stayed up until two. Netflix really should come with a health warning. As she reached for her eyeliner the phone rang. It had to be Granny Blue.

'I forgot to say, I've ordered something for you,' Gran said.

Bluebell glanced towards the hallway where a huge paisley-patterned suitcase was now blocking the light from the front door.

'It's already arrived.'

'I thought pink and purple was nice and jolly. Much better than your boring old navy case.'

Bluebell knew when she was beaten. Maybe Gran was right: she could do with a proper holiday and all her friends seemed to have other plans. And to be honest, although she couldn't imagine her future without Jamie, chatting to a group of nice old folk like Granny Blue might be more relaxing than spending a week trying to blend in with Jamie's pals from uni whilst they talked about property prices and people she'd never met in their loud, confident voices.

She took a deep breath. 'Thanks, Gran. It'll be just perfect for my Italian holiday.'

'It's nice and big so there'll be plenty of room for some souvenirs.'

Bluebell sighed. Some souvenirs? There was enough room for half the ruins from Pompeii. At least she would have no trouble picking it out at baggage reclaim. Who else would choose something like this?

She picked up her mobile and started scrolling. *The Amalfi Coast is renowned as the most romantic destination in Italy.* Romance: that was the last thing she needed right now. At least there was absolutely no chance of finding love on a coach trip with a group of pensioners.

'If you're sure . . .' Michela said.

'To be honest, you'll be doing me a favour.' Her flatmate grinned. 'I've been looking for an excuse to get rid of it. It's taking up so much space. And it's very . . .'

'Pink?' Michela suggested. She took the huge suitcase gratefully.

'Very pink, very purple, very large and very bright, but you'll never fit all your things in that old holdall of yours.'

Michela stuffed some socks into a pair of trainers and laid them in the bottom of the case. 'I can't believe I'm going home tomorrow. Italy's going to seem so strange after London.'

'I'm going to miss you like crazy. But I've got to run. Don't forget: half seven at The Frog and Trumpet.'

'See you there,' Michela replied. Her flatmate was halfway out the door already.

She picked up a pile of bright cotton dresses and laid them on top of her shoes. These old clothes held so many memories, but she couldn't imagine wearing them again even in the Italian sunshine. Within a few weeks of moving into her shared flat in Hammersmith she had become a complete convert to the London uniform of skinny jeans and ankle boots topped off with her long dark hair clipped up in a messy bun. After swapping a seaside town of less than three thousand people for a year in one of the busiest cities in the world, she felt like a different person. She certainly dressed like one.

Now she was going home. She wasn't sure how she felt about that. England was still so new and exciting, and her work placement as a sous-chef at The Golden Wolf was a once-in-a-lifetime experience she would never forget. She had learnt so much, but she wouldn't miss Aldo, the head chef. Aldo was a control freak who measured every spear of asparagus and stipulated the exact pattern of the balsamic glaze drizzled over the fashionable slates and sharing platters.

Michela couldn't wait to work with the friendly team at her cousins' bustling restaurant on the harbour at Positano where nobody counted how many olives were added to a salad, and generous portions of pasta were heaped up on plain white plates. With the tourist season already underway she would be far too busy in the kitchen to waste her time thinking about Stefano. After a year in London she should have forgotten all about him, but it wasn't that easy. It was pointless thinking about what might have been. Stefano was far away in Rome and she needed to get on with her life.

But before she started her new role, she would spend a few days in Minori. She was longing to see her family again. It had been months since her parents' brief visit to London. How small and out of place they had looked – bewildered by the noise, the crowds and *mamma mia!* the weather. It was even longer since she had last seen her beloved grandmother, Nonna Carmela, who had not left their little town of Minori for as long as anyone could remember.

She crammed in the last of her clothes, zipped up the case and leant it against the wall. The gaudy pink-and-purple design seemed to glow in the artificial light. At least there was no chance she would lose it at the airport; you could probably spot it from outer space.

Chapter Two

Bluebell spotted the girl from *Loving and Knitting* straight away. Josie looked about twenty-five with thick red hair caught up in a high ponytail and a friendly, open face sprinkled with freckles. She was standing by the luggage belt talking to a tiny, bird-like old lady in a knitted waistcoat who had somehow managed to retrieve her suitcase already.

Bluebell was about to walk over to join them when her attention was taken by a harassed-looking woman who was trying to juggle three small children and a pile of luggage that would give the Leaning Tower of Pisa a run for its money. The woman gestured helplessly as a pale blue holdall printed with the logo of the Naples football team slid to the floor. Bluebell found herself propping up one side of the luggage mountain as they worked together to balance the trolley's load.

She could only understand three or four words of Italian, but it was now obvious that the smallest child wanted the toilet and before she knew it she was standing guard over two little boys and a motley collection of bags whilst mother and daughter headed for the loos. By the time they returned and then went straight back to rescue the girl's lost cuddly bunny, Bluebell ended up running back to the almost deserted luggage belt.

Josie was still standing there patiently, holding up her *Loving and Knitting* flag. She was obviously used to waiting for waifs and strays. Bluebell felt slightly sick as she watched the few sad-looking bits and pieces still circling around and around on the black rubber belt: three neat, near-identical black cases, a khaki holdall split down the seam and a stray baseball cap emblazoned with the words *I Love London*. Then, at last, there it was: one large pink-and-purple paisley suitcase. She never imagined she would be so glad to see it. She grabbed it by the handle and hurried along behind Josie, muttering apologies as they zipped through customs and headed for the minibus.

'All these older ladies and it's the young one who gets lost,' Josie tutted, though Bluebell could tell by her smiling eyes and barely concealed grin that she was only joking.

Bluebell gazed out of the window as the minibus began its journey towards Minori. The sky was clear of clouds and the sea was calm and oh so blue. All her misgivings about the trip were evaporating as they travelled through the beautiful Italian landscape. Did it really matter if none of the other prizewinners were going to see sixty again? Josie, the trip leader, was a couple of years younger than her and seemed like she was going to be fun. Massimo, the bus driver, seemed a jolly guy too, though his habit of pretending to clap his hand over his eyes whilst he negotiated the twists and turns was causing a little consternation amongst the competition winners.

The minibus rounded yet another corner. The view ahead was obscured by an oncoming school bus. It was heading straight towards them. Massimo jammed on the brakes. The women clung to the hand rests, their faces tense. There seemed no way that these two vehicles could pass each other on the narrow road. Bluebell looked out of the window and instantly wished she had been sitting on the other side. Below them the cliff edge fell away in a sheer drop down towards the sea. She held her breath as the school bus slowly began to inch back bit by bit, its wing mirror scraping against the cliff side. Massimo was a picture of concentration, hunched over the steering wheel, as he moved them slowly forward.

Bluebell had never been particularly religious, but she found herself staring fixedly at the plastic figure of the Madonna perched on the dashboard. Surely with the blessed mother watching over them a coachload of innocent elderly ladies wasn't going to tip over and crash onto the rocks below. Bit by bit they moved alongside the bus. Then Massimo leant out of the window and began an animated conversation with the other driver. After several minutes of loud talking and gesticulating, their minibus somehow squeezed past.

'That was my friend,' Massimo announced, grinning broadly, as she realised that what had seemed like a near-death experience to her had been no more than a friendly chat for their ebullient driver. Then she looked down and realised she was holding on to the hand of the elderly woman sitting across the aisle.

'I'm Miriam,' the woman said.

Bluebell was relieved when they arrived in Minori and pulled up in the car park at the end of the seafront. Massimo hopped out and opened the door of the luggage space. For a small man he was remarkably strong, manhandling the cases two at a time. Soon a pile of sensible-looking navy and black luggage was sitting on the pavement dwarfed by one huge pink-and-purple case. Bluebell reached for her case just as Massimo unloaded the final piece of luggage with a loud thump. There, sitting on the pavement, was an equally large case in zingy shades of lime green and turquoise stripes.

'That's mine,' said Miriam. She and Bluebell looked at each other and burst out laughing.

'I think you and I are going to be great friends,' said Bluebell. 'We've already got something in common!' They walked side by side, wheeling their suitcases in the direction of the hotel. Josie took two cases and Massimo balanced the remainder on a wobbly luggage trolley. A few minutes later they were standing in the lobby of the Hotel Sea Breeze being handed much-appreciated glasses of freshly squeezed fruit juice whilst Josie checked them in.

Bluebell wrestled her suitcase into the hotel's tiny lift and down a long, tiled corridor. Her room wasn't large, but it was light and airy and had been furnished with care. The bed was made up with crisp white linens; above it hung a watercolour of the seafront in a light wooden frame. The walls were painted a tranquil lavender and a rickety but comfortable-looking rattan chair sat in the corner by the sliding door, which led to a small terracotta-tiled balcony furnished with two simple metal chairs and a round table just big enough for a cool drink and a book. Above the dressing table was a framed pastel drawing of the town of Minori. Her eye was drawn to a large yellow church. Behind it the town rose steeply, and on the hillside the artist had added a quirky little house, painted a soft marshmallow pink.

The low sun was still casting its warmth onto the balcony and she wasn't going to waste a moment. She took a book from her large shoulder bag and a cushion from the rattan chair and carried them outside. She laid her book down unopened. She felt deliciously lazy. She would sit here on the balcony in the late afternoon's sunshine and close her eyes, just for a few minutes. Her unpacking could wait until after dinner.

Chapter Three

Michela skipped straight over to the luggage belt, dodging past a pretty redhead holding a clipboard in one hand and a pink-and-white flag embroidered with the words *Loving and Knitting* in the other. The first item on the belt was her large pink-and-purple paisley case. How lucky was that? She quickly plucked it off and wheeled her way swiftly towards *Nothing to Declare*.

She walked straight through, past the newsstand and café bar then out through the exit. It was good to be in the fresh air again and even better to look up and see the grey sky of London replaced by the clear blue sky and sunshine of Italy. Her mood lifted. Even her case felt lighter than it had done that morning. She rounded the corner to catch the orange bus that would take her into the centre of Naples. It was about to depart but a tiny nun with a face like a little round button reached down and helped haul her case into a gap by the door. She squeezed in next to it. The bus was full and noisy. Everyone seemed to be talking at once. The silence of the commuters on the London Underground seemed light years away.

They pulled up near the central station. She grabbed her case, scrambled out and scanned the crowded pavement.

'Sofia! I'm so happy to see you!' Michela stepped forward and kissed her best friend.

'Michela! It's been so long!' Sofia hugged her, lifting her right off the ground. 'My goodness, you've got so skinny. There's nothing of you! Didn't they feed you at that fancy London restaurant?'

'The food there was amazing, but it was so busy. I barely had time to stand still.'

'So, no sitting gossiping with the regulars over a cappuccino and one of your mamma's pastries,' Sofia teased.

'Don't! You're making my mouth water. We made all these fancy little cakes at The Golden Wolf but I can't wait to taste one of Mamma's *sfogliatelle* pastries again.'

'Mmm. Maria's food is just the best. How I envied you growing up at Il Gattino. I used to wish my papa ran a café bar instead of a boring old garage. Come on, let's go and find my car. I'm parked in the underground car park.'

Sofia's baby-blue Fiat zipped along, driving too close to the cars in front as she tooted her horn and gesticulated. Michela never imagined she would feel nostalgic for the slow crawl of London traffic, and although she was pleased to chat to her old friend, she was rather relieved when they arrived in Minori and pulled up at the car park at the end of the seafront. Sofia was full of apologies that she could not stay longer and greet Michela's parents, Mario and Maria, whom she had known since childhood, but she had to get back to Naples. Michela was left to walk the short distance from the seafront to her parents' café bar.

She crossed Via Roma and wheeled her case through Piazza Umberto. The pink-and-purple design looked even brighter in the Italian sun and she noticed a small child smiling at her and pointing it out to his mother. She smiled back and gave him a little wave.

Minori had not changed a bit since she had last seen it. Piazza Umberto was the largest square in the small town and boasted three handsome restaurants looking out over the sea. On the left were the round tables and blue-and-yellow-striped umbrellas belonging to Trattoria di Napoli, the largest and most popular of the three. She was surprised there were no customers sitting at the outside tables as the evening was so pleasant, and there was no sign of Tommaso Amati sitting in his usual chair near the door. She had never actually tasted Mr Amati's cooking – it would have seemed disloyal to her family – but sometimes after school she and her brother Paolo had surreptitiously snuck up to the counter to buy ice-cream cones from his special display of homemade *gelati* and disappeared onto the beach before anyone could see them. And sometimes Stefano came too.

She turned off the square down a side road towards her parents' café bar. Il Gattino was a much smaller affair than the restaurants on Piazza Umberto. It seated just twelve people but during the warmer months they squeezed a couple of tables onto the pavement, even though passers-by had to step into the road to get past.

Her father Mario opened at seven every morning, serving tiny cups of espresso that most of his regular customers drank leaning against the counter. They munched homemade pastries from the display under the glass dome, their fingers wrapped in flimsy paper tissues from the metal dispenser. Later the café would be filled with men drinking more coffee or small glasses of beer whilst playing endless games of cards, arguing about politics or flicking through the football pages. Her mother Maria would be busy in the kitchen, a pot of her legendary *ragù* sauce bubbling constantly in one corner whilst she rolled out her fresh pasta dough.

Michela could almost smell Maria's cooking as she made her way up the road. She couldn't wait to see her parents and Il Gattino again.

As she got nearer, she could see the light shining through the windows, but no one was sitting at the two little tables outside. There was usually a couple of her father's old friends enjoying a beer, or a pair of tourists drinking bright orange Aperol spritz away from the busier places on Piazza Umberto. She felt surprised. Where was everyone this evening? Maybe it was still a little early in the season, though the evening was surely warm enough to sit out.

She went around the side of the building to the door that opened onto a steep staircase that led straight up to the apartment over the café and rang the bell. She heard someone running down the stairs. That was odd; both her parents moved with a leisurely gait. The door opened. Her brother Paolo was standing there. Michela threw her arms around him. 'What a wonderful surprise!' she cried. He embraced her tightly, crushing her against his chest. Then she looked up into his face and saw an expression she could not quite read.

'Paolo, what is it?' His pause alarmed her. 'Where are Mamma and Papa? What's going on? What's happened?'

Chapter Four

'Here, let me help you with that.'

Michela followed behind her brother as Paolo bumped her suitcase up the narrow, wooden stairs. She chucked her shoulder bag onto the back of the chair in the hall. Nothing had changed since she had gone away. The familiar scent of her house-proud mother's furniture polish mingled with the cooking aromas that had penetrated the wooden floorboards from the café's kitchen below. The *Bella Casa* doormat, her father's worn leather slippers and the green wicker shopping basket were all in their usual places, but the uncanny silence was unbearable.

'Something's happened. What is it? You've got to tell me.'

'It's . . . it's Papa.'

'What do you mean?'

Paolo fidgeted with the pocket of his jeans.

'What!' Michela almost shouted.

'Papa's in hospital. Mamma's with him. They think he's had a heart attack.' Paolo's words came out all in a rush.

'A heart attack. No!' Michela sat down heavily on the hall chair. She put her hands over her face. It wasn't true – it couldn't be. Not Papa. Not *her* Papa.

'Michela . . .' Paolo knelt down and put his hands on her shoulders.

'What happened?' she said.

'It was late this morning. Papa was clearing the outside tables. Mamma was in the kitchen making pastry when she heard the most almighty crash. She rushed outside; Papa had collapsed on the pavement. Mamma was screaming hysterically but no one was around. How I wish I'd been there. I arrived last night – I wanted to surprise you when you got home – but I'd gone out to see friends.'

Michela touched her brother's arm. 'It wasn't your fault, Paolo.'

'Mamma ran down the road to Piazza Umberto. Tommaso Amati was sitting outside Trattoria di Napoli in his usual place. As soon as he saw Mamma he knew something terrible had happened. He didn't hesitate to come and help. He sent Mamma inside to call for an ambulance and performed chest compressions until they arrived.'

'Thank goodness he was there. But it must have been quite a shock for him to see that happening to his old friend.'

'I just wish . . .' Paolo looked down at the floor.

'There's no point dwelling on what might have happened. Why are we still here? We must go to the hospital.' Michela picked up her shoulder bag.

Paolo put his arm across the door. 'No. Mamma has Tommaso with her. She insists we stay here and open the café as usual.'

Michela put down her bag. She desperately wanted to rush down to the hospital but when Mamma insisted on something, she knew that was the end of the matter. She allowed Paolo to lead her into the sitting room.

'Coffee?' Paolo said.

Michela sank down onto the old, brown couch. She listened to Paolo clattering around in the tiny kitchen. She had never felt so scared in her life.

★

The loud knocking at the door made Bluebell jump. She glanced at her mobile lying on the table next to her unopened book; it was nearly half past six. She must have nodded off. 'Just coming!' she called and padded quickly to the door.

She opened the door. Josie was standing in the corridor. 'I wanted to check you were okay. It's just that our welcome reception started twenty minutes ago. Of course, you don't have to come but I was about to run through the week's programme—'

'I am so sorry,' Bluebell interrupted. She felt her face burning. 'I just fell asleep. I don't know how.' She had held up the coach at the airport; now everyone was downstairs without her. Josie must think she was such an idiot.

'Shall I see you downstairs in a few minutes?'

'No, no, I'll come right now.' She hastily dragged her fingers through her messy, dark hair and followed Josie out to the lift.

'I am really sorry,' she said again.

'I knew you were going to be trouble,' joked Josie. She handed her a name badge as they walked into the hotel's small Vesuvius function room where Bluebell was greeted by a wave of excited chatter. It sounded as though there were a couple of dozen people in the room rather than seven. Everyone else seemed to have changed for the occasion, their comfortable travelling clothes replaced by crisp linen separates or bright cotton cardigans teamed with patterned sundresses that looked as though they had been freshly ironed. Bluebell ran a hand down her rather crumpled travelling trousers. She hadn't thought about changing. She hadn't even hung anything up. She was debating whether to run back upstairs when she noticed Miriam standing a little way apart from the others, twisting a silver bracelet around her wrist.

'I thought for a minute you weren't coming,' Miriam said.

'I nodded off.'

Miriam laughed. 'I won't tell anyone,' she said in an exaggerated whisper.

'Have they told us where we're going tomorrow?' Bluebell asked, but before Miriam had time to reply a waiter appeared brandishing a tray of flutes fizzing with a pale-apricot-coloured concoction.

'You like a Bellini, Bluebell?' he asked, reading her name badge. 'It is peach juice and prosecco. Like, you might say, sunshine in a glass.'

'Yes, thank you, *grazie*.'

'You speak Italian beautifully. *Complimenti*!' He beamed at her knowing full well that she probably only knew half a dozen words.

'Not really,' she mumbled.

The waiter handed a glass to Miriam, but he continued to hold Bluebell's gaze with a look of such appreciation that she could not help looking back into his long-lashed brown eyes. They were set beneath rather fierce brows in a deeply tanned forehead.

'I am Andrea. Let me know if there is anything you would like me to do for you.' There was an emphasis on *anything*, which made Bluebell wonder quite what he was offering. Andrea turned and walked smoothly across the room. She could not help turning to look at him. His wavy black hair lapped the collar of his white shirt; his black waistcoat just met a pair of slightly too tight trousers that stretched over the two full curves of his neat buttocks.

'I think he likes you,' said a tiny white-haired lady whose name badge identified her as Evie. She looked well into her eighties, but her bright blue eyes flashed with mischief.

'I think he's the sort of guy who likes anyone, as long as they're female with a pulse,' Bluebell replied, but despite this knowledge she couldn't help feeling stupidly flattered. 'And anyway, I'm definitely not looking for a holiday romance.'

'That's a shame. You should have fun whilst you're young and you've got all of us wingmen here to help you out. Isn't that what they call them nowadays?'

'You mean I've got a lot of competition,' Bluebell said. She surveyed her fellow prizewinners, causing Evie to giggle, but not unkindly.

'You don't meet many young people who are good at puzzles these days,' Evie continued. 'You've done ever so well. That *Loving and Knitting* crossword competition is fiendishly difficult.'

Bluebell went pink. She was about to explain how she had come to take Granny Blue's place on the trip, but she hesitated. The rules stated that competition prizes were strictly non-transferable. What if they made her turn around and go home? Her mini mishaps would pale into insignificance if Josie had to return an interloper to the airport, and despite her misgivings she was beginning to feel that this trip was going to be fun. And that had nothing to do with Andrea's cheeky smile and pert backside.

'Umm, yes, I've done a lot of crosswords with my gran,' she said. Luckily, she was rescued from the need for further explanation by Josie announcing that she was going to run through their programme for the week before dinner was served in the adjoining dining room.

A hush fell over the room whilst the six prizewinners listened intently as Josie described the activities that the team at *Loving and Knitting* had planned.

'Tomorrow we'll be visiting Ravello, high up in the hills. There's an ancient path cut into the hillside that links it to Minori but you'll be relieved to know that Massimo will be taking us there in the minibus,' she began.

Bluebell sipped her Bellini, the cool liquid fizzing on her tongue, as Josie described their planned visits to nearby Sorrento; the ancient, buried city of Pompeii; and a boat trip to the picturesque town of Positano where teetering rows of houses were piled up overlooking the sea. The week promised to be packed with activities. It sounded as if even she was going to be in need of the free day when they would get the chance to relax by the pool at the Hotel Sea Breeze or wander around the small town of Minori. It would set them up nicely for the trip she was most looking forward to: their last outing to the nearby island of Capri, a place that conjured up visions of movie-star glamour and unforgettable beauty.

'Don't worry if you can't remember it all,' Josie continued. 'I've pinned a copy of our schedule up on the noticeboard in Reception. If anyone's got any questions shall we do that over dinner? I'm told they're ready for us in the dining room.'

Bluebell had never seen a group of older ladies move so fast. She was just thankful they were having a sit-down meal not a buffet. She wouldn't have much chance of getting her plate filled with this bunch of fork-wielding pensioners.

Andrea ushered the ladies to their seats, pulling back their chairs, knowing that they were amused and flattered by his broad smiles and exaggerated courtesy. Bluebell took a seat next to Miriam. Evie sat on her other side, placing a tortoiseshell-handled tapestry bag on the spare chair next to her.

'Just a little something for my great-grandson.' She opened the bag for Bluebell's inspection.

'Very nice,' Bluebell replied, though all she could see was a tangle of rainbow-coloured wool and something that might be a half-finished bonnet or a bootie for a child with unusually large feet. Evie was clearly a devotee of the *Knitting* part of *Loving and Knitting*, but judging by her cheeky grin, Bluebell was pretty sure that she could tell some tales of *Loving* as intriguing as the romantic fiction found between its covers.

Silence fell briefly as the menu was studied. An English translation had been provided, making the choice of dishes slightly easier but the whole process took a little time, so Bluebell was glad of the generously filled basket of bread in the middle of the table to distract her from the enticing smell of garlic and fresh herbs that was drifting over. Fortunately, Josie was blessed with the ability to hurry people along without them feeling rushed for even a moment, so Andrea was eventually able to depart with their order. How he remembered it all without a notepad Bluebell would never know.

As she took her first sips of the local wine, a warm sensation washed over her. It was funny; she had come on this trip so reluctantly, knowing she would never hear the last of it from Granny Blue if she let the prize go to waste, yet almost as soon as she had taken her seat on the minibus from Naples Airport she had felt the beginning of a change for the better. The tension in her shoulders had slowly started to ease and the vague headache and knotted feeling in her stomach that had never quite left her since she had found Jamie with giggly, golden-haired

Carrie seemed to have melted away in the warm Italian sunshine.

The thought of spending a week on holiday with a group of *Loving and Knitting* readers who would almost certainly be of pensionable age had seemed like a penance for failing in the pursuit of love. Now she looked around and saw a group of happy faces, eager to explore and enjoy what this beautiful part of the world had to offer. These faces sported a good deal more lines than those on the faces of Jamie's uni friends, and little Evie showed off a full set of unnaturally white false teeth, but what these faces had in common were their genuine smiles. And nobody was going to be posting bikini selfies on Instagram.

Her thoughts were interrupted by the arrival of the first course, which was served after a degree of confusion when half the women could not remember quite what they had ended up ordering as everything had looked so delicious. A couple of hours and several courses later, six exhausted prizewinners bid each other goodnight, hoping that the excitement of the trip would be cancelled out by the wine and the travelling, and that a good night's sleep would await them.

Bluebell opened her large shoulder bag and took out the small washbag Granny Blue had given her. Gran had thought of everything. There was even a travel-size version of her favourite moisturiser and a pink folding toothbrush that packed away in its own little case. She washed her face quickly. She really should unpack her suitcase before she went to bed, but she just couldn't be bothered. Instead she flopped beneath the covers and was soon fast asleep.

She wasn't visited by the recurrent nightmares that had been haunting her these last few weeks. Instead of jumbled images of Jamie and Carrie kissing and laughing at her, she dreamt of whizzing around the hairpin bends of the Amalfi Coast road. But this time she did not reach out and take hold of Miriam's hand. The hand she took belonged to a dark-haired young man in rather too tight trousers.

Chapter Five

The knocking on the door grew louder. Michela sat up with a start, pulling her mother's old cotton dressing gown around her.

'Come in!' she called. Her voice shook slightly as she remembered the drama of the night before. How could she have slept so peacefully whilst her father was hovering between life and death?

Her brother, Paolo, entered the room. The question on her lips was answered by the broad smile on his face. 'Such good news! Mamma rang from the hospital. Papa's operation went well. It looks like he's going to make a full recovery but he's going to have to take it easy from now on.'

'Thank God!' Michela felt tears pricking her eyes.

'Why on earth are you crying?' Paolo asked.

'I don't know. Relief maybe?' She started to laugh; a whole crowd of emotions was pinging around in her head. Then she fell silent.

'Michela?' Paolo said.

'Are you sure he's going to be okay?' she said quietly.

'Yes, as sure as I can be. He's been through a major operation, but all the signs are good. Mamma says the doctors are very pleased.'

'I just didn't imagine anything like this could happen to him,' Michela said.

'I'm just so, so thankful Tommaso Amati was there,' Paolo said. 'Mamma is convinced he saved Papa's life.'

Michela reached for the glass of water on her bedside table. She took a large gulp and swallowed hard. 'I can't bear to think what might have happened without Tommaso. It was so good of him to go to the hospital with Mamma. I still feel terrible that I wasn't there.'

'I told you Mamma insisted Il Gattino must open as usual last night. It was one less thing for Papa to fret about. Talking of which, it's time you got out of your lazy pit. We'll have customers arriving any minute.'

Michela looked at her bedside clock: seven a.m. Normally she would be groaning at the thought of washing up dozens of coffee cups but today she couldn't wait. Papa was going to be okay. She would gladly wash up a thousand coffee cups. She swung a leg out of bed.

She threw on an ancient pair of jeans from the old carved chest in the corner. They were a bit too big around the waist now, but she cinched them in with a belt. Unpacking her massive suitcase could wait for another day.

The sun streaming through the white linen curtains woke Bluebell from a deep sleep. She reached for her mobile phone and checked the time. It was nearly half past seven – perfect. The hotel dining room would be open. Whether she could fit in breakfast after last night's four-course meal was debatable, but it was a challenge she was happy to accept.

She quickly showered, lathering her body with the honey shower gel that she had found in a small white basket filled with toiletries. She inhaled deeply as the heady fragrance filled the small room. Then she grabbed the white bathrobe left folded neatly on the bathroom stool and padded across the tiled floor. Her rumpled travelling outfit lay in a heap on the floor. A large, greasy, red smear was spread right across one trouser leg. Eating spaghetti with just a fork was clearly something best left to the experts.

She unzipped her paisley suitcase and opened the lid.

'What the—!' She was staring at a pair of black jeans – a very small pair of black jeans. Instead of being half full, as she remembered, the case was tightly packed. Her heart was racing as she started to toss clothes onto the bed. Out came black, grey and navy jeans, logo T-shirts and hoodies – all designed for someone no bigger than a size eight. The only part of Bluebell that would fit into a size eight was her feet. The rather faded, billowy maxi dress she'd been planning to wear might not be the most exciting holiday outfit but at least it fitted – with room for a couple of ice-creams too. Bluebell held up a pair of jeans. She might be able to get her arms inside these, but her thighs – no chance.

If Gran was here now, she would tell her to look at the facts. And the facts of the situation were as follows. The first fact: she had taken Granny Blue's place on an organised tour of the Amalfi Coast with five ladies at least twice her age. The second fact: she had none of her clothes with her except a spare pair of knickers and one rather substantial bikini which, thank goodness, she had stuffed into her hand luggage. The third fact: she was in possession of a large paisley suitcase containing someone else's clothes. The fourth fact: she was going on a trip to the hilltop town of Ravello in just over an hour. Forget the facts – what on earth was she going to wear?

She put her head in her hands. But then, out of the corner of one eye she noticed something bright orange lying in the case, just visible below a couple of dark jumpers.

26

She chucked the jumpers onto the bed and pulled out the most beautiful dress she had ever seen: an orange fit and flare dress patterned with white poppies, just made for a 1950s starlet. Below that was another stunning sundress: this one had a royal blue skirt and a bodice patterned with life-size golden sunflowers. Nestling beneath the dresses were a gorgeous pink-and-cerise-striped gypsy top with matching cropped trousers and a daisy-print, halter-neck dress folded around a handful of tops in bright yellow, emerald and lime green.

These colourful dresses looked as though they belonged to a completely different person. She would never fit into this skinny minnie's jeans, but these dresses – would she? Could she? She held up the dress patterned with sunflowers: it looked about the right size. She turned it inside out but there wasn't a label. The seams were a little wonky and the hem had been turned up by hand.

She slipped the dress over her head, smoothed down the skirt and looked in the mirror. To her astonishment a girl with a wide smile was looking back at her. The royal blue of the perfectly fitting dress contrasted with the dark hair that fell over her shoulders and the sunflowers seemed to cast a golden glow on her pale English complexion.

Bluebell took another look in the mirror. Her mind was made up. Today she would wear this beautiful dress. After all, she didn't have much choice unless she wanted to disrupt the trip to Ravello. Tomorrow she would get up early to ring the airport and try to sort out the mix-up. She did feel a bit guilty, but more than that, she felt very sorry for the other tourist who would open her case to find a selection of rather dull pastel-coloured maxi skirts, cut-off cotton trousers and a couple of not desperately stylish sundresses.

She slipped on the pretty flip-flops she had picked up at Duty Free and made her way down to breakfast where Josie presided at the head of a table in the large airy dining room. Her stomach rumbled at the smell of freshly baked croissants so after saying her *good mornings* she made her way to the groaning buffet table where she found fruit, cereals, yogurts and pastries. Next to baskets of plain and seeded white rolls she was stunned to see a whole array of sponge cakes and apple cakes, mini muffins and chocolate tarts. If this was the Mediterranean diet it was one she could wholeheartedly embrace.

She carefully filled her plate, hoping she was showing a suitable appreciation of the spread rather than undisciplined greed. She could always stick to fruit and yogurt on the other mornings.

'American coffee? Or can I get you a special cappuccino?' Andrea asked smoothly. His eyes made their way from the top of Bluebell's head to the tips of her toes, then right around her for good measure.

'A cappuccino, please.'

'*Bellissimo,*' he replied in a way that made it clear he wasn't just approving of her choice of drink. She blushed furiously as the other women smiled approvingly at his vanishing behind.

'He's right. You look beautiful,' said Miriam.

'*Bella!*' added Evie in a convincing Italian accent. 'That dress is just so cute on you.'

'Oh, this . . .' began Bluebell. She realised she was about to say *this old thing* – her default response when anyone (rarely) complimented her choice of outfit. Before she was tempted to explain, Andrea reappeared with her drink. As he leant over her to put it down a waft of lemony cologne reached her nostrils, mingling with the smell of the freshly brewed coffee. She couldn't help smiling.

'Enjoy,' he murmured as he set down the cup and saucer. He left to a flurry of smiles from the impressed ladies and a stage-whispered *he likes you* from Evie. Then Josie reminded them that time was ticking on and everyone started talking at once about their trip to Ravello.

Bluebell clambered aboard the minibus and took a seat next to Miriam.

'I feel like I'm back at school.' Miriam grinned. 'I always sat on the back row when we went on a trip. I spent so much time giggling and messing about it's surprising I learnt anything!'

'Me too, but I wish I'd been more of a swot, then I might have ended up doing something more exciting than working in a high-street bank.' *I might even have gone to uni like pretty, perfect Carrie and applied for that marketing job at head office*, Bluebell added silently.

The minibus began its slow progress along the winding road towards Amalfi. This time Bluebell avoided looking towards the sea; instead she leant back against the headrest and enjoyed the sight of blue sky and the anticipation of visiting a new place. She had deliberately not Googled the stops on their itinerary; she wanted to have the pleasure of discovering them with no preconceptions at all.

After about a mile and a half Massimo indicated right and they began to climb uphill away from the coast, turning and twisting around the narrow road that led up to Ravello.

The bus drew up just outside the town and Massimo waved them off after repeating the pick-up arrangements several times. Josie led them into Piazza Vescovado, a wide square lined with large continental cafés where people sat in faux-wicker armchairs shaded by large cream umbrellas. At one end a flight of steps adorned with bright flowers bursting from terracotta planters led to the cathedral. Above its main entrance a pair of elegant arched windows were set into a pale, plain façade. The mountains in the distance seemed to hang like a painted backdrop in an old Hollywood movie. Traces of snow could still be seen at the summits. The women started rummaging in their handbags, digging out cameras and phones to capture each other against the stunning scenery.

'It's difficult to imagine that something man-made could compete with this,' Josie said. She waved a hand in the direction of the mountains. 'But here in Ravello we are going to visit two famous gardens, which are a treat for the senses, even for those of you who usually prefer concrete underfoot. But first we'll take a look around the famous cathedral and its museum.'

Josie led them up to the eleventh-century cathedral where they admired the famous embossed bronze doors before stepping into the cool and simple interior, where six stone lions supported twisted stone columns, like giant sugar canes inlaid with dazzling mosaics. Two raised stands were decorated with more mosaics, one showing poor Jonah being swallowed by the whale. After what Bluebell considered a mercifully quick look around the cathedral museum, which housed sculptures, silver artefacts and the usual columns, urns and relics, they set off down a tree-lined street to the gardens of Villa Rufolo.

After exploring every corner of the gardens and enjoying a lunch of mouth-watering salads and fresh fruit sorbets on the sun-drenched terrace of a small restaurant just off the main square, they followed Josie past the church and convent of St Francis of Assisi to the entrance of Villa Cimbrone.

As the women looked around, Bluebell wandered away from the rest of the group. She could feel the sun beating on her back and shoulders, but there was a soft breeze on her face. When she lifted her arm near her face she could smell the salt on her skin. She looked at her arm in surprise; she could swear she was getting a tan already. She unfurled the mini map of the villa's garden she had picked up on the way in. She seemed to be heading for the Terrace of Infinity at the far end. After lingering for a few minutes in the cool of a small temple, she stepped through an archway and gasped. She was standing on the edge of the gardens where a balcony topped with white stone statues seemed to lead directly out into the air. In the distance the blue of the sky met the blue of the sea. This was surely one of the most glorious views in the world.

She paused for a while, conjuring up a picture of Andrea, imagining him leaning her against the stone balustrade and kissing her. She would be wearing one of the dresses from the case, perhaps the orange one with the white poppies. Her long dark hair would be wafting in a soft breeze. She felt dizzy with the heart-lurching thrill of what might lie ahead.

'Bluebell!' It was Miriam calling her name and holding up a camera. She tried to wipe the silly grin off her face and compose her features to look as normal as possible as she and Miriam took pictures of each other against the dazzling backdrop of sea and sky before they walked back through the rose garden to join the others by the exit.

To her surprise she was loath to drag herself away from the garden, but she was happy enough spending some time strolling around the shops with the other women. Bluebell fell into step beside Evie, though she had to make an effort to walk more slowly so that Evie's little legs could keep up. They bypassed the establishments selling ceramics and the local *limoncello* liqueur in a hundred different types of bottles and headed for some boutiques filled with linen tops, trousers and dresses.

'That's a lovely outfit you have on. I've been meaning to say something about it all day,' said Josie, admiring the sunflower dress that Bluebell had borrowed that morning.

'Oh, thank you.' Bluebell's face felt hot and she knew it wasn't the sun. She should have said something about the suitcase straight away and tried to reunite it with its rightful owner but as soon as she slipped into the sunflower-printed dress she wanted to put that moment off for at least a little while longer. She had wasted so much time dressing to please Jamie by blending into the background, but when she twirled in front of the mirror and the dress swished to and fro, she didn't feel like the frumpy assistant manager of a high-street bank, dumped by her ex. She felt like someone else entirely and she did not want to give that up. But what would the other women think if they knew the truth behind her flattering holiday wardrobe? She was sure that borrowing someone's clothes didn't count as theft, but they might still think badly of her.

She should take the opportunity to buy herself a few holiday clothes whilst she was in Ravello, but she would never find anything as lovely as the dresses lying in the case back at the Hotel Sea Breeze. She might as well just grab a couple of cheap sundresses from the local market in Minori. So, she waited outside in the shade of a shop's canopy with Josie and Evie whilst Miriam went in to try on a pretty, light-blue linen blouse with subtle embroidery around the collar that she could not resist.

After a few minutes Miriam emerged carrying a suspiciously large glossy carrier bag.

'That looks a large bag for one blouse,' Josie said.

'Well, it did go rather well with this skirt and this light jacket and umm, actually this coordinating scarf as well.'

'How clever to find all that so quickly.'

'Oh, I didn't find anything. The minute I picked up the blouse the woman behind the counter had me all kitted out. She was very persuasive. I have to hand it to her: it all went together beautifully and fitted perfectly, but that place should come with a hazard sign.'

'Financial crisis ahead?' Bluebell suggested.

'Let's say it's a good thing I've got a low rate on my credit card.'

Whilst the others *oohed* and *aahed* over the window display in another fancy boutique – none of them now dared go in – Bluebell's attention was drawn to a small higgledy-piggledy shop tucked away up one of the side streets. The narrow pavement outside was heaving with a variety of cheap household essentials such as plastic buckets, wipe-clean tablecloths and reduced-price cleaning materials. In the window two plastic dummies wearing some extremely uncomfortable-looking red nylon lingerie jostled with piles of beige stomach-controlling shapewear and nighties patterned with cartoon characters.

'I'm just going to look in there,' Bluebell said. Evie raised an eyebrow and exchanged glances with Miriam, but Bluebell just smiled. Amongst the piles of tat she had spotted a pearl: multipacks of cotton knickers in every size imaginable, all priced at a bargain three euros. Grateful that she was no longer going to be washing and rotating the pair she had travelled in with the one spare she had shoved into her hand luggage, Bluebell was as happy as if she had unearthed a double-choc biscuit from a mountain of rice cakes. As they walked back to the coach, she slipped her arm through Miriam's.

'I never thought I'd enjoy walking around those gardens so much,' Bluebell said.

'I could really picture Greta Garbo strolling through Villa Cimbrone with her lover. It was so romantic.' Miriam touched the smooth links of her elegant silver bracelet.

'That's pretty.'

'Thank you. It was a twenty-fifth anniversary present from Colin, my late husband.'

'Oh.' Bluebell wasn't sure what to say. She could see the sadness clouding Miriam's pale blue eyes.

'This is the first time I've been abroad since he passed away. I didn't think I'd ever get on an aeroplane again. It was pure chance I entered that *Loving and Knitting* competition. I've never even read it before.'

Bluebell dropped her voice. 'To be honest, I've never read it either but my gran, Granny Blue, buys every issue.'

'I almost didn't take up my place. It felt so weird – wrong somehow – to being going somewhere so beautiful without Colin. But life goes on, I suppose. At least that's what everyone says.'

'I'm sure he would rather you were visiting a lovely place like this instead of sitting home alone feeling sad.'

Miriam sighed. 'I suppose you're right, dear.'

Bluebell looked over her shoulder. 'You won't tell anyone if I tell you a secret, will you?'

'Of course not.' Miriam smiled encouragingly.

'It was Gran who won the competition, not me, but at the last minute she couldn't go. She insisted I take her place after my own holiday fell through. I was supposed to be going away with my boyfriend Jamie . . . ex-boyfriend, I mean . . .' Bluebell looked down.

Miriam touched her lightly on the arm. 'It's okay . . . you don't have to tell me.'

'He left me for his best friend's fiancée.'

'How horrible for you. Sometimes I'm glad I'm far too old to start dating again.'

'No, you're not!'

'It's very sweet of you to say that, but I can assure you romance is the last thing on my mind,' Miriam said with a laugh.

Chapter Six

Miriam drew back the sliding doors of the double wardrobe. Thank goodness the hotel had provided plenty of hangers. She had never quite managed to embrace the concept of the capsule holiday wardrobe. It was hard enough getting a swimming costume that fitted, let alone one that could supposedly double up with a maxi skirt for sightseeing then with cropped cigarette pants and chandelier earrings for cocktails. Would the other readers of *Loving and Knitting* even drink cocktails?

Trattoria di Napoli sounded like a fairly casual type of place but people might still change for dinner. She wished she had thought of asking one of the others. She didn't know what to expect.

She touched the silky fabric of her cerise pleated skirt. It still had the price tag dangling from the waistband. Why had she chosen something so bright? It wasn't her at all. The cornflower-blue one was better, perhaps, but it was knee-length; she preferred to cover her legs these days. She wasn't sure about some of the dresses, and the tie–dye blouse picked up on her last holiday abroad with Colin looked a little bit droopy, but at least she had plenty of choice. It was surely better to pack too much than leave things at home gathering dust.

She glanced at her watch; she still had plenty of time. She took a book out to her little balcony; it looked a lovely place to read. But after a few minutes she laid her book down and watched the comings and goings in the street below. Mothers squeezed their baby buggies past teenagers standing around in groups, chatting on the narrow pavement. A young couple were arguing, the girl's dramatic hand gestures almost knocking an elderly gent off his bicycle. Their voices were lost in the sound of a mint-green Vespa roaring past. A family of four were crowded aboard, the littlest child, clad in a red Mickey Mouse T-shirt, standing on the running board between his father's feet.

How different it was from her own small village. How lucky she was to be able to make this trip and see a little bit more of the world. Colin would approve of her holiday; she was sure of that now. She could hear his voice encouraging her: *Be brave, old girl. Go and see the places we didn't have time to see together.*

She stepped back into her room, freshened her make-up and picked out a floral frock. It was an old favourite of hers, one that had so many memories associated with it, so many meals and outings with Colin. Now it was faded from repeated washings, but the softened colours suited her pale complexion and silvery hair. It was one of several dresses that she had not worn since those happy times, but she was glad that some impulse had led her to add it to her already heaving suitcase. She would wear it for their dinner at Trattoria di Napoli tonight. It was time to give it an outing again and maybe create some happy memories of a different kind.

As she smoothed down her slip and carefully fastened the zip it slowly dawned on her: it wasn't just anxiety making her stomach flip over. There was something else – a tentative feeling of excitement. She opened her handbag and reached for her coral lipstick.

Michela caught sight of herself in the mirrored interior of the hospital lift. She was still wearing her uniform of white blouse and black skirt. She frowned as she rubbed at a small smear of ricotta on the black material. She had thought about getting changed, but she knew the sight of her uniform would reassure her father that she wasn't neglecting her duties at Il Gattino.

She exited the lift and walked down the corridor, stepping past a huge trolley piled with rolls of toilet paper and hand towels. The place smelt of bleach mixed with hospital food. As she approached her father's ward a sick feeling of fear lurked in her stomach. She wiped her clammy hands on her grubby skirt and swallowed, but her throat was dry. She stood motionless in the doorway. Then she spotted him, propped up in the hospital bed. He looked so pale, even against the stiff white pillows. She took a tentative step towards him. He looked up and blinked in the strong bluish light.

'Papa, it's me.'

'Michela!' His voice was weak, but his smile lit up his whole face.

She flung her arms around him.

Chapter Seven

Tommaso Amati handed each of the seven English ladies a large menu bound in burgundy faux leather emblazoned with *Trattoria di Napoli*. He had the feeling this was going to take quite some time. His local customers usually ordered quickly; in fact he found that they tended to order the same dishes on every visit. These lovely ladies would read through the whole menu two or three times over, examining his starters – trying to decide between the familiar Italian classics like Parma ham and melon or to brave the unfamiliar like the crunchy little blue fish caught nearby. Next, he had a whole page of pasta dishes to choose from. Perhaps they would like his *spaghetti al limone* made with the supersized knobbly lemons grown on the Amalfi Coast or Minori's speciality: *'ndunderi*, a type of gnocchi made with ricotta, milk, flour and egg yolks served with a sauce of cherry tomatoes, onion, basil and smoked cheese. Not to mention the second courses of grilled meat and whatever fish was landed that morning.

Tommaso answered all their questions courteously and with great pride in the traditions of his home town. He loved to explain the inspiration behind his dishes and talk about the local herbs and ingredients he chose to use. There was no rush at all. And the longer it took for the ladies to decide what to order the more wine they were likely to drink.

His eye was caught by two women in particular, one of whom was much younger than the other. The dark-haired girl with a beaming smile wore a colourful dress patterned with sunflowers. There was something strangely familiar about her, but it was probably just his imagination playing tricks on him. The older lady she was talking to was a fine-looking woman. Her soft, floral dress and gentle manner reminded him of his late wife. As he poured out her wine his eyes met hers for a split second before she looked away. Every so often he plucked up the courage to steal a glance in her direction; once or twice she looked back and smiled.

The next couple of hours passed in a blur of fetching, carrying and making sure everything was to his customers' satisfaction.

Despite declaring themselves far too full, the group of English ladies had all decided to enjoy a dessert after all. Tommaso busied himself organising tiramisu, fresh fruit and *delice di limone*, the soft lemon-flavoured dessert shaped like a woman's breast. As he put everything onto a tray, he could hear happy laughter coming from their table. Some of the group were several years older than he was, and witnessing their obvious enjoyment in kicking back and relaxing hardened his resolve to spend some of his remaining years taking it a bit easier. Perhaps it was finally time to move to the nearby island of Ischia where his younger sister, Silvia, and her husband ran a fish restaurant in the harbour. They could do with a helping hand. His two nephews worked on the tourist boats and seemed to prefer a life at sea to the hot and sweaty confines of the family's kitchen.

Tommaso thought of Mario lying in hospital. He knew his friend's heart attack was a wake-up call. The long hours he worked in Trattoria di Napoli were more wearying than people realised. Although he had the assistance of two local lads, he was constantly working morning, noon and night. Mario was lucky. He had his beloved Maria to help him keep the show on the road at Il Gattino. He knew there was no chance Mario would want to retire; he would want to keep working to leave something to Paolo and Michela. He, Tommaso, had no such impetus since the terrible car crash ten years ago that had robbed him of his wife and only child. And he would have no one to nurse him if he suffered the same fate as his friend.

The English party finally paid their bill and left, after being persuaded to enjoy a complimentary glass of the local *limoncello* liqueur – persuading them wasn't exactly a hard job. He went into the back room of the restaurant. He opened his desk drawer and took out a sheet of cream paper. Before he had chance to change his mind, he picked up a thick black pen and wrote on the paper in bold letters, then he propped it in the window: *VENDESI – FOR SALE.*

Darkness had fallen whilst the women had been eating and the piazza was illuminated by the soft glow of the old-fashioned three-armed street lanterns. Lights shone in the windows of the old houses, and above them the headlights of cars cast dots of light that moved across the hillside, tracing the movement of people driving up to the hill towns of Ravello and Scala. The dark expanse of the sea stretched away into the distance, but people of all ages still strolled along the pier and the seafront where a couple of bars were set up and doing a good trade. A crowd had gathered halfway along the front and lively music was drifting over.

'Shall we take a look, or do you want to get straight back to the hotel?' said Josie.

41

To Bluebell's surprise, the older ladies were in no hurry to go to bed. Revitalised by a rest before dinner and fortified by their excellent meal, they were curious to see what was attracting such a gathering. Miriam seemed particularly animated. She had been in no rush to leave the restaurant and seemed very keen to prolong the evening.

As they got nearer, Bluebell realised that the music was coming from an old-fashioned portable boom box sitting on a trestle table. A banner pinned along its length announced: *Sergio's School of Dance*. A man with sideburns straight out of the seventies and long dark hair pulled up in a ponytail, whom she assumed must be Sergio, was leading a group of dancers in a lively-looking routine. Young and old, small and large, they seemed to have boundless energy, stepping and shimmying in their matching *Sergio's* T-shirts as the boom box belted out the latest hits sung in Italian interspersed with the sort of seventies classics that were guaranteed to get Bluebell up on the dance floor at the bank's Christmas party.

Elderly women in floral tent dresses and thick black stockings stood simultaneously watching and gossiping. Old men with scrappy little dogs stood next to groups of teenagers leaning against their scooters, whilst passing tourists stopped to clap along. Mothers with babies in pushchairs, glad of a rest, watched the dancing with half an eye on small children who ran about despite the late hour. No one seemed to care when the toddlers threatened to cause havoc by running between the dancers' legs or diving under the trestle table.

Sergio was joined by an elegant woman in a leotard and full-length, peach-coloured tulle skirt. He stopped the music and handed her a microphone through which they took it in turns to make some announcements. Bluebell hadn't a clue what was being said, but judging by the reaction of those around them, it soon became clear that he was inviting the audience to participate in the next dances. The seventies grooves gave way to rock and roll as Bill Haley and his Comets played 'Rock Around the Clock'. Some of the teenagers began to shuffle around; a few middle-aged couples began to boogie, arms flailing wildly, whilst gangs of small children bopped around, getting under everyone's feet.

There was an appreciative murmur as a tiny old man, smartly dressed in button-down shirt, waistcoat and neatly pressed trousers, led a plump, equally elderly woman onto the makeshift dance floor. With one hand on her shoulder and the other on her forearm, the elderly gent began to lead his partner in time to the music, their movements becoming faster and more fluid the more they danced. The buckles on his shoes gleamed in the dim light; the substantial skirt of her rose-pink dress flipped up and down as she twisted and jived. At the end of the number there was a burst of spontaneous applause.

As the music switched to 'Jailhouse Rock' Bluebell gasped in surprise and delight as she saw little Evie heading for the gyrating group, clutching the hand of a heart-break-ingly handsome young man who looked rather familiar. Her eyes were bright, her wide smile showing off her new false teeth as she danced.

Bluebell laughed as she recognised Evie's dance partner: it was Andrea, the waiter from their hotel. Judging by his black trousers and crumpled white shirt, he had just finished his shift and had been on his way home completely unaware that he was about to be pounced on by an energetic octogenarian. The sight of Evie boogieing got the other women tapping their toes and one by one they all began to dance. Miriam swayed along to the music with a smile on her face. Every so often she glanced in the direction of Trattoria di Napoli.

Josie was soon partnered by a passing policeman who spun her around and around so fast that when he let go, she carried on spinning and almost collided with Miriam.

When she stopped laughing, Josie sidled up next to Bluebell. 'Pretty fit, isn't he?' she whispered.

'Andrea?' said Bluebell.

'Of course! I'm not talking about that old gent in the waistcoat,' Josie said.

Bluebell stifled a giggle as they watched Andrea twirl Evie around.

Evie could not keep up with Andrea for long and soon went to sit on a bench, leaving him with the choice of more than a dozen women to pick as his partner. Bluebell could not care less who he danced with but when he took her hand and they began to dance she felt a thrill of excitement. Andrea was a flamboyant dancer; he was the best-looking man on the seafront and he knew it. Bluebell could see more attractive girls amongst the dancers, but none were wearing a dress as colourful and flattering as the sunflower-patterned sundress from the mysterious suitcase.

Andrea and Bluebell were attracting plenty of admiring glances, but they were quickly outshone by the elderly man in the waistcoat and his plump partner in the rose-pink dress who had found a second wind and begun to dance again with a style that far surpassed their own.

The tempo changed, and Elvis switched from rocking with the jailbirds to urging them to love him tender. Bluebell found herself pressed up against Andrea's firm chest. His arms were wrapped around her a little lower than necessary and her nose was squashed against his neck, which smelt of his warm, golden skin blended with the lemony remnants of whatever aftershave or cologne he had applied that morning. She looked up into his eyes, which looked straight back into hers, seemingly daring her to kiss him. Her heart was pounding in her chest.

Conscious of the eyes of Josie and the other women on her, Bluebell loosened her grip slightly. She did not want to be known as the girl who threw herself at the waiter on their first night out, no matter how appealing he was. Andrea did not seem offended and they continued dancing, his come-to-bed eyes locked on hers. Then the microphone squealed with static feedback making Bluebell jump and Andrea laugh. The moment had passed.

Sergio and his tulle-skirted sidekick made another series of incomprehensible announcements, then a troop of half a dozen identically dressed teenage girls began a dance routine to a background of loud Italian rap music. This immediately halved the audience though those remaining, probably parents and relatives, applauded wildly. Josie suggested it was time they made a move and no one disagreed; it was nearly midnight. Bluebell looked over at Andrea, but he was talking to a man wheeling a scooter. He jumped on the back of it and sped away. She watched the tail light until it faded to a tiny red dot in the distance.

Chapter Eight

Michela entered the small stone church of Santa Lucia. She was the only person there this early in the morning, apart from Emilia Bellucci, the owner of the swimwear shop, who was busy with her duster.

As Michela stood for a short time in front of the gilded wooden triptych looking at the carvings of Saints Lucia, Agata and Apollonia, she felt her breathing slow down and a pleasing sense of calm enveloped her. She was in no doubt that the three saints had helped her father's recovery. She lit a small candle and gave thanks.

She walked back to Il Gattino with a new sense of purpose. The thought of going to work in her cousins' restaurant in Positano no longer excited her. This small village where she had spent almost all her life was where her future lay. She would stay here in Minori and work at Il Gattino for as long as her parents needed her. Their tiny café bar was nothing like the big restaurant she and Stefano had once dreamt about, but it was her father's pride and joy. And one day, when he and Mamma finally retired, she might take over the lease. It would make Papa so proud.

It was a blessing in disguise that she hadn't met anyone special in England. Imagine if she had decided to stay in London; it would be unthinkable to be hundreds of miles away from her beloved papa at a time like this. And now she was back home, the thought of settling down anywhere else seemed impossible. Perhaps one day she would meet someone here in Minori, if only she could get Stefano out of her head. He couldn't be the only attractive man on the Amalfi Coast, could he? And if it wasn't meant to be, she had her family. And that was the most important thing of all.

Michela pushed open the door of Il Gattino. 'Paolo, I'm back! Has it been busy?'

'No, it's very quiet at the moment. I wasn't expecting you so soon. Why don't you take a longer break whilst you have a chance? You'll be busy enough next week when I'm back in Naples. My firm's been very good about extending my leave but one of the other guys goes on holiday soon. So now Papa's on the mend they're expecting me back in a day or two.'

'If you're sure you're okay I'll go and see Nonna Carmela. I haven't had a chance to see her since I've got back, and I'd love to tell her how Papa's getting on.'

'Sure,' Paolo replied. He was holding a wine glass up to the light and frowning at a lipstick print on the rim. He reached for a cloth. 'Go on, before I change my mind. Go!'

Michela climbed the steep steps to her grandmother's front door. How the old lady managed to get up and down them at the age of nearly ninety she would never know. Though to be fair, Nonna Carmela was likely to have something sturdier on her feet than the spike-heeled shoes Michela had realised, too late, that she was wearing.

She found the key to the side gate in its usual hiding place inside the ceramic toadstool and let herself in.

'Michela! How wonderful to see you. Here, give me a hug. Oh, *mamma mia*, you are so thin. Like a piece of spaghetti. You must eat! Please fetch the cake tin – you know where it is.'

Michela fetched two plates and the round tin patterned with kittens that Nonna had used for her homemade cakes for as long as Michela could remember.

'Now, tell me, how is your father this morning?'

'Paolo rang the hospital. They say Papa is making good progress.'

'Thank goodness! What a thing to have happened. I could scarcely believe it. And your poor mother, how is she coping? She must be beside herself with worry.'

'Mamma has gone to the hospital to sit with Papa. She says she can't settle at home knowing he is there.'

'I thought as much. I told her not to try and visit me this week; she has far too much to do.'

'I am so sorry I did not come and see you straight away, Nonna. We have been so busy at Il Gattino,' Michela said.

'There's no need to be sorry. Your father will want you to keep the place going. That is the most important thing. But, Michela, I don't want you looking after other people if you're not looking after yourself. You must make sure to eat properly.'

'Yes, Nonna.'

'And besides, I can always find someone to tell me how Mario is getting along. You know what this town is like. It's impossible to keep anything quiet. Now, perhaps you could help me move that armchair and change the light bulb. Of course, I'm more than capable of doing it myself. It had just slipped my mind. But now you're here . . .'

'Is this where you want the chair?' Michela asked.

'Perfect. Now we'll have some coffee and you can tell me all about London. I want to know all about working at The Golden Wolf. I've read and reread your letters but there's nothing I'd like more than hearing all about it from you. Are you sure there wasn't a nice boy working there?'

Michela settled down in the rather lumpy green armchair whilst Nonna adjusted the position of a couple of crocheted cushions. She leant forward and told the old lady all her news, speaking as slowly and clearly as she could.

'I am both sad and glad that you did not fall in love,' Nonna Carmela said. 'I may be a selfish old woman, but I hoped that you would not find a new life so far away, even though I would like nothing more than to see you settled and happy.'

Michela smiled. England might as well be Australia as far as her grandmother was concerned. Carmela Gentili had spent her childhood in the neighbouring town of Maiori, brought up as the only child of a widow whose husband had died shortly after Carmela was born. Carmela had married and left home at nineteen, moving just along the coast to live in Minori, in the same little house where they were now sitting. The old-fashioned kitchen and cosy sitting room had changed little since the days when Michela's mother Maria had been born and were as familiar to the old lady as the contours of her own face.

'You heard your old boyfriend Fabio got married? I did not want to tell you in a letter,' Carmela said.

'Yes, I hear he married Daniela and is very happy,' Michela replied.

'He asked her out the week after you left for England and they were engaged six weeks later.'

Michela raised an eyebrow, but she felt relieved. She had felt bad about ending her relationship with Fabio and when she was feeling particularly hard on herself she felt guilty for even starting it.

Fabio was the son of the local fruit supplier. He had been a year above her at school and she had known him all her life. He had left school as soon as he could. Education wasn't much use to him; his life was already all planned out. He would work for his parents and eventually become an assistant to his brother when it was time for the older boy to take over the business.

Throughout her teenage years she had been conscious that Fabio always hovered for an unnecessarily long time when making his deliveries to the kitchen of Il Gattino. If she was the one to come to the door he got himself into quite a confusion, muddling up his order or dropping his boxes of produce. She had lost count of the times that she and her brother Paolo had chased after an errant melon rolling down the road or rushed to gather up cherries or raspberries from the doorway before they were crushed underfoot. Then one day it happened: blushing and spilling his tray of figs all over the floor, Fabio asked her out on a date. He was such a nice, kind boy she could not bring herself to say no and before she knew it, she had become his girlfriend. She was eighteen years old and he was her first proper boyfriend.

Michela knew her parents, Mario and Maria, would be happy for her to settle down with Fabio, but whenever she sat down and made a list of his good points there was something missing. Fabio was faithful and considerate, bought her thoughtful gifts, worked hard, got on with her friends and was unfailingly polite to her parents. She tried to tell herself this was more than most girls could dream of, but when she looked into his kind, open face and saw the love shining in his eyes she couldn't help feeling guilty. Guilty that she would never love him as much as he loved her. Guilty that when she dreamt of walking down the aisle of the church of Santa Lucia the face that would turn towards her wasn't his. It was Stefano's.

When the chance of working at The Golden Wolf presented itself, the excitement of moving to London was tinged by the sadness of leaving her family behind but provided her with the perfect excuse to finish her relationship with Fabio. She hoped that he would find it easier to get over her whilst there were hundreds of miles between them. Now it seemed that it had all worked out for the best. By all accounts Fabio was happy with his new bride and as one day she was due to inherit her parents' farm, his future was looking much brighter.

'Fabio wasn't right for you,' Carmela said. Michela frowned; she knew her grandmother had always liked the fruit supplier's son.

'But you were always so fond of him.'

'I was fond of him, and so were you. That's why he wasn't the right one. The right man isn't the one you are fond of, no matter how nice he is. The right man is the one you're in love with. And I hear he may be coming back home.'

'Who?'

'Stefano, of course. The boy you've always been in love with.'

'How do you know . . .'

'I haven't reached nearly ninety without having eyes in my head. Do you really think I didn't see the two of you sneaking around together? Do you think I didn't know your heart was broken the day he went to Rome?'

'So, what have you heard?' Michela asked. What a fool she was to get her hopes up. Why would Stefano look at her now, after all these years? There was no point getting excited, but her heart hadn't got the message; it was knocking against the wall of her chest. Her fingers tightened around the arm of her chair.

'I've heard nothing definite, I'm afraid, but my friend was buying a bikini in Casa Emilia and Emilia Bellucci said that her sister had heard in the market that Stefano was moving back to Minori soon. But you know how these stories go around. Now have another slice of cake. Let's see, what more news do I have for you?'

Michela sat back and listened as Nonna filled her in on various pieces of gossip. Or at least she tried to listen; her head was filled with thoughts of Stefano.

After hugging and kissing Nonna Carmela farewell, Michela made her way carefully down the treacherously steep steps leading from the house and wished once more that there was another route to and from her grandmother's. Although the land on the far side of the house sloped gently towards the main road, where an infrequent bus ran down into the town, it was made up of old, neglected farmland. A strong, high fence blocked off Carmela's house making it clear that trespassers would be unwelcome even if they did fancy picking their way over the rutted, uneven ground ridden with weeds and bits of broken farm machinery.

Michela was soon back in the main part of town, making her way back to Il Gattino via the main piazza, where she could see Tommaso Amati carrying a tray of drinks to one of his outside tables. She would be forever grateful to Tommaso; without his quick thinking things could have been so much worse for her father. He might not even have survived. She pushed the thought away; it was too painful to contemplate. Instead she tried to think about the forthcoming summer. Although it was only June, Minori was getting busier. That would be good for both Il Gattino and Trattoria di Napoli.

As she turned away from Tommaso's grander establishment, a bold but hastily written notice propped in the window caught her eye. It read *VENDESI – FOR SALE*. Suddenly she had a plan.

Chapter Nine

Bluebell pulled on the pink-and-cerise cut-off trousers and matching top. She glanced in the mirror on the back of the door and couldn't help smiling. Then she took off the trousers and top with a sigh and pulled on her old travelling trousers. The stain from the tomato sauce was still visible, despite her best efforts. Today she would contact the airport to arrange to return the suitcase and see if her own luggage was languishing there.

She picked up her phone and sent a message to the contact details on the airport's website. An email came back straight away. She clicked on *Google Translate: Thank you for your email. We will respond within ten working days.* Well, that was a fat lot of good. She dialled the phone number for Lost Luggage. The phone rang, and rang, and rang. She was never going to get through and get down in time for breakfast. Tomorrow would have to do.

Bluebell strode into the dining room, surprised to see that most of the *Loving and Knitting* ladies were already down for breakfast despite their late night, dancing on the seafront. When she returned from loading her plate at the breakfast buffet – her all-fruit breakfast could wait for day three – a cappuccino was already waiting for her. A small rosebud had been placed on the saucer.

'That waiter definitely fancies you,' said Josie.

'Stop it!' Bluebell blushed.

Evie hummed the tune to 'Love Is in the Air' as Andrea passed by their table. He paused for a split second and gave Bluebell a broad wink. To the astonishment of everyone, particularly herself, Bluebell winked back.

After breakfast the ladies assembled by the reception desk, chatting away, clutching a mixture of sun hats and cardigans just in case the fine June day turned out to be too hot or too cold. As Andrea appeared from the dining room and made his way over to Bluebell the noise level of their conversation fell.

'You like my rosebud?' He smiled, showing his perfect teeth.

'Yes, thank you. *Grazie*,' Bluebell replied.

'I see you are all eating in the hotel tonight.' He gestured to the *Loving and Knitting* itinerary, which was pinned to the hotel noticeboard. 'You will not be finished too late and it is my evening off. I would like to show you a nice place for a drink when you have finished your dinner, maybe.'

Men had been the last thing on Bluebell's mind when she had agreed to come on this holiday and after her experience with Jamie a relationship was the last thing she wanted. But Andrea was undoubtedly dangerously attractive even without the aid of a couple of glasses of wine and Elvis Presley crooning under a starlit sky. And it was only a drink – what harm could there be? The minibus to Sorrento was leaving in ten minutes and six expectant pairs of eyes were staring at her. She felt Josie's elbow digging into her. There was only one thing to say in the circumstances. So, she said it: 'Yes.'

Josie counted her six prizewinners before they boarded the minibus. 'Better safe than sorry,' she said.

'That's right, dear. You never know, I might take it into my head to run off somewhere.' Evie gave a mischievous chuckle as though she was already planning her escape.

'Have you ever lost anyone on one of these trips?' Miriam asked. She sounded a little nervous.

'I've never forgotten anybody but on last year's trip to Spain someone did almost give me the slip.'

'Really, why?' Bluebell said.

'I'm not sure I should really say . . .' Josie said.

'Oh, go on. We're not easily shocked,' said Miriam.

'It was on our trip to the flamenco dancing school. I eventually found her with a moustachioed instructor with a penchant for older women. He was volunteering to teach her a few moves that weren't in any dance class that I've ever attended.'

Evie giggled. 'I won't be getting up to anything like that, dear. I don't suppose I'll get the chance!'

'That's a relief,' Josie joked. 'I still have nightmares about that day, to be honest.'

Bluebell took a seat next to Miriam. Behind them, Evie sat on a double seat by herself, busy with her knitting needles and some extraordinarily vivid yellow wool. Apparently, this was her top-secret knitting project and no one was allowed to peek.

Once everyone was safely buckled up, Massimo set off for Sorrento, sounding his horn exuberantly as he turned the tightest corners along the coast road.

Miriam and Bluebell were soon chatting away. The older lady was so easy to talk to that Bluebell soon lost her earlier reticence and before she knew it, she had told her all the details of her three-year relationship with Jamie.

'But you are still very young,' Miriam pointed out.

'Twenty-eight. That's nearly thirty!'

'Are your mother and father worried that you haven't got married yet?'

'Heavens no! Mum's more worried about how my younger sister is getting on at uni and whether I'm going to get promoted at work.'

'It was different in my day. I met my husband, Colin, when I was just eighteen. He worked at the same place as my father. In fact, it was my mother who persuaded Dad to set us up on a date – she had heard so much about Colin. I was married by the time I was twenty. My parents were thrilled.

'These days people would say I was far too young, but it worked out for me. We were ever so happy together even though we never had the children we both longed for. I've got a couple of lovely nieces though, so really, I'm blessed. The younger is married but the older one's in her thirties with no sign of meeting anyone special. She seems perfectly happy though. Girls don't need to worry about being "left on the shelf" as they used to say when I was young. If I had been single in my thirties my mother would have been having kittens. But you know, even if my niece never marries, I think there are many different ways to be happy.'

'I do hope so. I'm not looking to get involved with anyone right now. In fact, I'm not too sure I really want another relationship,' said Bluebell.

'Except your holiday romance, perhaps,' Miriam said, with a twinkle in her eye.

'Oh, Andrea? We're only going for a friendly drink,' Bluebell said, but her cheeks were burning.

'I imagine our handsome waiter might have more than friendship on his mind.'

'Well, he won't be getting anything else.' The thought of being held and kissed by Andrea was rather appealing, but she certainly wasn't going to admit that to Miriam or any of the other prizewinners. Instead she said, 'Wasn't it strange, your parents setting you up on a blind date?'

'A little, I guess, but I think they did a better job than I could have done myself.'

'I think mine would have picked someone better than Jamie.' Her parents had always kept any opinions about Jamie to themselves, but looking back, she remembered that Granny Blue had made it clear she wasn't too keen on him.

'I don't think they'd pick Andrea either, even though he has got his charms,' said Miriam with a laugh.

'You're not wrong there.' Bluebell chortled. She couldn't quite imagine the tanned, tight-trousered Italian shaking hands with her dad. Well, she wasn't likely to need to worry about that; there was next to no likelihood of tonight's drink with Andrea turning into a long-term relationship.

The rest of the journey to Sorrento passed quickly as Bluebell and Miriam chatted away. Before long they had waved goodbye to Massimo, who went off to park, and they were following Josie into Piazza Tasso, a pleasant square lined with cafés and bars. They had been in the minibus for a little over an hour so a coffee stop with a spot of people-watching was definitely in order before their walking tour of the town.

Bluebell took a seat next to a woman with a broad, friendly face, framed by a thick steel-grey bob, who was dressed in a loose, striped, collarless linen shirt. A couple of leaflets from the hotel lobby were wedged under her water glass, no doubt in a quest to arm herself with even more information than could be found in the substantial guidebook that protruded from the emerald-green tote bag hanging from the back of her chair. Her name badge from the welcome party was still pinned to the shoulder strap: *Brenda*.

It was a beautiful day for sitting outside with a round of perfectly made cappuccinos accompanied by crunchy, almond-filled biscuits. The people on the other tables were mainly tourists, most of them talking in English. It was too early for the schools to have broken up, so most were older couples or people in organised groups like themselves. Everyone had the unhurried air of being on holiday with no fretful children wanting to rush off here and there. Everyone except Josie. She was studying her phone, frowning.

'Josie, is everything okay?' Bluebell said.

'I need to make a quick call. I'll just find a spot for a decent signal,' Josie said.

She returned a few minutes later looking worried. 'I'm afraid we have a problem.'

'Nothing serious?' Bluebell asked.

'It's the lady who is taking us on our guided walk of Sorrento. She texted me to say she's been taken ill. I just rang the company that takes the tours and they don't have anyone else they can send this morning.'

'You mustn't worry. I'm sure we will be fine just wandering around,' said Miriam.

'I'm a very good map reader,' said Evie. 'I could make sure we don't get lost. I've been looking at the sort of route I thought we might be taking.'

'It's such a shame. The lady who was going to take us was going to tell us about the places we were going to see. It makes such a difference when you have someone who's enthusiastic and knowledgeable about a place,' said Josie.

'I can't imagine she knows more than Brenda if she's been reading her way through that huge guidebook,' Evie joked.

'Well, I have been finding out a lot of interesting things,' Brenda said, blushing slightly.

'Could you tell us about some of the places as we walk around?' asked Miriam.

'I'm not sure that would be fair on Brenda,' said Josie, turning to her. 'Unless you'd like to, of course.'

'I don't want to bore everyone, but I'd love to try my hand at a guided tour, if you'll have me.' Brenda had hardly finished her sentence before she was drowned out by a chorus of enthusiastic agreement. With Brenda and Evie leading the way, they set off down Corso Italia in the direction of the cathedral.

'Now this would be top of my sightseeing list if I was a little bit richer,' Evie quipped, as they admired the chic designer boutiques that lined the wide street.

'I think we'd better leave any clothes shopping until after lunch, otherwise Brenda will have to take a crash course on Italian fashion icons.' Josie grinned.

'I don't know how they wear those,' said Brenda, pointing to a pristine white dress with long, floaty sleeves that reached the mannequin's fingertips. 'Imagine all the washing!'

'They're beautiful, but not very practical,' Miriam admitted. 'Oh, goodness, look at that.' She pointed to a window display of skin-tight leather dresses.

'Not for me,' Bluebell said, laughing.

'Not even for your date with sexy Andrea?' Josie teased.

'Definitely not! Anyway, I'd look far too fat in something like that. Jamie always said . . .' Bluebell's voice tailed away, remembering the day of Jamie's brother's wedding. She had felt so good in her new blue midi dress. It skimmed her curves in all the right ways; she couldn't wait for Jamie's face when she rang the doorbell. She would never forget the way he looked at her when he opened the door, then insisted she borrowed one of his sister's shapeless cardigans to 'make herself decent'. She blinked away a tear.

59

'Who's Jamie?' Josie said.

'My ex-boyfriend,' Bluebell said quietly.

'I bet you're glad you got rid of him.'

'Actually, he dumped me.' She liked Josie but she didn't really want to go through it all again.

'Well, that just proves what a total loser he is,' Josie said.

Bluebell could not help laughing at the look of utter disgust on her new friend's face.

'I had a boyfriend a few years ago who used to try and put me down like that,' Josie added. 'Leaving him was the best thing I ever did. Honestly, Bluebell, you're better off without him.'

Bluebell nodded. She had believed for so long that Jamie was The One, but after just a couple of days in Italy she was beginning to think that Josie might be right.

After a few minutes they came to the gate that led to the courtyard in front of the cathedral. The pale stone exterior in front of them seemed to glow in the June sunlight as Brenda gave them a few pointers as to what they would find inside. Bluebell had never been particularly interested in looking around old churches, but she found herself peering intently at the *intarsia* – the mind-bogglingly detailed inlaid woodwork, which Brenda pointed out. The women looked around in silence, taking it all in, then after stopping to admire the adjacent bell tower, Evie quickly consulted the map and confirmed that they were just a moment away from Via San Cesareo, which Brenda assured them was one of the most delightful streets in the old town.

Via San Cesareo was lined with shops, but they were nothing like the cool, minimalist boutiques of Corso Italia. Small cafés and shops crammed with rails of linen clothes competed for space with grocers whose boxes of soft peaches and oversized knobbly lemons were piled up beneath canopies hung with waxy red chillies. The scent of fresh pastries wafted invitingly from a bakery. Bluebell inhaled deeply.

Amongst the jostling crowds, traditional artisans were competing to attract their attention. One woman in a denim smock was painting her ceramic pots with big sweeping brushstrokes; a man was bent double, stitching the sole of one of a pair of leather sandals and a wizened elderly woman peered through stern spectacles at the bag she was weaving. Tourists bumped into each other and shouted at their friends to stop for a selfie whilst Italian mothers bargained with stall holders and remonstrated with recalcitrant children. Overhead, strings of colourful flags crisscrossed the narrow street. Josie took a couple of photos. They would be perfect for *Loving and Knitting's* Facebook page.

After wandering for a while, Brenda suggested they set off towards the Villa Comunale, Sorrento's public park overlooking the sea. On the way, they paused in the tranquil Piazza della Vittoria by a dramatic winged war memorial.

'This seems to be a monument to the First World War,' said Miriam. 'I don't know much about that period but my father-in-law, Jim, was in this area during the Second World War. He was part of the Allied landings in 1943. Operation Avalanche, they called it.'

'I was reading up about that the other day. About 100,000 British troops and almost 70,000 Americans landed along the Amalfi Coast. There was quite a bit of fighting on the Salerno plain before they were able to make their way up towards Naples,' said Brenda.

'Colin's father was in a battalion that landed at Maiori. He was lucky there weren't any German troops stationed in the town, though apparently there was fierce fighting on other parts of the coast,' said Miriam.

'Maiori is right near where we're staying. It's the next little town along in the opposite direction to where we've come today,' said Josie.

'I'll have to look it up,' said Brenda. 'What's so funny?' she added as everyone laughed.

Evie consulted the map again, and they were soon standing in the Villa Comunale admiring the spectacular view over the Gulf of Naples. The sun was sparkling on the blue sea and the bulk of Mount Vesuvius was clearly visible in the distance. Under this tranquil sky it was hard to imagine that the slumbering grey volcano had once erupted so fiercely. As Brenda gave a succinct summary of the dramatic destruction of the towns of Pompeii and Herculaneum, Bluebell felt a shiver run through her.

'Like someone walking over your grave, isn't it? One moment you're cooking or bathing or walking the dog; the next you're turned to ash only to be dug up by archaeologists hundreds of years later,' Josie said.

'No one knows what will happen tomorrow,' said Evie.

'That's why it's so important to make the most of today. And I suggest our next stop is lunch down in the marina if everyone's hungry. There's a lift that takes us straight down,' said Josie.

'Shall we just take a quick peek at the Church of Saint Francis and the medieval cloister first? Then we can head off for lunch if that's okay with everyone,' said Brenda.

They walked up a few stairs into the imposing church, which stood just outside the park. The end of each pew was decorated with a posy of pale pink roses and large spheres of roses interspersed with clouds of delicate white gypsophila were mounted on a pair of columns near the entrance. After a brief look around, they entered the adjacent cloister.

'Oh, look! A wedding party,' Evie said, pointing to the group gathered within the cloister's pale, arched walkways. A tall, slight man sporting a camera with a large telescopic extension, which hung from a wide canvas strap around his skinny neck, was corralling the guests into different groups. The men wore sleek suits accessorised with sunglasses and tan leather lace-ups or Gucci loafers. The female guests were extraordinarily elegant, wearing evening-style dresses of royal-blue chiffon, look-at-me scarlet ruffles or close-fitting trouser suits with towering heels. There was no sight of the floral dresses with cotton cardigans or sturdy pastel two-pieces worn at a typical English wedding for fear of upstaging the bride.

There was no chance of upstaging this bride: her long thick hair was loose down her back, accessorised with pearl-trimmed combs from which a sweeping scallop-edged train fell to the floor. The bodice of her dress was sewn from thick guipure lace over a nude underlay; her skirt was made from layer upon layer of soft white chiffon that fell to the floor. Her groom in his dark blue mohair suit, snowy white shirt and silvery blue tie was heart-breakingly handsome.

Bluebell smiled. She could just imagine Andrea wearing a well-cut suit like that, standing in front of the purple bougainvillea cascading down the walls of the ancient cloister.

'My next-door neighbour's daughter got married in Italy last year,' Miriam said.

'I couldn't get married abroad. I'd want to get married in the church near home where Mum and my gran, Granny Blue, both got married. Though I can't imagine I'll get married at all,' Bluebell added, quickly dismissing the fantasy she had been indulging in just a few moments before.

'You don't know what's around the corner,' said Miriam. She had a faraway look in her eyes.

'Like Vesuvius erupting again and wiping us all out as we're eating our lunch!' Bluebell quipped.

'Nothing like being optimistic! I think we're pretty safe from that. At least, let's hope so as we're off to Pompeii tomorrow.'

The Marina Grande harbour was lined with beach clubs and platforms overlooking the sea where restaurants served up fresh fish that had been caught from the local fishing boats that morning. Soon Bluebell was passing round a patterned ceramic dish loaded with *bruschette* fragrant with oil and garlic, topped by the brightest chopped tomatoes and shredded basil.

Josie helped herself to a third piece.

'You're so lucky. I don't know how you manage to stay so slim,' Bluebell said.

'Nervous energy.' Josie grinned.

'I can't imagine you ever being nervous. You never seem to get ruffled.'

'Really?' Josie looked momentarily stunned. 'I was totally stressing when I found out that guided tour lady wasn't going to show up.'

'You seemed pretty calm to me. I can't imagine ever organising a trip like this. I'd have enough trouble planning a day trip to Brighton.'

'Can't you just see us all eating sticks of rock and sitting on donkeys,' Josie said.

'Stop making me laugh!' Bluebell could feel her sparkling water bubbling back up her nose. 'But seriously, Josie, you're doing a fantastic job.'

'Thanks,' Josie said. She shot Bluebell a grateful smile.

The *bruschette* were followed by local fish accompanied by several serving dishes piled high with spinach, peppers and aubergines cooked until they were soft and velvety. They were soon demolished. The women did not dare look at the dessert menu, knowing that another generous meal would be waiting for them back at the Hotel Sea Breeze that evening.

Josie called for the bill. 'Everyone's free to do whatever they like this afternoon. We're not meeting Massimo for nearly two hours.'

Evie, the smallest and frailest of the party, declared that she needed a rest after lunch. She was quite sure the others would now manage to find their way around without her orienteering skills. What's more she had her special secret knitting project in her bag that she wanted to work on. Leaving Brenda to explore the old churches, Bluebell, Josie and the others set off for a general wander around that might, just might, entail a trip back down Corso Italia to window-shop in some of those tempting boutiques.

Sometime later, they made their way back to the main square where Evie was happily sitting on a bench by the clock tower. Nearby, a horse and trap waited in the shade of a tree whilst its driver took a nap.

Bluebell and Miriam sat together in the minibus whilst Massimo drove them back to the Hotel Sea Breeze. Everyone seemed to be looking forward to an early night. Everyone except Bluebell. She had her date with Andrea to look forward to. A holiday fling was just the sort of confidence booster she needed right now. What's more, she was dying to try on the prettiest dress of them all – the orange full-skirted number covered in big white poppies. She might even wear it tonight. Who was she kidding? She was definitely going to wear it tonight.

Chapter Ten

It was the first time Bluebell had been on the back of a scooter. Her heart was pounding in her chest as she leant into the bends as Andrea instructed. Her arms were around his waist, but her palms were clammy. The orange poppy-print dress probably hadn't been the wisest choice as it rode up her thighs as they sped along. But tonight she didn't care. She could feel the warm evening sunshine on the back of her neck as the breeze lifted her hair.

In just a few minutes they arrived at the neighbouring town of Maiori. Bluebell spotted an old convent on the left as they passed the sweeping port area full of little sailing boats. They rode along the seafront, which was separated from the sea by a tree-lined boulevard. The other side of the road was lined with small shops and hotels.

Andrea turned into a wide road leading away from the sea into the heart of the town. He parked his Vespa in a side street near the entrance to Bar Bruno, a dimly lit, old-fashioned bar. Bluebell peered inside to see an elderly waiter elegantly balancing a tray laden with drinks as he weaved between tightly packed wooden tables. Iron wall-lights cast a soft glow over the terracotta-coloured walls, which were covered with a series of faded colour prints of Vesuvius. Rows of mysterious, dusty bottles lined the shelves above the counter where patrons young and old perched on three-legged stools to drink and chat. She was entranced but Andrea led her further up the street to a doorway beneath a blue neon light spelling out the words *Bar Gino*.

Bar Bruno looked as cosy and welcoming as a trattoria in an old fishing village. Bar Gino, on the other hand, had a clinical, brightly lit interior dotted with white shiny tables decorated with odd, black curvy vases, each containing a single pure white bloom. The walls were covered with arty black-and-white photos in identical silver-coloured frames and there were far too many mirrors about for Bluebell's liking. Rather haughty-looking girls in tight red dresses poured drinks behind the bar and groups of fashionably dressed young people jostled each other as they waited to be served.

'My favourite bar. Much more modern than the one we just walked past,' Andrea said.

'It's great,' Bluebell said, though she was thinking how much more comfortable she would have felt in the unpretentious interior of Bar Bruno. Andrea left her sitting on a chrome, leather-topped bar stool and went up to the bar to get the drinks without bothering to ask what she wanted. At least she was excused the difficulty of having to choose. She did not recognise some of the brightly coloured drinks that people were sipping, and she tended to have a minor crisis of confidence if she was ever handed a wine list.

She noticed several girls checking out Andrea as he made his way to the bar, but tonight she did not have the old familiar feeling that people were wondering what she was doing with someone so handsome. It must be the effect of the poppy-print dress: the fit-and-flare style skimmed over her slightly ample hips and gave her a waist she did not know she had. Unlike the pastel colours she had worn for so long, it lit up her complexion with its sunny hue.

Andrea returned with two orange-coloured Aperol spritzes in large bowl-shaped glasses accessorised with old-fashioned paper cocktail umbrellas. Bluebell giggled but he did not seem to understand why she thought it was funny.

Their conversation wasn't exactly flowing, either. Bluebell had to talk quite slowly and Andrea, not surprisingly, could not always find the right words. He tried asking a few questions about her life in London, but after a while he gave up trying to find out anything about her and just talked about himself. She leant forwards trying to follow the thread of his stories, but she didn't care how very little they had in common as she looked into his dark eyes and his hand brushed lightly against her arm.

After a while she noticed that he had stopped talking and was looking over her head at something or somebody.

'Please excuse me. I must go and say hello to my cousin. She is sitting over there,' Andrea said. He smiled winningly, his white teeth sparkling under the fluorescent lighting. Then he leapt up so quickly Bluebell had to put her hand out to steady their table.

'My cousin, she speaks no English,' he added over his shoulder as if fearing that Bluebell would follow him. She watched him pick his way over to the far corner of the room where a rather attractive blonde girl who looked more Scandinavian than Southern Italian was sitting.

Bluebell sipped her Aperol spritz, opening and closing the pink cocktail umbrella, which was now lying on the shiny white table.

'*Scusi!*' The man's voice made her jump. She turned around. It was one of the three Italian guys who had been sitting on the table behind them.

'Yes?' she said, automatically speaking in English, though '*si*' was one of the few Italian words she knew.

'Oh, sorry,' he replied in perfect English, backing away slightly. 'I, err, sorry.' He pushed an untidy fringe away from his forehead. She noticed that his eyes were exceptionally blue.

'Sorry for what?' she said.

'I didn't realise you were English.'

'Oh, is that a problem?' she joked.

'Oh, not at all. I'm English myself. I've been staying here teaching English for a year. It's just I thought you were someone else. It's that dress, you see – she wore one just like that – and your dark hair. But when you turned around I realised you weren't her.'

'The dress isn't really mine,' she began but the boy was looking at her strangely and his friends were pulling on their jackets and gesturing for him to join them.

'I'm Bluebell,' she said, hoping to delay him, but he was warily eyeing Andrea's approaching figure, probably suspecting that a red-blooded Italian would not take kindly to someone chatting up his girl.

'David. Nice to meet you,' he said quickly over his shoulder as he and his two friends headed for the door.

Andrea glared in David's direction then purposely turned Bluebell's head towards him. He gazed into her eyes with an unwavering intensity. The appearance of another man seemed to have brought out his competitive instincts, the slim blonde apparently forgotten. He ran his fingers through her long hair, pushing it up away from her face. Then with one hand still entangled in her hair the other gripped her forearm as if to make sure that escape was impossible.

Bluebell felt her heart pounding as Andrea leant across the small table and lightly brushed his lips against her own. Then he moved his mouth over hers more forcibly, his tongue tracing the outline of her lips before pushing between them and kissing her with quite startling intensity as if they were two lovers in an old black-and-white movie. She felt her insides turn to liquid in a way they had never quite done with Jamie. Then just as quickly he released his grip. He leant back in his seat and picked up his drink, but he kept his eyes firmly focused on hers.

Bluebell drank her next Aperol Spritz a bit too quickly and was too slow to stop Andrea from fetching another. Was it just the effect of the alcohol that was responsible for her light-headed state or Andrea's eyes burning through her clothing as he mentally undressed her? She wasn't sure she could stand up without wobbling. How was she going to manage to stay on the back of his Vespa for the journey back to Minori?

As they left Bar Gino and made their way to where he had parked the scooter, she steadied herself by clinging on to his arm. She clambered onto the back in a rather undignified fashion, the orange poppy-print dress half caught up in her knickers.

When they reached the end of the road Andrea parked by the seafront then took her hand and led her along the promenade and down onto the sand. She ignored the warning voice sounding in her ear and relaxed into his arms as he kissed her. Her head was spinning; the holiday feeling and the effects of the Aperol Spritz were intoxicating.

'You like to swim?' he said. He took her hand and led her to the edge of the shore.

'You're not really thinking of going in, are you?'

'Why not? Don't you like the skinny-dipping?'

She wasn't sure if he was having her on or if he was really about to peel off all his clothes. The thought made her giggle but even after a few drinks she didn't think she was really the kind of person who would happily just throw her clothes off and run into the sea – she was far too English for that. And how on earth would they dry off? The cotton scarf knotted around her handbag strap wasn't much bigger than a hanky.

'It's too cold to swim. But like this, it's okay, I think,' Andrea said. He removed one of his shoes and dipped his toes in. Feeling relieved, she followed suit and they walked in the edge of the water for a few yards until he took her hand and led her up the sand away from the shore, where they used her little scarf to dry off their feet and put their shoes back on.

He put one hand firmly on her shoulder and the other on her back. Then he began to kiss her passionately, holding her so tightly that she could hardly breathe. Bluebell gasped as his hand began working its way up under the skirt of her dress and inched towards her knickers, the rather sturdy, unglamorous knickers she had bought from the household shop in Ravello. She felt a frisson of excitement, but unwelcome thoughts started to intrude on her conscience. It was dark, the beach was deserted and not a soul knew where she was. She couldn't get away from him even if she wanted to. But why would she want to? This was what she wanted, wasn't it: a thrilling, meaningless fling?

Andrea started to undo the buckle on his jeans. His shirt was hanging open revealing his smooth brown chest. Bluebell could hear the rhythmic pounding of the waves and as she looked up at the sky there was a chink of light as a cloud passed, allowing the soft light of the moon to illuminate his dark eyes glinting under strong brows and the determined set of his jaw. She was in the arms of the most handsome man she had ever kissed, on an Italian beach in the moonlight. So why did her stomach feel as though it was being kneaded by invisible fingers? What was wrong with her? Why couldn't she relax and have a bit of fun for a change?

As Andrea reached into her dress to unhook her bra, the still of the evening was interrupted by an increasingly loud barking coming from the promenade. A large furry dog threw itself at the pair of them, practically knocking Bluebell off her feet. Andrea leapt back as the fluffy white beast started leaping all over him, licking his arms and face.

'Quick, quick! Run!' he shouted wildly.

'It's okay, I think he's just being friendly,' Bluebell said.

'The dog, he is okay. The owner is problem.'

'Why?'

'My ex-girlfriend. We must run. Quick!'

'I'm sure she won't mind her dog saying hello to you,' Bluebell replied, trying to suppress a smirk at the look of panic on Andrea's face.

A woman's voice was calling from the promenade: 'Ludo, Ludo!' Bluebell looked up to see a woman in her fifties climbing down the steps onto the sand.

'Oh my God! Her mother,' Andrea whispered. 'Ludo – get down!' he hissed. 'Get down! GET OFF my leg!'

Andrea endeavoured to shake off the randy beast as Bluebell tried in vain to stifle a fit of the giggles, but she soon lost the battle and was doubled up laughing so hard that her stomach hurt.

'Andrea?' the woman shouted. Then as she got nearer and noticed Bluebell, her expression changed for the worse. 'Andrea, *che fai?*'

It was pretty obvious what Andrea had been doing, or trying to do, from the way he was hurriedly fastening his belt buckle. The mother was bearing down on them, but she turned away for a second, distracted by a girl shouting something from the promenade.

'Is that your ex?' Bluebell asked.

'Yes, my ex, but I have a big problem. She does not know she's my ex.'

'Oh,' Bluebell said, suddenly grasping the situation. A bust-up with some feisty Italian girl, let alone her formidable-looking mother, was the last thing she wanted in her wobbly state. She scanned the beach. Perhaps she could find something that would distract the dog. As the younger woman ran towards them, Bluebell spotted an old trainer lying in the sand. She swiftly grabbed it and waved it under Ludo's nose. The dog was immediately interested in the smelly old shoe, so she threw it as far as she could.

The dog hurtled down the beach. Andrea grabbed her hand and they legged it to the waiting Vespa. Somehow, she swung her right leg over the back and sat down with a jolting thud. She put her arms around Andrea's waist and clung on for dear life.

As they sped away, she turned to see two figures running after the scooter yelling and gesticulating. She could not understand what they were saying but she was pretty sure she had just learnt the Italian for *you cheating bastard*.

The scooter roared back down the seafront, past the convent and the tourist port then rounded the bend on the road back to Minori. A few minutes later they were pulling up outside the Hotel Sea Breeze. She thought Andrea might try to come up to her room but instead he paused outside the revolving door to try and kiss her, but she pushed him away. She wasn't going to do to another girl what Jamie had done to her.

Andrea didn't try to persuade her. He stepped back looking embarrassed, said goodnight and rode away. Perhaps he had a conscience after all. More likely he wanted to get home and lock the door before his girlfriend and her mother turned up.

Bluebell collected her room key from Reception, glad of the discretion of the man on the night desk who had pretended not to notice Andrea. She fell into the lift still feeling a little light-headed. Miraculously her room key worked first time despite her fumblings. She headed straight for the minibar, retrieved the bottles of still and sparkling water and glugged them down one after the other. She cleaned her teeth, to hell with removing her make-up, and fell thankfully into bed, alone.

Chapter Eleven

Michela and Paolo were both exhausted, not having a free moment between cooking and serving all day long in Il Gattino whilst Maria was with their father at the hospital. But when the last customer had left, and they finally sat down, Michela was bubbling over with the excitement of sharing her plan. It wasn't a plan she had really thought through, but the idea was intoxicating.

Her brother listened silently as Michela told him about the *For Sale* sign in the window of Trattoria di Napoli. 'If we all worked together, we could buy it, Paolo, I'm sure. Il Gattino has been Papa's life, but you know how he used to talk about owning a restaurant like Mr Amati's. Think what a boost it would be to him to have that at last. A new project would give him so much to live for when he's better. The flat above it is so much bigger too. Nonna Carmela could move in with us and I'm sure she would put the money in from the sale of her little house. She knows how much it would mean to him. And I'll work there. I don't need to go to work in our cousins' big restaurant in Positano; I can stay right here. And maybe you could move back here too.'

'I'm sorry, Michela,' Paolo said firmly. He reached across the table to hold her hand. 'It's a lovely idea but it's just impossible. Papa is going to have to slow right down. He might struggle to keep Il Gattino going. He can't start running a bigger restaurant.'

'He could if we all helped him. We could all work together. We could take on a couple of extra people at the weekend. We could keep on the boys who work for Mr Amati. They're going to want to keep their jobs, aren't they? I've got so much more experience after being in London and you were always a great cook.'

'Michela, I'm a lawyer now. I can't go back to working in a restaurant again. Papa wanted me to follow my dreams. Don't you remember how proud he was when I finished law school? He wouldn't want me to leave all that and move back here. I love Mamma and Papa and I love Minori. It's always going to be close to my heart, but my life's in Naples now.'

Michela was silent for a minute. He was right. Papa had been so proud that his son had been the brainy one of the family, the one to leave the hands-on restaurant business and start making a name for himself at the law firm in Naples. But she needed Paolo to make this work.

'But it would be perfect if Nonna Carmela moved in with Mamma and Papa. I don't know how she manages in that funny little house. All those steps! They're hard enough in the summer, but she can barely go out in winter it's so treacherous. Not having to imagine her breaking a hip will be one less worry for Mamma.'

'You know as well as I do that Nonna Carmela is the most wonderful granny in Minori but she's the most stubborn little lady who ever lived. There isn't a chance she is going to sell that house to come to live in a flat above a restaurant. Mamma has talked to her about moving so many times and she says she's only leaving that house in a box.'

Michela sighed. It had been such a wonderful idea. Perhaps Paolo was right, and it wasn't going to work out, but that didn't mean she couldn't try, did it?

Chapter Twelve

Bluebell shot upright. For a moment she wasn't sure where she was. Then her eyes alighted on the orange poppy-print dress tossed over the back of the rattan chair. Memories of the night before came flooding back but they were all in a jumble: riding a scooter with the wind in her hair. The beach. Andrea.

She remembered walking along the wide boulevard by the sea with his jacket wrapped around her shoulders. He'd suggested going skinny-dipping. Surely she hadn't. No, no, she remembered now. The sea had been too cold, thank goodness. Perhaps he thought she was disappointingly unadventurous. Then she remembered his mouth on hers, warm and insistent, how her lips had responded and that warm feeling spreading through her body.

It was no use, she wasn't going to fall back asleep again; she might as well be the first one down for breakfast for a change. She showered, lathering the honey-scented gel over her limbs, imagining Andrea's hands doing the same. She took a yellow halter-neck dress with a pattern of white daisies out of the case. She looked at the seams – another dress that looked homemade. Again, it fitted her perfectly.

She was just dragging a brush through her hair when another memory came out of nowhere: the English boy in Bar Gino who thought he recognised her until she turned around. He'd introduced himself just before he left. Did he say Darren or Damien? No, David – that was it. Now she remembered it all: David was working as a teacher in Maiori. And he almost certainly held the key to finding the real owner of the orange poppy-print dress, the owner of the suitcase that she really ought to try to return.

She picked up her mobile and checked her emails. Not surprisingly, no one from the airport had responded to her message. She rang the airport's Lost Luggage room again. It rang and rang . . . Then somebody answered.

Bluebell tried in vain to explain the situation but the worker at the other end of the line wasn't much help.

'So, madam, I still no understand. You lose a big case, or you find a big case?' Roberto sighed.

Bluebell tried again. 'Yes, that's right. My name is Bluebell Virginia Baker and I have lost a big, paisley-patterned, purple-and-pink case and I have taken by mistake a big, paisley-patterned, purple-and-pink case belonging to someone else.'

'Okay, okay,' Roberto said wearily. 'You find a big case. Yes? Big purple-and-pink case. Yes? And you lose a case too. This one a big purple-and-pink case, yes? You are sure this big case you find is not the big case you lose? Okay, okay. We no have any big cases, pink and purple.'

Roberto thought it all sounded very fishy. Two purple-and-pink, paisley-patterned cases. In all his years at Naples Airport he had never seen luggage like that. And one case was supposedly owned by this person calling herself Blue Bell. 'Okay, lady, when you fly back you bring to the airport this big case and we put it here in the lost luggage. Then we look for the other.' That would get rid of her. Crazy English people. He was going to have to deal with them all summer.

Bluebell stuck the phone back in her bag. There was nothing more she could do. She couldn't help feeling a little bit pleased that she didn't have to give up the flattering clothes just yet. She walked down to breakfast feeling gorgeous and guilty.

The hotel dining room was quiet. Bluebell wondered where Andrea was before remembering it was his day off. She was quite relieved that she did not have to talk to him. She had to admit she had been enjoying the evening until Andrea's girlfriend and her mother appeared – it had been good to flirt with someone and feel desirable again – but that was enough. She was going to have plenty more fun on this holiday without wasting any more time on a guy like that.

She made her way over to the *Loving and Knitting* group's table where Miriam was sitting.

'No one else here yet?' said Bluebell.

'No one else is mad enough to be up early today. We had a bit of a late night after all. You missed a fun evening; we all ended up walking down the town and having a nightcap outside Trattoria di Napoli. The owner is such a lovely, hospitable man.'

Bluebell thought she detected a smile playing at the corners of Miriam's mouth when she mentioned the smartly dressed proprietor and wondered whose idea it had been to return to the restaurant. 'He's rather handsome for an older man,' she said encouragingly.

'Oh, I hadn't really noticed,' Miriam said, but she did not sound very convincing. 'But by the way, don't you have something to confess?'

Someone was bound to work it out eventually. This yellow daisy dress was designed for a young Sophia Loren not a pale English girl like her. Miriam must have put two and two together.

'I have been feeling a bit guilty. I know I should have said something about the suitcase before, but the clothes are just so perfect, like they were made for me, well, a more attractive version of me.' Bluebell stopped talking, realising Miriam was looking completely bewildered.

'I meant a confession about your night out with Andrea. But what's all this about your clothes and your case?'

Miriam listened wide-eyed as Bluebell explained the whole story and told her about the strange encounter with David, the English boy at Bar Gino.

'I've got an idea,' said Miriam. She raised a finger in a silencing gesture as the other women came over to join them.

Brenda was clutching a well-thumbed copy of Mary Beard's *Pompeii*. 'I'm so excited. This is the highlight of my week,' she declared.

Bluebell wasn't sure wandering through the ruins of a buried city was quite her thing. Maybe she was just lacking in imagination. Her slight hangover wasn't helping either, despite another hearty and not entirely cake-free breakfast.

The women were soon assembled in the lobby chatting excitedly about the day ahead. As they made their way towards the exit Miriam toppled forward, missing Brenda by millimetres. Bluebell put out her arm to break Miriam's fall, but it was too late – she was left clutching at thin air.

The others could only watch in horror as Miriam let out a strangled cry and fell – straight into the back of a substantial sofa.

Bluebell gasped as Miriam grabbed on to the solid piece of furniture. Worst-case scenarios flashed through her mind: an ambulance; hours waiting in Casualty; hospital doctors who didn't speak English.

Josie went white. 'Oh, Miriam! Are you okay? Are you hurt?'

'Oh, no, I'm fine, but my ankle – it's . . .' Miriam bent down slowly and rubbed it.

'Sit down for a moment,' Brenda suggested.

Miriam sank into the squidgy cushions on the striped sofa. 'That's better.'

'Shall we get someone to take a look at it?' Josie said.

'Oh, no. It's nothing serious but I don't think I'll be up for walking around Pompeii. I'm going to have to stay here, I think. Bluebell, would you be a dear and keep me company?'

Bluebell quickly agreed before anyone else had the chance to volunteer. She tried not to look too pleased. A day by the pool was much more appealing than tromping around ruins and if Miriam's ankle improved they might take a little stroll into the town.

After plenty of well-wishing and a chorus of *oh dear what a shame* the others set off to meet Massimo by the minibus.

No sooner had they departed than Miriam leapt to her feet with no sign of any injury. Bluebell was momentarily lost for words. She could only gaze at Miriam in astonishment.

'Don't look so shocked, Bluebell. I told you I had a plan and the sooner we get going the better.'

'Going where?'

'Back to Maiori, of course. You said this David character was teaching at a school there. If we can track him down we're bound to find out more about the owner of your mystery case.'

'And get mine back,' Bluebell said gloomily.

'We don't even have to get the bus. I looked at the boat timetable in Reception and there's a ten o'clock boat to Maiori. It's only a few minutes away by sea.'

Bluebell looked at the clock behind the reception desk. 'It's nearly nine,' she said.

'That's perfect. We've just enough time to discuss tactics over a coffee at Trattoria di Napoli.'

They set off straight away, pausing only for a couple of minutes so that Miriam could pick up a handful of postcards at the newsagent on the square.

The silver-haired owner of Trattoria di Napoli was sitting at one of his outside tables, but he leapt to his feet as Bluebell and Miriam approached. He seemed delighted to see the two women. He ushered them to one of the larger tables, pulling out a chair for Miriam.

'*Grazie*. I'm Miriam. *Mi chiamo Miriam.*'

'I am Tommaso. Like Thomas. *Piacere* – pleased to meet you,' he replied, his brown eyes softening. Miriam ordered two cappuccinos whilst Bluebell took out her phone and started Googling. Soon they were looking at a list of schools in Maiori.

'There seem to be a few different schools, but it shouldn't take long to work our way round them,' said Miriam.

'But what will we do? Hope someone speaks English and ask if someone called David teaches there?'

Before Miriam had chance to reply Tommaso returned, carrying a tray with their drinks along with a small terra-cotta pitcher of water and two glasses.

'Perfect, thank you,' said Bluebell. He placed a cup and saucer in front of her. She noticed he had dragged the surface of the milky froth to make a pretty swirl on it. Then she suppressed a smile when she saw that he had created a delicate rose on the surface of Miriam's. It was just the sort of thing Andrea would do, but she couldn't imagine anything else the playboy waiter would have in common with this courteous man.

They took a few sips of their drinks and then Bluebell said, 'I think David might have been searching for this girl for a while. He seemed really disappointed that I wasn't her. If he's been looking all this time what chance have we got of finding her even if we do manage to track him down?'

'He may have been too busy with his pupils to look for her properly and anyway three heads are better than one,' Miriam said.

'I guess so.'

'Would you excuse me a moment?' Miriam pushed back her chair. 'I'm just going to pop inside and pick up a snack to put in my handbag in case I get hungry when we're out and about. I'm sure I noticed some of those wafer biscuits by the till.'

'Okay.' Bluebell picked up her teaspoon and toyed with the remnants of her cappuccino. She was surprised Miriam wanted something else to eat after the substantial breakfast they served at the Hotel Sea Breeze.

The minutes ticked by. Miriam was taking an awfully long time to purchase a packet of biscuits. Bluebell was about to get up and follow her inside when she saw Miriam and Tommaso in the doorway. One of them must have said something very funny because they were both laughing quite loudly.

Miriam hurried back to the table. 'We'd better go,' she said. She turned and gave Tommaso a wave. He returned her wave, smiling broadly.

They bought two return tickets at the wooden kiosk at the top of the pier and made their way to join the small crowd who were waiting for the boat for Maiori to arrive. As the boat was pulling in, Bluebell took the opportunity to take out her phone and send a text to Granny Blue: *Having a wonderful time. Busy solving a real-life puzzle!*

'Maioooori! Cetaaaara! Salerrrno!' a very suntanned fellow in tight pink shorts bellowed as he ushered the small crowd down the gangplank. They climbed the stairs to the top deck and sat on one of the wooden benches in the sunshine. Miriam glanced around, satisfying herself with the number of lifeboats. She had watched *Titanic* far too many times to be complacent.

The boat trip from Minori to Maiori was only a five-minute hop. It was mainly tourists who took advantage of the service, the local people preferring to take the cheaper bus that ran along the coast, too busy thinking about their daily tasks to luxuriate in the view of sea and sky that Miriam and Bluebell were now enjoying. For a moment they were tempted to stay on the boat to its final destination of Salerno, the sailing was so delightful.

They disembarked and made their way along Maiori's seafront, following the route that Bluebell had travelled on the back of Andrea's Vespa. This time she walked on a wide pavement laid with grey stones in which white stones were interwoven to form an attractive fan pattern. Benches were scattered around, and leafy trees provided a shaded canopy. Out beyond the beach, small rowing boats and pedalos were entertaining other tourists on the sparkling blue sea. Other tourists who weren't on a crazy mission to search out a boy one of them had met for all of two minutes, a boy who might lead them to an unknown girl who owned an orange dress printed with white poppies.

'We haven't really got a lot to go on,' said Bluebell, but she kept practising the sentence they had learnt from *Google Translate*, which was now written on the back of a spare postcard next to their list of schools. *Un inglese di nome David lavora qui?* Does an Englishman called David work here? They soon had it learnt off by heart, no matter that neither of them knew how they would be able to continue any such conversation once it was started.

'What's the worst that could happen?' said Miriam.

'We get chased off the premises because they think we're a pair of crazy Englishwomen.'

'They'd be right, then.'

'Speak for yourself!'

They turned off the seafront into the main street, ignoring the temptation of a leather-goods emporium brimming with handbags of all sizes and colours. As they headed up the road, Bluebell pointed out the turning that led to Bar Gino where she and David had met so briefly. They paused outside the Palazzo Mezzacapo, taking a moment to glance through the old iron gate leading to the formal gardens within, but there was no time to waste on tourist attractions, so they hurried on.

The sound of children playing drifted towards them. It seemed to be coming from behind a high wall. They followed the noise until they came to a gate leading to a playground where several dozen children in blue smocks dashed here and there whilst the odd loner leant against the wall with a book. A painted sign confirmed they were at the town's *Scuola Primaria*, which they guessed must be the equivalent of a primary school, judging by the age of the children running about. Bluebell's hands felt sweaty as she pushed open the door.

The entrance desk in the grey and rather gloomy hallway was unmanned but there was a large brass bell. Bluebell was just wondering whether this would summon a receptionist or accidentally announce the end of break time when a rather stern-looking lady of a certain age appeared. The woman wore a pair of spectacles on a chain around her neck and sported a thick, striped cardigan despite the warm weather. She looked like the sort of teacher who could quell bad behaviour with a raised eyebrow. Bluebell was instantly transported back to standing in the corridor outside the head teacher's study.

'May I help you?' the teacher enquired with the air of someone who assumed that the two intruders were tourists who couldn't tell the difference between a primary school and an ice-cream parlour. Relieved that they could speak in English, Miriam and Bluebell both started to talk at the same time, eliciting a rather withering look. Bluebell clammed up and let Miriam do the talking.

After ascertaining that they were searching for someone who was not only English but also taught English, the woman was quick to disappoint them. The school employed two people who taught English: a Miss Dell'Olio and a Miss Berlusconi, both resolutely Italian and definitely female. No Englishman was present on the premises and the women were left in no doubt that the appearance of such a fellow would be most unwelcome. Glad to leave the rather oppressive atmosphere inside the school for the sunshine outside they made a hasty departure and were soon heading back to the main street.

The two adventurers turned right into Via Roma past the Convent of San Domenico then headed away from the sea, stopping only for a quick detour to climb the steps to the square in front of the church of San Pietro in Posula. Soon they came to a blue board stating the name of the second school on their list. This time there was no shrieking or laughing coming from the playground. Break time here was over. The children would be back at their desks. Was there any chance at this very moment one group was being taught English by a man called David? They paused outside the entrance to practise their question in Italian then pushed open the sturdy wooden door.

A man of around David's height and build was standing with his back to them reading the school noticeboard. Could it really be him?

Chapter Thirteen

Bluebell's heart was pounding, her mouth was dry and she swallowed noisily but as soon as the man turned around she knew it wasn't David. It was crazy to think they would find him so easily. But there was something familiar about this boy and he was looking at her as if he was thinking the same thing.

'*Buongiorno. Un inglese di nome David lavora qui?* Good day. Does an Englishman named David work here?' Miriam asked as Bluebell continued to wonder why the fellow looked so familiar.

'David? An English teacher called David?' he replied in English. 'I'm an Englishman called Oliver if that's any help. Are you sure you're in the right place? I've got a friend called David who teaches English, but he doesn't work here.'

'To be honest, we're not sure at all,' Miriam began.

'But we are definitely looking for David,' Bluebell said. She looked at Oliver expectantly.

'I knew I'd seen you before. I'm right, aren't I? You were the girl David started to chat up in Bar Gino. You were with your Italian boyfriend so we all scarpered quite quickly.'

'Oh, he wasn't chatting me up. He thought I was somebody else because of the dress I was wearing. I didn't get the chance to explain to him that the dress wasn't mine.'

'Whose dress was it, then?'

'I don't know. That's why we're looking for him.'

'You're looking for David because you don't know whose dress you were wearing? If you don't mind me saying that's more than a little weird. I've got a free period before my next class. I should be doing some marking, but I'm tempted to pop out for a coffee. Why don't you both join me then you can explain a bit more and if you can convince me you're both not crazy stalkers I'll tell you where David's teaching.'

'That's fair enough and I could do with a sit-down, to be honest,' said Miriam.

Oliver led the two women to some rickety seats outside a small café hidden in a back street, the sort of place no tourist was likely to find. 'My new local. I love the way the cafés here sell beer and wine as well as coffee. It means you don't have to decide what you feel like until you're actually sitting down. I shouldn't have a beer though as I'm teaching so I'll have an espresso. You know the Italians never drink cappuccino after eleven, but don't let me stop you.'

'No one's going to stop me having my cappuccino. It's so delicious here,' Bluebell said firmly.

Oliver leant forward, his espresso untouched, as Bluebell explained the whole story of the suitcase mix-up and the colourful homemade dresses she had found inside.

'So that's why we're looking for David,' she concluded.

Oliver was silent for a moment. His brow creased in thought. 'You do realise this is a very serious matter,' he said.

'Serious?' Miriam said. Her voice quivered slightly.

Bluebell gave a nervous laugh and smiled at Oliver. He wasn't smiling back.

'This is theft. You can't just take someone else's clothes and go around wearing them.'

'But I'm going to give them back,' Bluebell said. Her voice sounded curiously high-pitched.

'This sort of behaviour may be acceptable in England but in Italy it's a police matter.'

'Police. Oh my God!' Bluebell said.

'Yes. I'm afraid I'm going to have to turn you in.' Oliver's jaw was set tight; his eyes were flinty.

Bluebell's hand flew up to her mouth. She looked at Miriam for support. Then she looked back at Oliver. He had dropped his head and was looking down at the table. His shoulders started to shake with laughter.

For a moment, Bluebell was completely bewildered. She glanced at Miriam who was looking equally confused. Then a feeling of blessed relief washed over her. 'I can't believe you tricked me like that!' she gasped.

'I am so sorry. I just couldn't resist it.' Oliver wiped his eyes. He took a sip of his espresso. 'Ugh, it's gone cold.'

'That's the least you deserve,' said Miriam primly, though she was trying not to laugh.

'Now you really do owe us,' Bluebell said.

'Here, let me get you something to eat, then I promise to tell you where David's working.'

He unfolded Miriam's pocket map of Maiori. 'See, just here. This is where David is working.'

They leant forward to see where he was pointing. 'Thank goodness we ran into you. That wasn't on our list of school addresses at all,' said Miriam.

'That's because you probably weren't looking for a *liceo scientifico*. A *liceo* is a type of vocational school. A *liceo scientifico* focuses on physics, chemistry and natural sciences,' Oliver said.

'A science school is the last place I'd expect to find an English teacher,' Miriam remarked.

'Italian schools are more specialised than English schools once you get older but pupils at a *liceo scientifico* still have to study a foreign language and English is really popular. It's a shame I can't come with you to see David, but I have to run. I'll just point you in the right direction. I'm sure he'll be interested to hear your story and I guess there's a chance you'll end up finding this girl between you. Tell him he owes me a drink if you do!'

'He was a nice boy,' said Miriam.

'Hmm. When he wasn't threatening to have me put away,' said Bluebell. She inhaled the aroma of her focaccia sandwich. 'Mmm, smells delicious.' She took a bite. Soft mozzarella oozed from the salt-sprinkled golden bread. It was perfect. She wiped some grease from her fingers with one of the flimsy paper napkins from the metal box on the table. She couldn't help lingering over every melting mouthful even though part of her wanted to bolt it down as quickly as possible so they could head off and find David.

Bluebell felt her heart thumping as they walked up a flight of stone steps into the imposing old building where David taught. He might provide some vital clues to tracking down the girl in the poppy-print dress. That must be why she felt so excited at the thought of seeing him again.

Once again, they were greeted by someone who looked them up and down and immediately spoke in English. Bluebell was secretly relieved that she hadn't got to try out the Italian question they had been practising but rather disappointed that she looked so obviously like a tourist despite wearing a dress that almost certainly belonged to an Italian girl.

'We are looking for David, the English teacher. We understand he works here,' Bluebell said.

'Yes, you are correct, madam. David has been teaching English for us this year. Sadly he is returning to England at the end of term. The school year finishes next week. We have a nice long summer holiday in Italy.'

'Would we be able to speak to him between classes today?'

'I am afraid not, madam. Our school days here are just from 8.30 until 1.30. David sometimes teaches up until the last lesson but today he has finished. I am afraid you have just missed him.'

'Would you mind telling us what time he is here tomorrow?'

'*Allora,* umm, tomorrow I am afraid, madam, he is not here. He works here just a couple of days a week. I believe he teaches some private English lessons to adults on other days. He will be teaching here, at the *liceo*, the day after next.'

'Would you be so kind and let us have his telephone number?' Miriam asked, giving the woman her most winning smile.

'I'm sorry, madam, that is against the rules. You must understand that we cannot give the personal details of our staff. It is forbidden.'

'We quite understand. Thank you for your time. Perhaps we will come back another day.'

The sky was as blue as ever as they walked back to the centre of town, but a grey cloud was hovering over Bluebell. They were so near but yet so far. Why on earth hadn't they just asked Oliver for David's number?

'At least we know where to find David now,' said Miriam. 'Perhaps we will try to come back when we have our free day. It's the day after next, isn't it? I must admit I am rather glad he isn't teaching tomorrow. I would hate to miss our trip to Positano. I'm looking forward to it so much.'

'We're going to Positano, David or no David. I certainly wouldn't let you miss out, not after having missed Pompeii today on my account.'

'I couldn't fake a twisted ankle two days in a row. I would feel far too guilty.'

'You were very convincing though. Shall we try to visit the Palazzo Mezzacapo before the three o'clock boat leaves? I'm determined you'll get to see more of Maiori than the seafront and a not very scenic tour of the town's schools.'

The entrance to the Maiori's biggest tourist attraction was firmly closed. They were out of luck. Bluebell studied the noticeboard fixed to the railing. The palazzo would reopen at four o'clock. She was about to turn away when she noticed that the padlock on the iron gate to the gardens had been left open.

Bluebell glanced around. No one was watching. She pushed open the gate; Miriam needed no encouragement to follow her in. Once they were inside, Bluebell spotted a low building marked with the international information sign, which appeared to house the town's tourist information office. Not surprisingly this was also closed, but an array of pamphlets had been left lying, perhaps by accident, on a table outside.

Miriam picked up a leaflet. '*Inside the Palazzo there is a mirrored salon and some beautiful frescoed ceilings.* What a pity we can't go in.'

'Good afternoon, ladies.' A small man with a luxuriant black moustache had appeared seemingly out of nowhere. He bowed theatrically.

'We're terribly sorry, we know you're closed. We just couldn't resist having a quick look round,' said Miriam.

'Sorry. No need to be sorry. I am always glad to see two beautiful ladies. Have you enjoyed looking at the gardens?' He gestured at the neatly manicured borders and pink rose bushes.

'Yes, but it's a shame we can't get to see inside the palazzo,' said Miriam.

'Nonsense, nonsense, just follow me. I have a key and there is one room that you must see. There is one thing us Italians like more than making rules and that is breaking rules.'

'If you're sure you won't get into trouble with your boss.'

'I am the boss.' That sounded unlikely but as he was equally unlikely to be a serial killer they exchanged glances and followed him through the shady entrance then through a large door and up a dramatic, wide stone staircase. 'The most beautiful room in the Amalfi Coast,' he announced.

It was a room fit for the grandest of parties. The walls were painted a blend of rich pink and terracotta, broken up by ivory panelled doors decorated with gold leaf and tall mirrors decorated with more gold. A heavily frescoed ceiling soared above their heads; mermaids rode on breaking waves; angels blew long trumpets and chubby cherubs frolicked amongst billowing pink-and-white clouds that covered the soft blue sky. Bluebell was momentarily lost for words.

'Magnificent, isn't it. Many people get married here, even the English,' he said. He looked meaningfully at Bluebell.

'It's a beautiful place for a wedding,' Miriam said.

'We had one here yesterday, a local couple. You can see they have left some of the flowers behind, here on this table. It was our oldest couple so far, I think. She was ninety-two and he was three years older than that.'

'Goodness,' said Miriam.

'They met at the hospital, in the outpatients department, and soon as they saw each other they immediately felt much better! Love can strike at any age.' Now it was Miriam's turn to receive a meaningful glance.

'Stories like that are so lovely,' said Bluebell. To think she had once felt washed up at twenty-eight. Yesterday's newlyweds probably could not even remember back that far. Not that she was remotely interested in getting married, though perhaps she might feel differently if she was ninety-two.

'There are some rooms along the corridor where we hold art and photography exhibitions. Please feel free to look around for as long as you like. You do not need a key to get out; just lift the handle on the door we came through.'

As Bluebell admired the local artists' watercolour seascapes Miriam was lost in her own thoughts. Since Colin had died she had just assumed that she would be on her own forever. The love story of two old folk marrying in that beautiful room after meeting in such unpromising circumstances had touched her. For the first time since her husband's death she dared to wonder if it was possible to find love again. It was said that the Amalfi Coast was one of the most romantic places in the world; it must be casting a spell over her.

As they walked back from Minori's port towards the Hotel Sea Breeze, Bluebell was quiet, pondering the day's events. It had been too much to hope that they would manage to track down David. They had come so near to finding him. She walked slowly, looking down at her trainers.

'Look at those!' Miriam said. Bluebell looked up. Miriam was pointing at some flamboyant bikinis in a glass case on the wall. Next to that was the entrance to a small shop. A sign above it read *Casa Emilia*.

'Shall we take a look inside?' asked Miriam.

'Why not?' said Bluebell. 'But I don't really need anything; it's not as though we are spending all day by the pool.'

'I don't think need really comes into it, do you?' said Miriam.

It took a couple of minutes for their eyes to become accustomed to the dim light in the small shop. Most of the interior was taken up by a long L-shaped, built-in counter behind which were rows of wooden glass-fronted drawers that reached up to the ceiling, whilst below the counter several long drawers filled the space right down to the floor. In one corner three headless shiny white mannequins stood in a small group. One sported a zigzag-patterned tankini in six or more shades of blue; another showed off a plunging halter-neck costume patterned with parrots and a matching chiffon sarong; the third wore a teeny red bikini trimmed with small wooden beads. Other bikinis in a bewildering variety of shapes and sizes were pinned onto one of the walls. A short sale rack of oddments was squeezed up against a curtained alcove, which looked to serve as a rudimentary changing room. A woman standing behind the counter greeted them with a beaming smile.

'Good afternoon. I am Emilia. Please do take a look around. I have most of these designs in other colours.'

She did not add the inevitable *can I help you?* No doubt she had the sense to realise that those words were likely to send anyone English scurrying back out the door in a trice.

They looked around and thumbed through the items on the sales rack, until Bluebell's eye was caught by a polka-dot bikini. It was simple but stylish, with an unusual edging of dainty white pom-poms.

Emilia obviously didn't miss a trick. She spotted Bluebell's admiring glance. She opened one of her many drawers and pulled out the bikini in Bluebell's size, along with others in the identical style but with the background in mint green, navy and a bright sunshine yellow.

'Pick the one that makes you smile,' she said.

Bluebell hesitated. Up to now she had been quite happy to wear the trusty, rather substantial bikini that she had fortunately packed in her hand luggage. It was typical of the type of holiday clothes she packed for her summer holidays with Jamie: sensible, inoffensive and rather safe. Jamie had always hated anything that he considered too skimpy or showy, though that certainly hadn't stopped him from being attracted to Carrie's lithe figure when she pranced around the holiday villa's pool in her sequin-trimmed string bikini.

Emilia was still holding out the bikinis, smiling. Bluebell smiled back. She reached for the daffodil yellow with its penny-sized white spots. It was perfect. Perfect for someone else – someone younger or thinner or prettier or with more of a tan. Emilia pulled back the curtain into the changing area. There was no harm trying it on, was there? She wasn't really going to buy it.

'And for you, madam?'

Miriam shook her head and Emilia did not try to persuade her otherwise. She probably knew from experience that any attempt to push someone like Miriam into trying something on before they were ready would only have one result: they would never come back.

Bluebell looked in the mirror. A week ago she wouldn't have dreamt of purchasing one of Casa Emilia's vibrant creations but now here she was trying on a yellow polka-dot bikini that said: *here I am*, not: *don't look at me I'm hiding in the corner*. She had left London feeling dull and dispirited; being twenty-eight and single had seemed like a failure when all around her friends seemed to be announcing their engagements. Now she could see herself how Miriam, Evie and the other prizewinners saw her – young and energetic with her whole life ahead of her. She might not be conventionally beautiful but she had thick, wavy hair and eyes that sparkled with life. Her figure was far from slim but instead of being hidden under saggy dresses it was now flattered by the fifties styles she had borrowed. And this bikini was just as lovely.

She emerged from the changing area with a smile on her face, which dipped only slightly when Emilia told her the price.

'This is a quality item and a classic design, which you will enjoy wearing for years to come, I hope. I think you are worth it, yes?'

She handed over her credit card, feeling only slightly sick.

Bluebell and Miriam stepped out of Casa Emilia, blinking in the sunshine. There was just time for a short spell by the pool before Josie and the other four prizewinners returned from their outing to Pompeii. And sure enough, the other ladies found the two of them enjoying the last of the sun by the pool, books in hand and looking like butter wouldn't melt in their mouths.

'We've had such an exciting trip,' said Brenda. A hefty guide to Pompeii was protruding from her overloaded green shoulder bag.

'It was a lot of walking,' said Evie. 'Very interesting but my feet are killing me. I managed a couple of little sit-downs but I must admit there were moments when I envied you two lolling by the pool all day.'

Bluebell felt her face glowing. She made her excuses and was just heading for the lift to go back to her room and have a bit of a snooze when Josie appeared. 'Would you like to go for a walk? I sometimes take a stroll out before dinner. It must have been a bit dull hanging around the hotel all day.'

Bluebell tried not to look too guilty. She couldn't really refuse. Especially as Josie believed she hadn't moved ten yards all day. Anyway, it would be nice to spend a bit of time with the indefatigably cheerful young woman.

After changing back into her trainers – thank goodness she had travelled out in them – she met Josie in the hotel reception.

Josie led her down through the town to Piazza Cantilena. They went through a small arch next to the imposing yellow basilica of Saint Trofimena and up some stone steps. Then more, more, steps each seemingly steeper than the last.

Fortunately, they stopped part of the way up to rest on a bench.

'Now are you going to confess?' asked Josie.

'About Andrea or about the case?'

Josie frowned. 'I'm dying to hear about your date with Andrea, but I didn't mean that, and I don't know anything about a case. I'm talking about your little outing with Miriam today.'

'Oh, how on earth did you find out about that?' Bluebell said. Had the party of ladies stopped off at Trattoria di Napoli on the way home and been tipped off by Tommaso?

'I realised I had left my phone in the room and when I nipped back to get it I spotted you and Miriam hightailing it out of the hotel heading for the seafront and neither of you looking remotely incapacitated.'

Josie listened as Bluebell stammered over her words and confessed the whole story. 'It really is a bit cheeky of you, Bluebell, though I guess there's a chance this other tourist is wearing *your* clothes right now. I suppose there's nothing we can do now 'til we get back to the airport but you should have said something earlier. I'm not sure you'll be able to claim anything on your insurance you've left it so long.'

Bluebell sighed. She hoped it wouldn't come to that. She had always assumed that she would get her own case back eventually. She tried to put it out of her mind as they continued their climb, looking down on the exquisite little town below them and out to the sea beyond. On the other side the rugged hillside was dotted with small houses; above them lay the town of Ravello. They paused for a while, then having got their breath back they walked towards the road that sloped back down towards the town centre. To their right a steep flight of steps led up to a small, narrow, old house painted a soft marshmallow pink. For a moment Bluebell assumed it was uninhabited. Who would live in such a place up that treacherous-looking set of steps, isolated from near neighbours by what looked like old farmland that had long since fallen into disrepair?

'Look at that quaint, deserted old house,' she said.

'I think someone's still living there. Look, there's an open window at the side,' said Josie.

The two women climbed a few of the steps towards it, egged on by curiosity. As they got nearer, they looked at each other in disbelief. The curtain flapping at the upstairs window was made from a piece of orange cloth patterned with white poppies.

Chapter Fourteen

Bluebell and Josie stood staring at the poppy-print curtain wafting in the evening breeze. 'It's just a coincidence,' said Bluebell, though she could feel her heart racing faster. They looked at each other and without further ado climbed the rest of the steps and walked around one side of the house. Bluebell peered through the rather smeared window glass into an old kitchen. The interior looked straight out of a period drama. A long wooden work surface, stretched along one wall, was cluttered with old crockery. Above it hung a variety of pots, pans and colanders on a series of metal hooks. And there, beneath the slightly chipped old butler sink, was a gathered cotton curtain made from a piece of material patterned with life-size sunflowers, just like the dress that she had worn on their trip to Ravello.

'But this can't be the house where the mystery girl lives,' Bluebell said. 'No one in their twenties or thirties would live somewhere like this. It looks like someone elderly lives here.'

Before she could say any more, Josie picked up the large door knocker and banged it three times against the chipped green paint of the old front door. They waited and waited but there was no reply. Then Josie looked at her watch and gasped. It was less than half an hour until dinner. They hurried back down the steep steps, thankful for the old iron handrail.

As they started to walk down the sloping road leading back towards the main part of the town, Josie turned to Bluebell. 'Now you can tell me about your date with Andrea.'

'Why don't we grab a drink at the hotel bar after dinner one night and I'll tell you all about it?'

'You're on. I can't wait!'

Bluebell picked up a forkful of *caprese* salad; it looked and tasted delicious. The chef at the Hotel Sea Breeze had done them proud. The soft, fluffy buffalo mozzarella seemed to melt in the mouth, the local tomatoes were such a startling red they seemed to be glowing and the plate was brightened further by the green basil leaves. The spaghetti with clams that followed was equally moreish but for once she couldn't wait for the meal to end. She was dying to tell Miriam about the marshmallow-pink house with the poppy-patterned curtain.

She tried to focus on the conversation going on around her. The women were full of enthusiasm about their outing to Pompeii. Brenda, in particular, was buzzing with excitement and recounted the tour in so much detail that Bluebell felt certain she could not know any more about the place if she had been there herself.

She looked across the table. Miriam was twirling the same piece of spaghetti round and round on her fork. She had a dreamy, half-smile on her face and her eyes were focused on something in the distance.

Bluebell hardly tasted her grilled sea bass. At last the final course arrived – a densely rich chocolate torte decorated with some tiny wild strawberries. No matter how much she wanted to talk to Miriam this was worth taking her time over. Everyone stopped talking and attacked the dessert with gusto. At this rate they would be in danger of sinking the boat to Positano tomorrow.

Worn out by a long day walking around ruins, the other women made their excuses and headed to the lifts for an early night. Bluebell and Miriam were left alone. At last, Bluebell could tell her about the pink house on the hill.

Chapter Fifteen

Michela wrapped her mother's old striped apron over her jeans. After only a few days back in Minori she did not need to do up the belt so tightly. Maybe she would end up wearing all her homemade dresses again. She thought guiltily of the pink-and-purple suitcase hastily dumped in the corner of her childhood bedroom, but she hadn't found a spare minute to unpack since arriving and hearing the news of her father's sudden heart attack. There had been no need to sort her things out straight away. Her work uniform of black skirts and a set of freshly ironed white blouses were, as always, hanging in the cupboard at the back of Il Gattino and she had either been working in the café bar or rushing around doing other chores in her old jeans. Now she was busy cleaning and scrubbing. Papa was coming back from the hospital tomorrow and everything must be spotless.

She fetched the wicker waste basket from the back room and the plastic bag from the kitchen bin and dragged them round to the large dustbin in the alleyway. A thin tortoiseshell cat peeked out from behind the row of bins. Although Michela spoke to him softly, he shrank away, waiting for her to go before he nosed around looking for scraps. Another bolder, slightly fatter cat sat on the step of her neighbour's storeroom further down the alley.

Those concrete steps held so many memories. So many hours sitting there, reading a picture book or playing with her doll. In later years she sat there with her schoolbooks, pretending to be working whilst she watched her brother and Stefano kicking a ball along the alley. On rare occasions she was permitted to join in their games, but they soon grew tired of her fumbled attempts at keeping goal and lack of tackling skills. Best of all were those days when Mamma or Papa called Paolo away to attend to his homework or run some errand and for a short while she and Stefano were left alone in the alleyway with only the stray cats for company. Sometimes he would insist that all girls were boring and go off home or into the kitchen to help Mario or Maria, but as he got older he did this less and less. By the time she was thirteen or fourteen they often sat together in the shade of the doorway chatting and writing their names in the dirt on the step.

Stefano surprised everyone with the amount of time he spent at Il Gattino, seemingly preferring the dark and rickety kitchen to the much more glamorous surroundings of his parents' home behind the Basilica of Saint Trofimena and the grand hotels they owned on Maiori's seafront. He spent hours perched on the rickety stool in the corner of the kitchen and after much begging Maria had finally allowed him to give her *ragù* its regular stir with a long-handled wooden spoon. He was even happy to help scrub clean the pots. Both her parents became very fond of the young lad. She had never felt more content than when they sat together doing chores handed out by Mamma and Papa, though she was usually too tongue-tied to speak.

One day she had crept out of school early and was skulking around the alley, kicking a stone, when three local boys appeared. She recognised them immediately as regular troublemakers, so she folded herself up as small as she could in the very corner of the doorway. She was so quiet that a thin, dirty white cat bravely padded over and sat by her, batting at her skirt with its grubby paw. Its loud meow alerted the three boys who chased it into the corner of the alley, throwing small stones at the terrified creature.

'Do you like that, cat?' the tallest boy said, his mouth twisted into a sneer. He picked up half a brick and looked at the other two boys who nodded approvingly. As he raised his arm, Stefano appeared out of nowhere and knocked the brick to the ground, swiftly followed by the boy himself. 'Sorry,' the boy squeaked feebly as Stefano held him in a headlock, whilst his two cowardly friends legged it. Then Stefano made it quite clear that under no circumstances would the bully or his mates be seen walking down that alley again. After checking the cat was okay, he put an arm around Michela. She pretended that she was still scared so that he would keep it there a little while longer.

And then it happened. Her first kiss. She could remember it like yesterday: his soft, warm lips, his strong arms wrapped around her, the sweet-salty scent of his sun-warmed skin. She had never known anything like it; she only knew that she wanted to kiss him again and again.

After that they would meet in the alley after school and sometimes down on the pier. How wonderful those times were, talking and kissing and dreaming about the future. 'We'll have a big house one day and our own restaurant right by the sea,' Stefano had told her. And she had believed him.

Then one day, Paolo and his other friends caught them together. They teased Stefano mercilessly. There was nothing less cool than kissing your friend's little sister. Stefano stopped coming to the alley; he hung around with his mates instead. When he was older he dated a series of local girls whose heads were turned by his money and trendy clothes. Michela did not care less about those things or what model of Vespa he rode around the town. She didn't want a candlelit dinner in Trattoria di Napoli. She just wanted to be with him.

By the time she was about to turn eighteen, Stefano was embroiled in an on-off relationship with a girl from Amalfi. So, Michela agreed to go to the pizzeria with Fabio. She did not have the heart to turn him down; she knew how much courage it had taken him to ask her out. She still saw Stefano around the town. He rarely stopped to talk but that did not stop her thinking about him. Despite all the evidence she always believed that they would be together one day. It was fate. She swore she could see it in his eyes in the rare moments when they were alone together.

Then one day Stefano landed a job as a waiter at Chucky Joe's, an American chain that served up cheap burgers and pizzas that were delivered frozen and heated up rather than cooked in the traditional wood-fired ovens of the Italian south. Mario was horrified; he could not believe that his protégé could commit such crimes against food. Michela was even more upset when she found out the job was in Rome. It might as well have been on the moon. Stefano was gone and he was never coming back.

From time to time she still allowed herself a little fantasy. She would be walking down by the sea and she would suddenly see him sitting on a bench overlooking the beach or leaning against the end of the pier watching the small boys with their rods and buckets by the *No Fishing* sign. He would turn towards her, pushing that thick, dark hair away from his chocolate brown eyes and say . . . Well, who cared what he would say; he would look straight at her and tell her he wanted to be with her and her alone.

Three years had passed. It was about time she faced the facts. Nonna and the gossips in the market were wrong. Stefano would never return to this small seaside town when he had the whole of Rome at his disposal. And, more to the point, all the girls in Rome to choose from.

She replaced the dustbin lid; she had enough to do without wasting her time daydreaming. She went back inside the house and picked up a duster. Three hours later she proudly surveyed her handiwork. The whole place looked tidy and the smell of wood polish mingled with the fresh flowers brought by well-wishers. Tomorrow she would wear one of the dresses her grandmother, Nonna Carmela, had made for her – perhaps the orange one with the white poppies. It might still be a little loose but it was one of her father's favourites. She would hang it up before she went back to work so any creases would drop out. She dragged her neglected suitcase onto the bed and unzipped it.

Michela stared blankly at the contents of the suitcase. Inside there were no skinny London-girl black jeans, no bright fifties-style dresses, just a collection of pastel maxi skirts and saggy-looking tops. And it was only half full, too. No wonder she had thought it was lighter than she remembered.

She cursed herself for not attaching a luggage tag, but what on earth were the chances that someone else on the same flight would have such an unusual piece of luggage? This case probably belonged to one of the English tourists on her flight, but as people flew into Naples to stay in Capri, Ischia, Sorrento and the whole of the Amalfi Coast, not to mention the holiday towns down on the Cilento Coast, the owner could be just about anywhere. There was a chance her own case might still be at the airport, a very small chance. There was only one thing she could do. She picked up her mobile, called the airport and asked to be put through to the lost luggage desk.

Roberto picked up the phone reluctantly; he was busy checking the racing results. Would you believe it! Another crazy woman phoning up about purple-patterned cases. This was definitely a wind-up. 'Not again! I tell that other lady, I have no pink cases, no purple cases, no paisley cases and no blooming blue bell cases! Bring this lost or found case or whatever it is when you come to the airport and don't call again.'

Michela put down her phone. She couldn't deal with this strange fellow, not today of all days. She would ask Paolo if he could take the case out to the airport for her when he returned to Naples and hope and pray that he would find her own case languishing somewhere in the lost luggage room. There was still a chance it could be there. She just hoped someone else would be on duty when Paolo got there.

Chapter Sixteen

Bluebell looked up as Josie joined her at the breakfast table, looking radiant after her morning jog. Josie was clutching a fresh peach in one hand and a natural yoghurt in the other, making Bluebell feel guilty that her portion of fresh fruit was once again sharing her plate with a *cornetto con marmellata* – a soft brown croissant filled with a deliciously sticky apricot jam. At least she was getting plenty of vitamins with her daily glass of blood orange juice, which had plenty of healthy-looking bits floating in it.

Andrea was back on duty and brought her cappuccino with a smile. She was startled to discover that she had almost forgotten him in the excitement and intrigue of the last twenty-four hours. She gave him a cursory smile.

As they left the dining room, Bluebell noticed a very attractive blonde girl sitting in the reception area nonchalantly leafing through a glossy magazine, which definitely wasn't a copy of *Loving and Knitting*. She looked familiar. Of course, it was the girl in the bar Andrea claimed was his cousin. Judging by the care she had taken with her appearance she certainly wasn't here for a family catch-up.

The old Bluebell, the self-conscious assistant manager of a rather unexciting high-street bank, would have been mortified to have been replaced by this girl with her model figure and classic good looks. The new Bluebell was surprised to discover that she didn't feel the slightest bit put out. She just felt sorry for Andrea's long-suffering girlfriend.

Bluebell had more exciting things to think about than romance. She had a mystery girl to track down, and there was David, the English teacher, too. It would be such a shame if they couldn't find him as well. He might know something about the strange pink house with its orange poppy-patterned curtain. But all that would have to wait until their free day tomorrow. Today they were taking the boat trip to Positano, one of the places she was looking forward to seeing most of all.

Josie did a quick head count. All the six ladies were assembled and ready for their next outing. Walking two abreast they headed down through the town towards the pier. As usual they left in good time, but their progress was continually impeded by the pedestrians and vehicles going about their business. Mopeds whizzed past, motorists pulled up across junctions to stop for a chat. At one point they all had to press up against a wall to avoid being crushed by a three-wheeled truck, the open back loaded with crates of oversized fruit.

'Look over there, Bluebell,' Josie said. She pointed down one of the narrow side streets at a slightly rusty sign cut in the shape of a sleeping cat. Written in italic letters were the words *Il Gattino* and below that *Café Bar.* 'I noticed it when I was out jogging this morning. We're supposed to be going to the big pizzeria opposite the hotel this evening, but I was wondering whether we should try that cute-looking place instead. I don't know if it will be any good; it's just a hunch.'

'Sure. Why not? It will be fun to go somewhere off the beaten track. It'll probably be a bit less touristy,' Bluebell said.

'That's what I thought. It's such a good group of prize-winners this year. When we were in Seville last year most of the ladies loved the leisurely pace of Spanish life, but I had two who kept complaining about the slow service. They couldn't bear all the garlic-laden tapas and lack of a full English breakfast so we ended up eating in all the safest touristy places where they could order chips with everything.'

'What a shame. I'm sure you can be more adventurous this year. Everyone seems to be embracing the Italian way of life already. We all loved that evening at Trattoria di Napoli. The owner was so charming.'

'You're right. I'll cancel the pizzeria and see if we can get a table in that little place tonight.'

As Josie ushered her charges across Piazza Umberto, the proprietor of Trattoria di Napoli leapt to his feet with a small wave. Bluebell wasn't sure if it was her imagination, but she could have sworn she saw his eyes linger on Miriam for a few brief seconds.

Josie had organised the boat tickets the day before, so the women went straight down to the bottom of the pier. Brenda, as usual, was busy with her guidebook, looking up the history of their destination. According to Brenda it was a roller-coaster tale of dramatically rising and falling fortunes: a story of nomadic hunters, Greeks and Romans, seaquakes, pirates, great wealth and abject poverty. Fortunately for the people of Positano its recent history was less traumatic. A modern road linking the town to the bigger cities of Naples and Salerno had brought a gradual influx of tourists so that by the 1950s it had become a fashionable destination. Elizabeth Taylor and Picasso were amongst the beautiful, rich and famous visitors. Today, six readers of *Loving and Knitting* magazine would join that illustrious roster.

The short hop to the port of Amalfi went without a hitch and Josie quickly found the correct spot on the pier for the boat that would take them to Positano. The once-blue sky started to cloud over and a splash of rain landed on Brenda's guidebook. They all looked up in surprise. Rain certainly wasn't part of the plan and no one was dressed for inclement weather.

'Just the odd shower, I expect,' Josie said brightly. No one noticed the old boatman gesture at the sky and shake his head.

'The average rainfall on the Amalfi Coast in June is only thirty millimetres so there's no need to worry,' Brenda said. She was proved quite right, as after a few half-hearted drips the rain vanished as they walked up the gangplank onto the larger vessel.

The boatman checked their tickets and gestured towards the internal lower deck. '*Piove*. It rain,' he said grimly. 'You want to sit indoors? No? Okay. You get wet.'

Bluebell wasn't going to let the odd splash of rain wreck her boat trip. She was looking forward to sitting on the open deck and looking at the scenery, and little Evie was more than happy to take the risk and sit with her. Bluebell looked around for Miriam, but Brenda was leading her inside.

The boat began its slow passage following the coast back in the direction of Naples. To their right they could see the beaches between Amalfi and Conca dei Marini. They rounded the cape of Conca and had just passed the entrance to the famous Emerald Grotto when a few drops of rain started to fall. Evie was keen to go back inside, and a kind gentleman helped her down the steep staircase back into the boat's interior. Bluebell declined to follow her; she was determined to complete the journey from the best vantage point, right at the front of the boat. What harm would a light sprinkle of rain do, especially in this weather where you would dry off in no time? She noticed that someone had vacated one of the white benches opposite, leaving a large red-and-white-striped golfing umbrella behind. She got up to get it. Now she was prepared for anything the weather could throw at her. She wondered why so few people were willing to risk a light shower; the top deck was all but deserted.

The sky turned an ominous slate grey and a splattering of rain hit the bench beside her. Bluebell fumbled with the golfing umbrella. The button was stiff but she managed to force it open. Within a few seconds the rain had become heavier and the view of the iconic coastline was obscured by a heavy mist. *The rain will be gone again in a minute,* she told herself, but she was glad of the umbrella as the downpour grew heavier and heavier. The wind began to whip up and any pleasure she had gained from her vantage point on the upper deck had completely vanished. She might as well go in, but as she stood up to walk the length of the deck back to the steep metal stairs a massive gust of wind nearly knocked her off her feet and turned the umbrella inside out.

She sank back down onto the bench, wrestling in vain with the umbrella as she was buffeted by the wind. It was now sheeting down in monsoon-like quantities but without the warm air that she guessed would accompany a tropical downpour. Suddenly an almighty gust ripped the umbrella from her weakening grip and it sailed through the air like Mary Poppins before landing in the sea where it bobbed about like an injured swan.

She clung on to the bench as the wind got stronger. The hairs on her arms were standing on end from the cold and the rain was soaking right through her dress and running in rivulets down her bare legs. She lurched from side to side, clinging on to the railing, trying to make her way towards the back of the boat. A final gust battered her backwards, banging her knee painfully against the side of one of the benches. An invisible hand seemed to grip her stomach as she noticed that there was no one else left on the top deck. She sank back down onto a bench, exhausted, drenched and shivering.

Miriam watched the raindrops as they trickled down the window. Surely it would not stay like this all day. The Italy of her imagination was always bathed in sunshine. Still, they'd make the most of their visit, whatever the weather; that's what women of her generation did.

The boat's crew were now shutting all the windows and ordering the passengers to sit down. As Miriam looked out into the gloom she saw something go flying past the window into the sea. It looked like a giant origami crane, but then she realised it was just an umbrella. She instinctively reached into her shoulder bag. Her little telescopic brolly was in there, tucked in next to her cardigan. She never went anywhere without either to hand; after all she was English. She wondered how young girls of Bluebell's age managed with their tiny cross-body bags. Oh. My. Word. Bluebell. She had noticed Evie come inside but Bluebell must still be out there.

Miriam could hear the wind and rain crashing against the boat. Her mind conjured up a picture of Kate Winslet clinging on to a chunk of the sinking *Titanic*. Without a moment's hesitation she got up and started to make her way towards the back of the deck. Luckily Josie seemed to have taken in the situation and swiftly followed her. A burly crewman put out his arm. 'Sit down! No one to go on deck. Is dangerous.'

'There's a woman out there. She's stuck on the deck. We must go and help,' Josie said.

'She might be in trouble. She could be swept overboard,' said Miriam. Her voice came out in an old-lady quiver, but she didn't care.

'Please,' said Josie. She fixed her big green eyes on the man and batted her lashes.

The crewman shrugged. He folded his arms and turned away.

'Can I help?' asked a polite English voice.

Miriam turned to see a young man. He was in his late twenties, possibly thirty. His dark hair was in need of a cut and a fringe fell into bright blue eyes. He was wearing loose trousers, a short-sleeved linen shirt, probably bought locally, and he had a tan, which suggested he had spent quite some time in the area despite being obviously English.

'Oh, please. If you can. Our friend is stranded on the deck, but this man won't let us pass,' Miriam said.

As Josie continued to plead with the unbending crew member the stranger ducked past the crewman out the door and onto the outside deck.

Bluebell hunched over in a vain effort to protect herself from the elements. The wind was making her eyes run and water dripped down her back. The daisy-print dress, now sopping wet, clung to her body.

Suddenly the wind dropped. A moment later the rain stopped as quickly as it had started. The mist lifted; she could even make out a faint shaft of sunlight trying to force its way out from behind the clouds. She could see the port of Positano in the distance.

She stood up slowly. As she did so, she could see the top of someone's head as they climbed up the ladder from the lower deck. A male voice called out, 'Are you okay? Let me help you down.'

A young man made his way towards her, pushing his rain-soaked fringe off his face. Drips of water ran down his forehead and pooled on his eyelashes. He blinked them away. He stretched out an arm to take her hand.

'Hang on a minute. I know you, don't I?' he said.

She stared at him in astonishment. 'David?'

'Bluebell? From Bar Gino? What on earth are you doing out here?'

Chapter Seventeen

'Come on, let's get you inside,' David said.

Bluebell did not need asking twice. David held out a tanned hand, which she took in hers as she tentatively climbed down the stairs. In less than a minute she was inside but still shivering. He handed her a grey cotton jacket that was lying across the back of one of the seats. Realising her dress was now completely see-through she did not need much encouragement to put it on. The other ladies flocked around him, introducing themselves and treating him as a hero although he insisted he had done nothing more than climb a few stairs.

'You must join us for our morning coffee as a way of saying thank you,' said Josie.

'Yes, we insist,' said Miriam, though he did not seem in any hurry to leave them.

As the boat pulled into the harbour at Positano they made their way out of the cabin into beautiful sunshine. There was a collective gasp as they took in one of the most beautiful sights of the Amalfi Coast and rummaged for their phones and cameras.

The harbour was lined with colourful small boats and to the right stretched a long beach covered with loungers and parasols. Built into the rock face behind the seafront were row upon row of colourful houses stacked up on the hillside climbing higher and higher towards a bright blue sky.

Vivid flowers cascaded over sea-facing balconies. Painted shutters led into unseen rooms behind the white, yellow and pink façades. Between the rows of houses the dark shapes of cars sneaked along the road, which wound around the cliff face. Below them boutiques and restaurants promised untold delights. Most beautiful of all was the majestic dome of the Church of Santa Maria Assunta with its green, blue and gold majolica tiles shimmering in the sunlight.

To Bluebell's relief and delight a large boutique with racks and racks of summer dresses was positioned just along the seafront. Although David's jacket was preserving her modesty, getting into dry clothes was the most blissful thing she could imagine. Once she was certain that he had definitely accepted the invitation to join their group for morning coffee, she and Miriam headed for the boutique.

As soon as the others were out of earshot she grabbed Miriam's arm. 'It's him! The guy I met at the bar in Maiori! It's David! The one who thought he recognised me.'

'Oh my goodness! He's the key to the mystery. We can't let him escape. Quick, quick, try these.' Miriam grabbed three dresses from one of the rails, thrust them into Bluebell's arms and pushed her towards the changing room.

There was no time to waste and even without the incentive of talking to David again Bluebell was in no mood to dally. She was desperate to get out of her clammy, wet dress and into something dry with a hot cappuccino within reach. She dismissed the first dress Miriam had grabbed – it was covered with real seashells and had *Positano* spelt out in diamanté around the hem. The second dress was a simple, pale linen – pretty but designed to blend into the background. Exactly what the old Bluebell would have chosen. The third dress was shocking pink with a turquoise bodice. It was a looser fit than the dresses she had found in the case, but the colour combination was bold and confidence-boosting.

Exiting the changing room wearing her new purchase and clutching the soggy outfit she had removed, Bluebell unpeeled two twenty-euro notes and handed them to the astonished woman behind the counter. Moda Antonia's customers usually left with their purchases wrapped in tissue and placed in glossy, branded carrier bags. They certainly did not walk out wearing them whilst dripping a trail of water from the changing room to the door. And as for this girl's tangled, windswept hair, Antonia could only hope a comb was her next purchase.

Clutching her soggy dress and David's jacket, Bluebell and Miriam hurried to find the others at The Old Fishermen. They knew that Italian waiters did not tend to rush about at the drop of a hat so there was every likelihood that their companions would still be sitting waiting to be served. Luckily, they arrived just as the waiter did so they were able to give him their orders immediately.

Bluebell was desperate to sit next to David but the seats either side of him were already taken. She squeezed in next to Josie instead. Josie tilted her head towards David and gave Bluebell a quizzical look. 'Is it him? The guy from the bar?' she whispered.

'How did you know?' Bluebell was astonished.

'He mentioned he was teaching English. There can't be that many English teachers called David round here.'

Bluebell nodded.

'I won't breathe a word,' Josie said. She sipped her coffee in silence whilst the other ladies chatted to their new companion. They seemed delighted to make the acquaintance of this rather good-looking young man who had been willing to risk the wrath of the boathands, let alone his own neck, to rescue Bluebell. He was disarmingly modest, insisting that he had merely climbed a few steps in a bit of wind and rain.

Bluebell hoped that her fellow prizewinners would soon find David's conversation less appealing than the attractions of Positano. She and Miriam must get him alone to see if he knew anything that would help them get closer to finding the owner of the poppy-patterned dress. She wanted to keep it a secret from the other prizewinners. She was sure that one or two of their party would disapprove if they found out she had purloined a stranger's wardrobe for the trip. And they would certainly disapprove of Miriam faking an ankle injury to excuse them from the outing to Pompeii. But for now she could only sit and listen, and hope they could get David alone.

Fortunately, Brenda was so keen to see all the churches in the town that as soon as her coffee was put on the table she gulped it down with indecent haste. One of the other ladies agreed to set off with her, happy to be dragged left, right and centre in the name of culture. The two empty seats next to David were quickly filled.

'So, how did you end up working in Italy?' Evie was asking him.

'It's a bit of a long story, so I'll try not to bore you,' David said. 'I studied French and Italian at uni then went to work at a bank in the City. I was on the international desk but I didn't get to use my languages much; our clients usually spoke perfect English. It was fun for a bit but the guys I worked with were fixated on making loads of money. It all just seemed a bit pointless after a while.

'I wanted to do something more worthwhile so I retrained and took a job teaching French at a big comprehensive in South London. I enjoyed the challenges; well, I enjoyed most of them. I ran the French club after school and in the holidays, but the school wasn't interested in offering Italian lessons. They had enough trouble getting most of the pupils to take one foreign language, never mind a second.

'When I spotted an advert to teach English in Italy I jumped at the chance. I've been teaching part time at a school in Maiori since September and giving private lessons to adults in my spare time.'

'So, is there no school today or are you playing hooky?' teased Evie.

'I am skiving off a little bit. I'm still teaching at the school 'til the end of term but I've dropped the private lessons, so I can do a bit of sightseeing. It seems daft to have been here nearly a year and not seen Positano or Capri.'

'I can't believe you haven't been to Capri! We're going the day after tomorrow. Why don't you join us if you're not teaching?' Josie could not help noticing how animated her competition winners had become in David's presence. Several of them were widows and clearly missed the chance to have some male company and conversation, and David's friendly demeanour and genuine interest was a real tonic. She also thought she caught him glancing at Bluebell slightly more than necessary. He was certainly a better bet than the smooth-talking Andrea. Bluebell had said she didn't want a serious relationship so soon after her break-up with Jamie, but Josie wasn't having any of that. You couldn't be the editorial assistant on *Loving and Knitting* and not be an expert on romance.

'That's very kind of you,' said David. 'I've been spending far too many hours wandering around by myself.'

'We'll really look forward to seeing you again,' said Josie. 'Everybody ready? If we set off now we'll probably catch up with Brenda.'

Bluebell lifted her empty coffee cup to her lips. She needed to buy some time. There was no way she was going to leave David before she had the chance to ask him about the girl in the poppy-print dress. She caught Miriam's eye. Miriam gave a little shrug. What could she do? She couldn't fake another ankle injury to delay them.

'Perhaps you should have another coffee, Bluebell. You need to make sure you warm up properly before you go back outside,' said Josie.

'I was thinking about ordering another cappuccino – this is one of the best I've tasted. What about you, David?' said Miriam.

'I can't think of anything better.'

Bluebell crossed her fingers under the table. And it worked. None of the other ladies had any desire to stay for a second drink. The sun was shining; the Church of Santa Maria Assunta was more enticing than any café.

Josie picked up her bag to leave. She touched Bluebell lightly on the shoulder. 'Good luck,' she said quietly. 'And by the way, that dress looks great on you.'

David stared at Bluebell and Miriam, his coffee untouched, as Bluebell recounted the story of how she had come to be wearing the orange dress with its distinctive white poppies. It seemed certain that the dress must belong to the girl that David had mistaken her for. She and Miriam were bursting to know about this stranger. And they were dying to tell him that they had a potential clue to her whereabouts: the curtains in the marshmallow-pink house on the hill.

'So, who is she?' said Miriam. 'Who is the real girl in the poppy-print dress?'

'You are going to think I'm crazy, but I don't even know her name. We didn't even speak. But she's part of the reason I ended up in Maiori.'

'Tell us more,' Bluebell demanded.

'The summer before last my parents had their thirtieth wedding anniversary. My mother had always wanted to see Italy, so Dad went a bit mad, booked a three-week holiday and hired a red Italian sports car. They drove from Pisa to Florence then on to Rome and Naples and ended up staying a week in Amalfi. I managed to get a couple of days off work and took a long weekend to meet them. We took a boat from Amalfi to Salerno so Dad could look at the famous cathedral – he's a bit of a culture buff. It suffered a lot of damage in an earthquake a few years back but there were plenty of medieval churches in the old historic centre for him to visit whilst Mum had a browse round the shops.

'The boat stops in Minori and Maiori on the way and it was there that I saw her. I was sitting on the top deck – Bluebell's favourite place! – with Mum and Dad and we were watching people getting on and off at Minori. People-watching – you know how it is. Dad suddenly said *there's a girl for you, son!* It's a bit of a running joke in my family about fixing me up with a nice girlfriend.'

Bluebell smiled. She wondered why. David seemed so nice it was surprising he hadn't been snapped up long ago. And the way he pushed that slightly too long fringe out of his eyes was rather endearing, not that she was interested, of course. A kiss on the seashore with a philandering waiter was quite enough for her this holiday. She needed something frivolous that could be forgotten a few minutes later, certainly not a relationship and all the complications that entailed.

'Go on,' said Miriam. David had paused; he was looking rather embarrassed.

'Well, I looked up and saw this girl getting on the boat. She was wearing this beautiful, fitted orange dress covered in white poppies that made her look like a fifties film star. She had long dark hair and she was obviously Italian. She had that golden skin of someone who lives in a place where the sun shines for months at a time. There was an old-fashioned glamour and an elegance about the way she moved. She sat outside on the lower deck, so I was able to watch her as the boat moved away. Dad was busy photographing Mum leaning against the ship's rail so I was able to watch her undisturbed. She had a couple of bags with her, which she put down on the bench beside her. She must have been shopping in Minori. There was something captivating about her; she seemed to embody the Italian *bella figura*, the art of presenting a beautiful face to the world. I suddenly felt this desire to go and talk to her.

'A few minutes later we docked at Maiori. A lot of people started getting up and I couldn't see her anymore. Then I saw her disembarking and walking through the port. I wanted to run after her but what would my parents think? Anyway, I knew it was crazy. As we sailed away towards Salerno, I could see her walking along past the old monastery. She was easy to spot, you see, with that vivid orange dress.

'Well, I kept my eyes open for the rest of the trip but of course I never saw her again. We had a great day in Salerno though and spent the next day pottering around Amalfi. The cathedral there is stunning.'

'Did you come back here to look for her?' asked Miriam.

'To be honest I tried to forget about her; it seemed so daft. I dated a girl called Sam, but it didn't work out. She kind of forgot to tell me she was still dating her so-called ex. It was more of an ego dent than a real broken heart, but it gave me another reason to leave London for a while. When I saw the advert for teaching jobs in Italy I did hope that I would somehow see her again. Most of the teaching posts were in the big cities, but I wanted to be somewhere less hectic after London and when I saw one of the vacancies was at a school on the Amalfi Coast I clicked on the link for more details. I couldn't believe it when the address was in Maiori. It seemed like fate, somehow, but of course I never did see her again. I'd given up hoping when I saw you that night in the bar. I couldn't forget that dress and with your dark hair for a moment I thought it was her. But as soon as you turned around . . .'

'I was a disappointment,' said Bluebell.

'Not at all,' he said, blushing. 'I hadn't really seen her face and yours is perfectly lovely. I just knew as soon as you spoke that you were English, and I could see that you were too pale to be living out here. It made me realise what a crazy idea it was to search for someone I didn't know just because they looked so captivating.'

'It's not crazy at all. I think it's very romantic,' said Miriam firmly.

'Well, whatever it is, I realised there's no chance of me running into her now. I'm leaving Maiori in a week or so. That's why I decided to get out and about and see a few more places instead of spending my spare time chasing after some silly fantasy. I'm going to live these last days to the full. After all, if I had decided to hang around in Maiori today I wouldn't be here in Positano having such a great time.'

'Well, we're both very glad you're here,' said Miriam.

'Actually, we've got a confession to make. We've been looking for you,' said Bluebell.

'You've been looking for me? Really, why?'

'We wanted to see if you could help us find the owner of the poppy-print dress. And anyway, it gave us a good excuse not to trek around Pompeii in the heat,' said Miriam.

'You seriously bunked off a trip to Pompeii to look for me?'

'Miriam faked a twisted ankle, so we didn't have to go.'

'That's outrageous!' David laughed. 'There's definitely more to you two than meets the eye. Maiori's not a very big place but it's not exactly tiny. How on earth did you think you'd find me?'

'Bluebell remembered you were teaching English so we started walking round the schools. We weren't having much luck 'til we ran into Oliver.'

'Oliver? I'm surprised he hasn't messaged me,' said David.

'He probably wanted to spare you from two crazy women,' said Bluebell.

'Crazy? That sounds about right . . . Ouch, no need to punch me!'

'Oliver did tell us where to find your school, but you'd already left for the day,' said Miriam.

'But then we bumped into you today. It just goes to prove that sometimes you only find what you're searching for when you stop looking for it,' said Bluebell.

'Like love,' said Miriam. Her eyes went all dreamy for a moment.

'Talking of which, I think I might have found the house where she lives,' said Bluebell.

'No! In Maiori? Where?'

'No, it's a house in Minori. Maybe the girl wasn't getting off that boat to go home. Maybe she was just visiting Maiori and has been living in Minori all along.'

'But if you found her case at the airport she must have been coming from London.'

'You're right. I assumed all along that the person who lost their case must be another tourist. I didn't think of it being someone returning home to Italy – someone who might live here – until I saw the curtain.'

'The curtain?' David frowned. Then Bluebell told him about her walk with Josie and the orange curtain patterned with large white poppies hanging at the window of the old pink house on the hill.

'We knocked on the door, but no one was there. The two of us were planning to go back tomorrow and try again. We've got a free day to chill out in Minori before our last big trip to Capri, so we thought we'd give it a try. There's just one thing though: when Josie and I looked in the window it didn't look as if anyone young lived there. It looked like the house belonged to a very old person.'

'It's worth a chance though, isn't it?' David said. 'Let's meet up tomorrow. I'm not teaching 'til eleven so if we meet at the big basilica at nine that should give us enough time.'

Bluebell was surprised how excited she felt at the prospect of meeting David the next day. She was so nervous with anticipation she actually felt quite queasy. She hadn't realised how much finding the girl in the poppy-print dress meant to her.

Chapter Eighteen

Michela was delighted that her father was out of hospital and making such good progress but now she had her mother to worry about. Maria looked worn out. She spent hours sitting with Mario and keeping his spirits up but she still insisted on making many of her signature dishes. Her stout legs took her up and down stairs all day from the kitchen of Il Gattino to their bedroom in the flat above where Mario, despite protesting his fitness, was currently confined. Michela and Paolo tried in vain to get their mother to slow down. Michela had taken over some of the cooking; it was a real pleasure to roll up her sleeves and work with the fresh, seasonal ingredients of the Amalfi Coast, but Maria refused to relinquish complete control. She insisted, quite rightly, that no one made a *spaghetti al limone* or a *ragù* sauce like she did.

At last, at about half past three, when the café bar was at its quietest, Michela managed to persuade her mother to sit down in the big armchair upstairs and take a rest on the condition that she and her brother took it in turns to take a break. They had a party of seven English ladies booked in for half past seven that evening so they all needed to be fresh and ready for what could be a long night. Soon the sound of Maria's gentle snoring wafted down the stairs.

Leaving Paolo in charge, Michela hung her apron on its usual brass hook and made her way down the street, across Piazza Umberto and down to the seafront. Although it was still early in the season, some stallholders had set up tables there selling a variety of handmade jewellery, handbags and eclectic collections of bric-a-brac. She browsed around the stalls, wondering about the tourists who bought these old prints in chipped frames, cups without saucers and trays of old bone-handled cutlery. Would they regret their purchases almost before they unpacked their cases, or would they become treasured mementoes of their holiday? She drifted aimlessly, picking up a handbag here, a hairslide there, then she stopped to speak to an old neighbour, the mother of a friend of hers who she had known all her life.

'Michela, I am so sorry to hear about your papa,' the woman said. 'I have been lighting candles in the church of Santa Lucia for him. How is he?'

'He is home now and making good progress.'

'Praise the Lord, I knew he would answer. He is a good man, your papa.'

'Thank you,' Michela replied. She was touched by her neighbour's simple faith and promised to pass on her best wishes to her father.

'I don't suppose we will see him behind the counter of Il Gattino for a while, though I expect he will be back there sooner than the doctors want him to be.' The old woman chuckled. 'And how are you? Are you staying for a while? Your mother told me that you were going to move to Positano to work with your cousins at The Old Fishermen when you came back from London.'

'Yes, I'll be staying here as long as Mamma and Papa need me. It's lucky the owners of The Old Fishermen are family, so they understand why I've had to let them down.'

'It will be lovely to have you back in Minori, my darling. And it looks like you're not the only one returning. Have you seen Stefano yet?'

'I heard a rumour he was coming back here but I don't think it's likely to be true. I hear he is doing very well in Rome, so I can't imagine he is going to return to this little place.' She had been doing so well to stop daydreaming about Stefano and get on with her life, not allowing herself to believe that Nonna Carmela might have been right about his imminent return. Trust her friend's mother to bring Stefano's name up just as she was trying her best not to think about him.

'Well, I heard he is definitely planning to move back to Minori and guess who told me.'

Michela tried to compose her features into a neutral expression. 'I don't know. Tell me.'

'Stefano himself. I saw him walking past just ten minutes ago. He didn't stop for long; he said he was meeting someone. I thought it might be Paolo. I know what good friends they were.'

Michela hurriedly made her excuses and left. This was so unexpected; she needed a little time alone for the news about Stefano to sink in before she made her way back to work. There would be no time to think once the party of seven English ladies arrived and if they had a couple of other bookings Il Gattino would be full.

She knew deep down that there was no point getting excited. Even if Stefano were coming back, why would he be interested in her now? It had been a long, long time since they had sat on those dusty steps sharing their hopes and dreams. Would he even remember the thrilling, clandestine kisses that still meant so much to her?

She started to walk down the pier – it wasn't much of a detour, but she always found it relaxing to walk its length, looking out to sea. To the left the coast led round to the neighbouring town of Maiori; to the right she could see the buildings of the old town clinging to the cliff edge.

A large man with a small fluffy dog at his feet was sitting on one of the white benches. She couldn't help smiling; the little fellow was no bigger than the man's shoe. It was then that she saw Stefano. Could it really be him? Of course, it was; she would know him anywhere.

She allowed herself the luxury of watching him from afar for a few moments. It had been more than three years since she had last seen him. She had dreamt of this day for so long she was going to savour every moment. He was standing at the end of the pier, dressed in dark trousers and a light-coloured linen jacket, leaning on the railing and looking out to sea. His nut-brown shoes shone in the last of the day's sun. He still had the same thick, dark hair but he looked a little less boyish than when he had left Minori. He had grown into his strong features and it suited him.

She couldn't bear to wait another moment. He turned his head. She took a step forward. A wide beam spread across her face as she anticipated his answering smile. Then she realised he wasn't looking at her but at someone else – a tall girl in a chic, coffee-coloured wrap dress who was striding down the pier towards him.

She watched the girl greet Stefano with a warm embrace. Half of her wanted to run back to Il Gattino, the other half wanted to stay and watch the scene unfold like a car crash at the side of a motorway. She couldn't move even if she had wanted to; her feet felt like two paving slabs cemented to the pier.

Stefano turned away and put one arm on the girl's shoulder and with the other pointed to a building further along the coast as if she was a visitor who had not been to the town before. The girl's dark corkscrew curls cascading over her shoulders wafted gently in the soft breeze. She was laughing as he pushed them out of her eyes.

How could she be such a fool? With all the girls in Rome to choose from Stefano was never going to come back to Minori and take up with the little sister of his old friend. He had brought this beautiful, chic girl home from Rome with him. Now he was showing her the town where he had spent so many happy years. He had probably introduced her to his parents already. They would be having dinner in one of his father's hotels in Maiori tonight.

Michela looked down; she was still wearing her restaurant uniform. Her make-up, which had run in the heat of the kitchen, needed reapplying. Her hair was scraped back in a scrappy ponytail. How could she think he would look at her twice? She felt tears pricking her eyes. Now the girl was throwing back her head and laughing at something Stefano had said. Michela turned and fled.

Michela stopped running when she got to Trattoria di Napoli. Despite her brother Paolo's less than enthusiastic reaction to her plans she decided to pop in and see Tommaso Amati and ask him about the FOR SALE sign in the window. Talking to the old man might help take her mind off Stefano and his sophisticated new girlfriend from Rome.

Tommaso Amati listened as Michela outlined her plans for her family to buy the restaurant. He knew that his old friend Mario had once talked about running a place like Trattoria di Napoli, right on Piazza Umberto, overlooking the sea. Mario and Maria's cooking deserved a wider audience and now they had Michela to help them. Tommaso could think of no one better to buy out the business and do justice to the marvellous location. He would have loved to sell the restaurant to his old friend's family; he would even have taken an offer below the market price. But he knew better than anyone the stress and strain that lay behind the apparently effortless success of his restaurant. And he knew Mario's talk had been a young man's dreams. Mario had found true contentment running Il Gattino. And now he was pushing seventy he would want to slow down and finally find some spare time to enjoy life with his beloved Maria, not work himself into an early grave.

It was typically thoughtful of Michela to want to make her father's old dream come true, but Tommaso could not be responsible for burdening him with the extra responsibilities and stress after his illness. Besides her plan was full of holes. Mario would never want to be responsible for Paolo quitting his promising career as a lawyer in Naples and he was convinced that there was no way that Maria's mother would ever move from her old house up on the hill, no matter how convenient and logical it might seem to everyone else.

Michela was disappointed. Tommaso had seemed less than enthusiastic about her scheme, but he hadn't actually said no, had he? Her job at The Old Fishermen in Positano was on ice; Stefano, the love of her life had come back to Minori with a new and serious-looking girlfriend; even all her new London clothes, not to mention some of her old dresses, had gone missing. Her own life was a mess, her dreams in tatters, but maybe she could somehow make her father Mario's old dream come true and build up something for her future, too. If her family could take over Trattoria di Napoli she would be far too busy to think about Stefano. Why, oh why, did he have to come back to their home town? She ducked into the alley behind Il Gattino and let her tears fall.

After a while she pulled herself together, blew her nose and approached the door of Il Gattino. She could smell the delicious flavours of her mother's cooking wafting from the kitchen. She went around to the side of the building, climbed the stairs to the family's flat and crept into the bathroom to splash water on her face and wipe off her smeared mascara with a tissue. Then she peeked into her parents' room where Mario sat propped up in the matrimonial bed. The robust carved headboard seemed to emphasise his frailty. He had lost a fair amount of weight over the last few days and some of the colour had gone from his face. His hair and eyes looked paler too. She moved her mother's mending from the bentwood chair by the bed and sat down. Mario reached and took her hand. She tried not to show her shock at the way his once-strong fingers lay weakly in hers.

'How are you feeling, Papa?'

'Good. I'll soon be up and about, but you know these doctors: they insist on treating you like an invalid.'

'You mustn't rush yourself, Papa. You've had a major operation.'

'It's your mother I'm worried about, always so busy and now having to fuss around after me, too. The sooner I'm back downstairs the better.'

'If you try to rush back to work that will worry Mamma even more. If you do what the doctors tell you she'll be a lot less worried.'

'I suppose you're right. Could you pass me that newspaper? I'd have no trouble getting up to get it myself, of course, but as you're here . . .'

She fetched the paper, handed it to him and topped up his glass of water from the jug on the bedside table. They sat quietly for a minute or two, then the silence was broken by the sound of his snores. She picked up the newspaper, which had slipped to the floor, and crept quietly down the stairs.

She brushed her long dark hair and pulled it away from her face with a large silver clip, then put on a fresh white blouse. She replaced her scrubbed-off eye make-up and added a touch of blusher to put some colour back in her cheeks. She was determined to put on her best and brightest smile to greet the party of English ladies booked in that evening. She wondered why the women had chosen her family's small establishment. Organised tours rarely came into Il Gattino, usually preferring to eat in their hotels or at the bigger restaurants where they could consult multilingual menus, minimising the chance of anyone risking ordering something they hadn't already tried out at the local Italian back home. There was no menu at Il Gattino let alone an English one, just the names of a few specials that were scribbled on the blackboard on the far wall to supplement the usual dishes, which their customers knew by heart.

Two local couples were also booked in. It looked as though they were going to be full tonight. Michela was glad. She was desperate for something to keep her mind off Stefano and the beautiful girl from Rome with the corkscrew curls. But above all else she was determined that all their customers would enjoy their visit tonight. She would not let Mamma and Papa down. No one would guess that earlier that evening this smart, friendly, freshly made-up girl had been crouching in the alley behind the café sobbing her heart out with only the mangy stray cats that skulked around the bins for company.

Chapter Nineteen

Miriam was planning to sit out on her little balcony and read before dinner, but she was conscious that there were only two full days of the holiday remaining and she wanted to do and see as much as possible.

She picked up the phone and keyed in Bluebell's room number. Luckily, her young friend was more than happy to wander into the town and mooch around for a bit.

Minori was busy with people of all ages encouraged out of their homes and hotels by the light, pleasant evening. It was hard to believe that the coast had been battered by such a downpour just that morning.

The two women strolled along the seafront, enjoying the gentle warmth on their bare arms. Bluebell's brightly painted toenails, visible in her beaded flip-flops, clashed merrily with her turquoise-and-pink dress from Moda Antonia. Miriam had paired a simple white blouse with her cerise pleated skirt. She wondered why she had thought the colour was too bright for her. Maybe it was the Italian sunlight that made the difference.

On the pier, children were playing happily whilst old men and women sat on the benches gossiping and teenagers fiddled with their mobile phones, jostling and giggling.

'Oh, look – that's new!' Bluebell said.

Tinkling music was drifting over from the end of the promenade. Prancing horses in ice-cream colours were gently rising and falling as an old-fashioned carousel spun slowly. The two women could not resist taking a closer look.

'It must be more than sixty years since I rode one of those,' Miriam said.

'Let's have a go.' Bluebell stepped forward as the carousel slowed to a halt and a stream of children and parents dismounted. Two teenage girls brushed past them, pink-cheeked and laughing.

'*Buonasera*. Two tickets?' The ride's operator tore a couple of tickets from his pad.

'No, it's for children.' Miriam laughed.

The man's gold tooth gleamed in the sunlight. He pointed to a small painted sign: *Ages 3–103*.

'Come on, it'll be fun,' Bluebell said.

The man put his hand under Miriam's elbow and guided her forward. She held on tightly as the music started. Her painted steed rose and fell in time with the music. She started to laugh. She could not remember when she had last felt so happy and free.

The music finished as the ride came to a halt. Miriam dismounted as elegantly as she could in the circumstances. 'That was such fun. What shall we do now?'

'Let's get an ice-cream.'

'But it's only an hour 'til dinner!'

'So what? There's no one to stop us.' Bluebell headed purposefully towards the gelateria.

'Well, if you insist . . . I suppose I could manage a small one.'

Miriam was thankful the ice-cream shop was in the opposite direction to Piazza Umberto. She didn't really want to walk past the Trattoria di Napoli with her face glowing bright pink and her pleated skirt all crumpled up.

'This is so good,' Bluebell mumbled through a mouthful of strawberry ice-cream.

'Mmm.' Miriam was busy concentrating on spinning her cone around so she could catch each drip before it fell on her open-toed sandals. She licked the last remnants from her sticky fingers as they strolled back to the Hotel Sea Breeze.

Josie's instincts were spot on. The other prizewinners were delighted to find out that they would be visiting Il Gattino that evening rather than eating in the large, rather brash-looking pizzeria. They were even happier when they walked past the pizzeria and saw that half the tables had been taken up by a crowd of local teenagers noisily celebrating someone's birthday. They followed Josie up a side road until they came to a small café bar with two tiny sets of aluminium tables and chairs crammed onto the pavement. Above their heads hung a metal sign in the shape of a sleeping cat.

Brenda consulted the pocket dictionary that she kept in her big green shoulder bag. 'Il Gattino means the kitten or the little cat,' she said.

'They certainly couldn't call it *The Big Cat.*' Miriam peered through the window into the small interior. The room wasn't very spacious, but it was light and cheerful, simply furnished with peach-coloured cloths spread over the wooden tables and rough whitewashed walls decorated with brightly coloured hand-painted ceramic plates.

'At least there won't be room to squeeze in a party of teenagers,' said Evie. She found it rather difficult to hear these days when lots of folk were talking at once.

'Are we early?' asked Miriam. There did not appear to be anyone around, but just at that moment a girl in her twenties dressed in a crisp white blouse and black skirt appeared from behind the door leading into the kitchen and welcomed them in. Soon they were all seated. Bluebell was squeezed into a corner seat, next to Josie. It was a bit of a tight fit; she hoped she wouldn't have to get out in a hurry.

The girl's English was nearly fluent, so they had no trouble at all understanding the various menu options, and they were happy to follow her suggestion to start with shared platters of mixed *bruschette* topped with tomatoes, black olives and artichokes. Then she ran through the main dishes and specials, smiling when Evie said, 'I didn't quite catch that, dear. No, don't repeat your specials. I'll have it anyway. I like a bit of a surprise.' Brenda chose a mushroom risotto and the others plumped for the local *scialatielli* pasta with seafood or Il Gattino's ever-popular spaghetti with clams or red prawns. The girl took their orders and returned with a couple of baskets of fresh bread, which she placed on the peach linen cloths that covered the three wooden tables that had been pushed together to accommodate the party. Then she came back with three full jugs of water, two for the Englishwomen and one for a local couple who had just arrived.

Silence fell over the table where the *Loving and Knitting* group were seated. The women were now so relaxed in each other's company that they did not feel at all embarrassed about stopping their conversation in order to tuck into the crunchy *bruschette* with their tasty toppings. Bluebell, who was used to Granny Blue's bird-like appetite, was amazed at how much food the group managed to put away, especially little Evie who had surely eaten her own bodyweight in spaghetti on more than one occasion.

The huge pile of *bruschette* was finally demolished and the women sat chatting and drinking the local wine, which the waitress poured from a large terracotta pitcher, whilst Brenda sipped a glass of lightly sparkling water.

'It's a relaxing day tomorrow,' Josie reminded the group, when there was a lull in the conversation. 'You might want to make the most of some downtime, pottering around here. We're going to have a full-on day, the day after that. The boat to Capri will leave at eight thirty and we're going to pack a lot in.'

'Is that nice boy who rescued Bluebell from the storm still coming with us?' asked Brenda.

'David? Yes, the boat to Capri calls at Maiori before it stops at Minori, so he said he would get on there and see us on board,' Bluebell said.

'Oh, good. I'm glad he's coming. He seemed like such a nice person,' said Brenda.

'If only I was fifty years younger,' said Evie with a comical sigh. 'Though I might have some competition from Bluebell.'

'We're just friends, and I know for a fact even if I was interested in him, which I'm not, he's not at all interested in me,' Bluebell said.

'I'm so looking forward to going to Capri,' said Josie, changing the subject, obviously conscious that Evie might have touched a nerve. Bluebell shot her a grateful look.

'There's going to be so much to see. There's a huge section on Capri in my guidebook,' said Brenda.

'I expect you'll be able to tell us a lot about it,' said Miriam.

'Oh, I feel awful. I must be really boring everyone.'

'Absolutely not. You saved the day in Sorrento, telling us all about the places we saw,' said Josie.

'It wouldn't have been nearly so good without you; you were really professional,' said Miriam.

'Have you ever been a blue badge guide or anything like that?' Josie asked.

'Oh, no, I wouldn't have dared, but everyone on this trip is so nice and easy-going I thought I could give it a go. I've always loved history, you see, and sharing it with people. I wanted to teach but it was never to be.'

'Why not? You would be ever so good, I'm sure,' said Miriam.

'I was one of those children who didn't enjoy school very much, then one day we got a new history teacher. I'd hated history up until then but Miss Wright . . . I'll never forget her. She changed everything for me. She had this gift of bringing the stories alive and she encouraged everyone no matter how much or little talent they had. I started to work harder and decided I wanted to follow in Miss Wright's footsteps when I grew up. I thought my future was all planned out. I was going to be a teacher, and then by the time I was twenty-five I'd have met someone. I'd get married, have a couple of children and return to teaching part time but none of those things happened. Just before I was due to take up my place at teacher-training college my mother became seriously ill and I stayed at home to help my father. I had two older brothers but it didn't really affect them. They had their careers and got married and had children but I spent the next five years looking after my mother. After she died I was a full-time carer for my dad. By the time he died I was in my fifties and took an admin job locally.'

'What a shame,' said Bluebell.

'Oh, I didn't have time to feel sorry for myself. It was just expected in those days, if you were the only girl in the family and weren't married. I don't expect I'll ever marry now and it's too late to be a teacher. I've got lovely nieces and nephews and great friends, but I would have loved to have helped some children the way Miss Wright helped me.'

'I'm not sure it's too late,' said Miriam. She furrowed her brow with the air of someone quietly cooking up an idea.

Bluebell was silent for a few minutes thinking about Brenda's story. It made her doubly determined to get as much out of this trip as she could. You could never tell what the future had in store. She looked up to see the waitress coming towards them carrying two plates of spaghetti and clams. She wondered if it was choice or duty that led the girl to spend her days in this tiny café bar in a small coastal town.

Despite declaring themselves to be rather full, the girl somehow persuaded them to end their meal with refreshing lemon sorbet served inside hollowed-out lemons, followed by tiny cups of espresso and glasses of *limoncello*. By the time Josie called for the bill Bluebell was feeling extremely glad she had decided not to get changed. The bright-pink-and-turquoise dress she had picked up that morning in Moda Antonia had plenty of room for expansion.

Happily fed and watered, they set off for the Hotel Sea Breeze. Even though the hotel was on one of the bigger roads in Minori the narrow pavement did not allow them to walk more than two abreast, so they formed a little caterpillar behind Josie, walking in pairs like children on a school outing. The local townsfolk were used to making their way slowly up and down the street, stopping to let each other past; no one was in too much of a rush in the sleepy little town.

Suddenly a young woman hurtled past in the direction of the seafront, almost bowling Evie over. Despite her spindly high heels she was travelling at quite a rate of knots, her pale blonde hair streaming behind her. Josie put out an arm and just caught Evie before she fell.

'*Scusi!*' the girl shouted over her shoulder. Bluebell recognised her as the Scandinavian-looking beauty waiting for Andrea in Reception that morning. Then she'd been languidly flicking through a magazine as though she'd had all the time in the world. Now she was running from the hotel as though she had a pack of wolves at her heels.

Evie got herself back on an even keel just as a second figure came flying down the street: a young man dressed in a white shirt and black trousers with a half apron tied over the top, which flapped comically as he ran. They all jumped to one side to get out of the way. It was Andrea, the waiter, and he was rapidly gaining on the escaping girl. The women stopped and turned to stare after his departing figure, Evie because she needed to get her breath back and the others because the unfolding drama promised an unscheduled moment of entertainment.

Andrea soon caught up with the girl and spun her around to face him. Her beautiful face was twisted in anger. The ladies did not know what he might have done to upset her, but Bluebell was willing to hazard a guess it wasn't anything to do with the service in the hotel dining room.

The girl took a step back. Andrea dropped his hands and it looked as though they were now calmly talking. An almighty slap across the face sent him flying backwards through the air. The girl turned and stalked off, indignation radiating from every pore. Bluebell was desperately trying not to laugh. There was a chance Andrea could be seriously hurt. She and Josie rushed to his aid as he lay sprawled across the pavement, but apart from an angry red mark across his cheek only his pride seemed to be hurt. They helped him to his feet, he gave them a *what can I do, these women are crazy* shrug and walked back with them to the Hotel Sea Breeze to finish off the last of his duties.

The older ladies bid each other goodnight. Bluebell and Josie headed for the hotel bar.

Michela allowed herself a small sigh of satisfaction. Everything had gone without a hitch. At least one thing in her life was going well. She had been a little apprehensive about tonight's party of English ladies, but she was relieved to find that they were obviously planning to have a long, leisurely meal, allowing her mother plenty of time to prepare everything and judge the cooking of her pasta to *al dente* perfection. Maria worked to her own timescale; the preparation of her dishes was rushed for no one.

Michela wondered about the relationship between the women. The pretty girl with the red hair who had made the booking seemed to be in charge. Perhaps she and the other girl with the long dark hair were the daughters or granddaughters of one of the older ladies. The one with the dark hair was wearing a bright linen dress, which Michela guessed came from one of the shops in Positano down on the harbour near The Old Fishermen. The vibrant turquoise-and-pink colourway was just the sort of thing she would have chosen for herself before she moved to London. Those days now seemed light years away.

She thought back to her conversations with Paolo and Tommaso. Maybe there was still some way of buying Trattoria di Napoli without Nonna Carmela selling her little house. She was sure it would give her father a new lease of life. And it would give Michela a chance to develop her cooking without leaving her family in the lurch. Maria's dishes were popular with locals and tourists alike, but Michela was itching to try out some of the new techniques she had observed at The Golden Wolf and give some of their old classics a modern twist. She knew better than to raise the subject with her brother tonight.

She needed time to think things through. But if Paolo was determined to stay at his law firm in Naples they had next to no chance of selling Il Gattino and taking over the prestigious site on Piazza Umberto. She did not know what the future held. She just knew it wouldn't include Stefano.

Chapter Twenty

Tommaso Amati looked around. The coffee cups were washed up and the last crumbs of his fresh *cornetti alla crema* were brushed away. The early morning breakfast rush was over. The bank workers, shop staff and other local customers had all gone to their various places of employment. Outside, under the blue-and-yellow-striped parasols, the blue cloths were spotless, the metal ashtrays clean and the blue-and-yellow napkin holders were filled to capacity. Everything was to his satisfaction. He sat on a three-legged stool by the counter, next to his large grey cash register, and put on his reading glasses.

The morning's post contained the usual motley collection of bills and unwanted catalogues from restaurant suppliers, but amongst the small pile was a handwritten envelope made out of thick cream paper. He was astonished to see that the letter was from Stefano Bassani.

Stefano's father Benito was a well-known figure in the area. He had once owned a small bar in their home town, at the far end of Via Roma, but he had sold it on at a handsome profit and now owned two large and lucrative hotels on the seafront in the neighbouring town of Maiori. Benito Bassani sometimes used Trattoria di Napoli to entertain local dignitaries and businesspeople and was fond of ordering the best wine on the menu and not stinting on the quantity. He was a valued customer, but

Tommaso did not have a personal friendship with the man. He did, however, know his son, Stefano, a little better. As a young boy, he and Mario's son Paolo would come running into Trattoria di Napoli to buy ice-creams to eat on the seafront. Sometimes they brought Paolo's little sister Michela with them.

When he was older Stefano occasionally stopped by and ordered a beer, sitting at one of the outside tables. Sometimes he came by himself, sometimes with some pretty girl or other in tow. He was a handsome lad with plenty of admirers. His father's wealth paid for the latest moped and the best clothes, and he was one of the few teenagers in town who could afford to impress his dates with a meal at Trattoria di Napoli. But Stefano was no fool. He was savvy enough to know which girls were only drawn to him by the cash in his pocket.

When he wasn't out on a date or busy at school, Stefano spent all his spare time in the kitchen at Il Gattino helping Paolo's mother, Maria, with the cooking. Tommaso had heard that the boy had a fascination with the whole process, helping to choose the best vegetables and the tastiest fruit and transforming it into the simple peasant-style cooking of the Italian south. And then he moved to Rome.

Stefano surprised most people when he left the little town of Minori but he had not surprised Tommaso. With a successful businessman like Benito for a father it was hardly surprising that the young man's ambitions were too wide to be contained in a small town of less than three thousand people. He quickly found a job with Chucky Joe's, an American-style fast-food chain, and swiftly rose to the position of deputy manager at the flagship branch on Corso Vittorio Emanuele. There were rumours that with the good impression he made and his head for business he would be able to rise to the very top of the management chain. Tommaso wished him nothing but good luck, though he understood Mario's horror that a boy who cared so much for the colour and freshness of the seasonal vegetables prepared at Il Gattino could apparently sell his soul to an organisation whose bestselling greenery was the lettuce sandwiched between bun and burger.

Tommaso had visited a branch of Chucky Joe's in Naples once. Never again! Chucky Joe's didn't have daily specials; it served the same food all year round with no concession to what was fresh or in season. Its pizzas weren't topped with a rich tomato sauce, fluffy buffalo mozzarella and silky, silvery anchovies; they were made by slapping watery tomato mush and cheap cheese onto pre-frozen bases. The burgers were even worse – and yet they sold thousands. Frozen patties of cheap mince were delivered each morning from a big industrial unit in the suburbs and were slapped between soft white doughy buns, which lasted several days – unlike the breads from Minori's bakery, which were hard by the evening. Tommaso shook his head. How could such businesses thrive?

According to his letter, Stefano had now decided to leave the big city and return to Minori. With the experience he'd gained in Rome and a large interest-free loan from his wealthy father he had plans to open his own restaurant. It seemed that his sights were set on buying one of the restaurants on Piazza Umberto and Trattoria di Napoli was number one on his list. According to his letter, Stefano had been due to arrive in Minori yesterday afternoon and would call in at Trattoria di Napoli at nine o'clock that very morning. He hoped that Mr Amati would find that convenient.

He certainly did. The boy's letter could not have arrived at a better time.

Tommaso glanced at the clock, picked up a pen, fiddled with it and put it down again. He knew that a good offer from Stefano would enable him to move to the island of Ischia and begin the next chapter of his life.

Tommaso greeted the son of Benito Bassani with a warm embrace. Stefano was the image of his father though standing a few centimetres taller and possessed of a more relaxed demeanour. Tommaso could understand how the well-dressed and well-spoken young man had been tipped for the top at the Chucky Joe's chain. But it seemed from his letter that life working for a large American-owned restaurant chain did not appeal to Stefano, however lucrative it might be. The boy was lucky to be able to turn his back on the promise of a large salary and a raft of share options. Not many people in the area had the privileged upbringing afforded to the son of one of the Amalfi Coast's leading hoteliers.

Tommaso led him through to the back of the restaurant. Nine o'clock was a quiet time of the day when he usually worked single-handed, but after receiving Stefano's letter he had arranged for one of his casual staff to come in and work a morning shift. Now they would be able to talk without fear of any interruptions.

A few minutes later a very attractive young woman appeared in the doorway. She was tall and slim with golden, almond-shaped eyes outlined in kohl below carefully shaped and painted brows. A cascade of natural dark curls fell over her shoulders almost reaching to her tiny waist. She was dressed in a plain olive-coloured dress and had a small, structured, mock-crocodile handbag nestling in the crook of her arm.

Stefano rose to greet her and introduced her to the older man. 'This is Nicoletta. Unfortunately my business partner,

Alberto, is unable to be here today but we will be able to give him our personal impressions of the site.'

Tommaso wasn't sure how he felt about Trattoria di Napoli, his pride and joy for more than thirty years, being referred to in such an impersonal manner, but he decided to listen to the details of their proposition with an open mind.

Stefano talked passionately about his plans and had clearly done his homework on the financial cost of the project. He had a vision of a restaurant that would be visited not only by the local people in Minori and its tourists but by folk from all the surrounding towns. He spoke of websites and apps and *Facebook* and *Instagram*. Tommaso knew very little about these things and he was glad that he found his own customers by word of mouth or by dint of his prominent position on Piazza Umberto. Stefano by contrast was looking to embrace all the help the internet could offer him. These new ways of communicating would help him to generate the publicity needed to turn the venue into the one of the most popular eateries on the whole of the Amalfi Coast.

When the young man had finished outlining his plans, Tommaso took them through to the back of the restaurant so that he and Nicoletta could assess the state of the large kitchen with its traditional range cooker, two sinks and walk-in larder. Next, he showed them the simple tiled lavatories and the capacious storeroom. Then they went up the staircase at the back of the kitchen, which led to the three-bedroom flat overhead. Nicoletta was full of praise, sure that Alberto would be more than happy with the proposed purchase. There was now little more to discuss than the price that Stefano and his partner were willing to pay.

Tommaso was shocked at the amount of money on offer. He was tempted to agree the sale straight away but he felt it more prudent to say that he would think it over and advise his decision in the morning. He did not want Stefano to think that he had been far too generous and start to backtrack on the deal. He shook hands with him and kissed Nicoletta. He would call first thing tomorrow with his answer. When the couple departed he made himself another coffee. He was doubly glad that he' asked one of his waiters to work that morning. He had a lot to think about. The sum of money that he was being offered was more than enough to wind up his affairs at Trattoria di Napoli and make a new start.

Now he must contact his sister Silvia in Ischia to see if he could come and stay whilst he started looking for a property on the island. An email or maybe even a proper letter would be best – it would enable her to reply in her own time. He was just about to take a seat in the back of the restaurant and start composing his words when he noticed a customer approaching the outside tables and chairs. It was the lovely English lady who had stopped there for coffee the other morning with her young friend. Writing his letter could wait.

Chapter Twenty-One

It was a free day in Minori for the competition winners, but Josie agreed to lead an optional excursion to nearby Amalfi. Brenda was up early, keen to be climbing the sweeping steps to the town's famous cathedral, but Bluebell, Miriam and Evie declined to join the party. They each made a different excuse. Only Evie was telling the truth: she was a little frail and wanted to rest before the highlight of the holiday, the day trip to Capri. Bluebell was keeping quiet about her plans for the day ahead; only Josie and Miriam were in the know.

Bluebell was bursting with excitement at the thought of retracing her steps to the marshmallow-pink house with the poppy-print curtains. It would be fun to meet David and try to hunt down the mystery girl, so she was not too disappointed when Miriam declined to join them, claiming she did not fancy climbing all the steps. It would be rather nice to have David all to herself, even if it was only for an hour or so before he had to go back to the school in Maiori to teach a couple of classes. She wasn't at all interested in him in a romantic way, but he made a nice friend. In fact, she could not remember when she last felt so at home with someone. But even if she was looking for a new relationship, David was a non-starter. He was clearly in love with the girl they were searching for.

She hurried down the street. She was running a little late. For some reason she had found it difficult to decide what to wear, eventually picking an orange top and yellow skirt from the case. She had also fussed around with her long dark hair for an uncharacteristically long time, pinning it this way and that. Goodness know why; she was only meeting David.

She looked at the time on her phone. Maybe he would think she wasn't coming. Maybe he wouldn't wait for her. The thought of that made her feel quite sick. She broke into a jog as she crossed Piazza Cantilena towards the steps of the Basilica of Saint Trofimena. Thank goodness she had travelled to Italy in her trainers; there was no way she could run in flip-flops.

As she got nearer to the basilica, she could see a male figure at the top of the steps leaning over the stone railings. As David spotted her and waved, she could not help breaking into a massive grin. 'You look great,' he said.

'Thanks, umm, so do you,' she said. She glanced sideways at him, taking in his dark trousers and simple, light-blue shirt.

'I thought you might turn up in the orange dress with the poppies, but I guess that would be a bit weird.'

'Yes, can you imagine if she opened the door to see some stranger wearing her clothes. She might freak out. I know I would. That's why I chose this top and skirt. They aren't so distinctive, and they're from an Italian chain, not homemade. These could belong to anyone, though I guess not many people would choose such bright colours.'

'And not many people would look so good in them.'

She blushed. Considering David was only a friend she felt unaccountably pleased at the compliment. 'Are you ready? It's not far,' she said.

'It's a shame I haven't got time for a coffee first.' David's eyes strayed to the small café by the side of the basilica where a group of men were engrossed in a game of cards. 'I wonder what they're playing. I used to love card games until all my friends got into Xbox.'

'I used to play poker with my gran. It's a good thing we played with Smarties or else I would have lost all my pocket money.' Bluebell laughed.

'I'll have to take you on sometime,' David said.

'It's this way.' Bluebell led David round the back of the basilica to the same set of steps she had discovered with Josie. He chatted away but Bluebell was too puffed out to say much. She was glad when David insisted that they pause to take in the view looking down onto the town and out to sea.

'That must be it!' David pointed out the sheer flight of steps that led to the small, narrow marshmallow-pink house where an orange poppy-print curtain could be seen hanging at the upstairs window.

The steps were as steep as Bluebell remembered. She was glad when David reached and took her hand as they climbed. Luckily it was a warm, dry day. She could not imagine climbing up here in bad weather even with his added assistance. Eventually, they reached the top of the steps. They stopped and looked at each other. Then David knocked firmly on the old green front door.

Chapter Twenty-Two

Miriam couldn't help feeling a little bit guilty about lying to Bluebell that morning, but it was a little white lie for the right reason. She knew she would be quite capable of walking up the stairs to the pink house; she felt full of energy since coming on this trip. She was avoiding this morning's outing for another reason. She wanted to leave David and Bluebell alone together. David had some crazy crush on a girl he had never even spoken to, but as far as she was concerned, he just needed to get his head out of the clouds and see the gorgeous girl right in front of him. Bluebell seemed to be unwilling to have her heart broken again, thinking that a brief fling with a totally unsuitable, though admittedly very good-looking, waiter was all she deserved. She just hoped that they wouldn't find anyone when they visited the pink house. She didn't want Cupid firing his arrow at the wrong girl.

The others had gone off to Amalfi with Josie, but she would stay in Minori and spend the morning exploring more of the delightful little town. This decision, she told herself, had nothing to do with a desire to return to Trattoria di Napoli and chat to that charming man Tommaso. And the thought that she would soon be sitting under one of his blue-and-yellow umbrellas had nothing to do with her happy mood.

She walked slowly towards the seafront. As she entered Piazza Umberto she looked over at the place where

Tommaso usually sat and saw him rise to greet a dark-haired young man. The visitor was dressed as if for a business meeting in smart trousers and a linen jacket. He wore brown suede loafers and carried a tan leather document holder. He was strikingly handsome, but she thought Tommaso was quite his equal, with his kind brown eyes, luxuriant silver hair and neatly trimmed beard. She did not have time to admire either of them for long as the two men disappeared inside the restaurant.

She took a seat on a slatted bench on the seafront where she had a perfect view of the pier. She had plenty to look at: mothers strolling holding hands with young children, some clutching ice-creams, and locals walking small dogs of indeterminate breeds. In the distance the rich blue of the sea met the lighter blue of the sky, which was dotted with wispy white clouds.

As she sat watching the townsfolk and the tourists wander past, she felt a real happiness – a true contentment – that she had not expected to feel again. She still thought about Colin and all that they had shared – of course she did – but now her thoughts were nostalgic rather than red raw with pain. This holiday had done her the world of good. It was the first time since her twenties that she had holidayed with a group of strangers. Here she wasn't somebody's wife or somebody's aunty as she had been in the years since Colin died. She was just Miriam, a woman on holiday with a group of very nice people.

It was fun to share the experience with the others, especially Bluebell, who had become a rather special friend. The late addition of David as a sort of part-time honorary member of the party had provided a boost to them all, and the other people she was meeting along the way, like Massimo the minibus driver and even Andrea, the philandering waiter, had enlivened the trip. And it had all come about because she had picked up that copy of *Loving and Knitting* magazine in the kiosk at the railway station.

It was developing into quite a warm day. An hour had gone past; she could do with a cold drink. She would walk along to one of the beach bars directly overlooking the sea. Who was she kidding? She would go back to Piazza Umberto and sit at one of the round tables beneath the blue-and-yellow umbrellas of Trattoria di Napoli. Tommaso would surely have finished his meeting and she knew he would provide a warm welcome. There was no reason to believe that he didn't give the same treatment to all his customers. Even so, she could not help comparing him to the men that friends and acquaintances had tried to push in her direction once they felt a suitable interval of time had elapsed since Colin's passing. So far they had all fallen into one of four categories: the permanent bachelors whose strange obsessions, dubious dress sense and erratic personal hygiene had failed to attract a mate back in the days when they still had the advantage of a full head of hair and a full set of teeth; the confident, successful men who made it clear, in not so subtle ways, that they were fighting off women twenty years younger than her; the divorced men failing to hide their bitterness behind their sarcastic quips about their exes; and the sad men still in love with the memories of their late wives, gamely trying to dredge up a renewed enthusiasm for the opposite sex in order to put a stop to the constant interference from their concerned families.

The owner of Trattoria di Napoli was as far removed from those sad stereotypes as his homemade ravioli was from a cling-filmed ready meal. *And as far removed as I am from a sexy, tanned, Italian* signora, she told herself sternly.

'*Buongiorno,*' Miriam said. He found it charming that she made the effort to greet him in his own language.

'*Buongiorno.* Good morning, madam.' Miriam, he thought she had called herself, but he did not want to be overfamiliar, or worse, call her by the wrong name.

'Miriam. Please do call me Miriam.'

He smiled, relieved. 'Then you must call me Tommaso. What would you like to drink? A cappuccino, perhaps?'

'So delicious, but first I would very much like a cold drink. It's really rather warm.'

It was indeed unusually hot for the time of year so he suggested a refreshing bottle of peach iced tea. He was back a few minutes later carrying the drink on a small tray along with a couple of complimentary lemon biscuits. Miriam was fanning herself with the menu and did appear a little pink. As he put down the tray he caught a waft of her perfume. It was subtle and gentle like fresh flowers in an English summer garden.

'Perhaps today you might like to sit inside. It is nice and cool.'

'It seems a shame to hide from the sun when we spend so much time in England longing to see it,' she replied, but she agreed that she would find it more comfortable to go inside. Besides he wanted her to have a proper look at the restaurant's interior. When the *Loving and Knitting* group had gone there for dinner they had been dining outside in the gentle warmth of the evening.

Tommaso ushered Miriam inside and showed her to a corner table then busied himself behind the counter. He saw her looking around and hoped that she liked what she saw. Although the interior was smart it still had a pleasingly informal air. Comfortable seats and upholstered benches flanked plain wooden tables, which in the evening would be covered by thick linen tablecloths. A small narrow vase on each table contained a single flower bud whilst a glass-and-metal tealight holder held a candle ready to supplement the light cast by the old iron wall-lamps. The floor was tiled in a striking geometric pattern of blue and terracotta whilst the walls were painted a simple warm cream. Hanging from the walls was a selection of cake moulds and other kitchen paraphernalia. Below these were dozens of old framed prints and photographs and it was these that seemed to attract her interest.

After what he considered to be a decent interval, he wandered over to her table and offered to tell her a little about the people and places portrayed in the photographs. Some she might recognise: here was Piazza Umberto where the restaurant was situated, here a view of the sea. One old photo showed the road where Casa Emilia now stood. The swimwear shop was easily identifiable but instead of swimsuits and sarongs it displayed pots and pans of every size. Brooms, bins and old chairs were piled high on either side of the doorway.

'These are so interesting,' Miriam said. 'Do you have any other old photos of the town.'

'Yes, I've got quite a collection.' Tommaso took a buff-coloured folder from the drawer of the dresser in the corner. He sat down beside her and spread some of the pictures across the table.

'These are two old paper mills. You can still see the ruins on the outskirts of the town. And here are some workers harvesting lemons.'

'And what's this one? I can tell it's the seafront, but it looks like there are sheets or towels spread out to dry on the ground.'

'Pasta.'

'Really?' Miriam laughed.

'No, seriously. Minori has been famous for its homemade pasta since the nineteenth century. In those days small boats travelled down the coast to buy the best quality wheat they could find. Dozens of small factories produced sheets of pasta and spread them out to dry on the seafront . . .'

Tommaso paused, maybe he was talking too much. He did not wish to bore her, so after amusing her with a few old family photos he gathered up the pictures. As he reached for the image of the old paper mills his hand brushed against hers.

'So, what brings you to Minori?' he said quickly.

Miriam took a sip of her iced tea. 'This is the first time I've been abroad since my husband died five years ago. For the last few years I have been visiting my nieces in England. I might not have plucked up the courage to fly again but by chance I saw a competition to win a holiday to the Amalfi Coast in a magazine I picked up at the railway station. It was a real surprise when they wrote to say I was one of the winners.

'It seemed like fate that I should come here, especially when I looked at a map to find exactly where Minori was. My late husband's father, Jim, was with one of the American regiments that was sent out to this part of Italy in the 1940s as part of the Allied landings. Apparently, he didn't get to do any fighting, which was a terrible disappointment to Colin when he was a child. The kids at school loved to tell tales of their hero dads' daring adventures, though no doubt a lot of it was exaggerated.

'Jim didn't like to talk about the war, but Colin later found out from his mother that after landing in Maiori he was injured as his unit was making its way up the high street. He was a rather bookish lad whose head was in the clouds and I believe he was gazing up at some architectural detail that caught his attention when he tripped over, landing so awkwardly that he broke his ankle. He was very embarrassed about it. It wasn't the sort of wartime injury you could boast about. She told me that a local lady who had done some nursing volunteered to take him in. He never did get to fight after that because his ankle was still weak, you see. In fact, I believe it always gave him trouble. I think it was a big disappointment to him that he hadn't done more for the war effort. And he wished he had done something to make his son really proud of him.'

'Extraordinary! There is an old lady who lives in Minori who once told me a tale like yours. She moved here when she got married but she grew up in Maiori. I remember her telling me that when she was quite young, maybe about twelve or thirteen, an American soldier stayed with them. He was a young man, no more than twenty. He had broken his ankle marching up the main street and her mother, who had done some nursing, had taken him in.

'She believes her mother kept him there a little longer than she really needed to. She hated the thought of young men having to fight. I think she had a word with someone at the hospital they set up in the old convent and church in town and persuaded them he would be an ideal person to help with the admissions there and that's where he ended up.'

'That's amazing! What a wonderful coincidence.'

'If you aren't busy this afternoon we could pay the old lady a visit, if you would like to. She does not get many visitors these days and I am sure she would love to meet you. I got the impression she had a bit of a schoolgirl crush on your father-in-law though she would never admit to it.'

'I'd love to. What time shall I meet you?' asked Miriam.

'Four o'clock would be perfect, after the lunchtime rush. It's fairly quiet here that time of the day.'

Miriam left Trattoria di Napoli, assuring Tommaso that she would be back at the allotted time and made her way up the road to the Hotel Sea Breeze. She slowed down. Her heart seemed to be racing. She must be walking too fast in the heat.

She paused outside Casa Emilia and looked again at the wildly colourful beachwear in the glass case affixed to the wall. The first time she had been inside was when Bluebell bought that yellow-and-white bikini; she was far too old and sensible to purchase something like that for herself. But when she walked along the seafront in Maiori she noticed the Italian women had no such qualms. Small, wrinkled, elderly ladies and soft, round mammas wore small bikinis with a casual self-confidence. They loved their bling too: diamanté clasps, jewel-trimmed straps and metallic finishes were worn without apology. Before she had time to talk herself out of it, Miriam pushed open the door and entered the small boutique.

Emilia greeted Miriam with a ready smile. 'Good afternoon, madam. You are alone today. Your friend is enjoying the sun in her new polka-dot bikini, perhaps?'

'How clever of you to remember.'

'I remember everyone, even those who come here on their holiday, just once a year. But of course it is my job. I will leave you alone to look around but if you need any advice, that too is my job. I see you are looking at that bikini on the counter with – how do you say? – horror.'

'Not horror exactly . . .' Miriam felt herself redden. She didn't want to insult this kind lady, but this bikini – who would choose it? The skimpy green-and-white design featured snakes slithering over shoulders and around buttocks and was finished off with a metal clasp in the shape of a serpent's head, which sat between moulded bra cups.

'My *serpenti* design. No, Emilia thinks it is not for you. But I am thinking of putting it on the mannequin in the corner, though maybe in a different colour.'

'It will look very striking, but for me, perhaps a swimsuit . . .'

'*Certo*. Certainly. But it is not necessary to wear a one-piece when one is no longer a teenager. I have some marvellous bikinis with wider straps and a good uplift. Now let me see. Black is always smart but perhaps something just a little brighter to flatter the complexion.'

Emilia slid open a long drawer beneath the counter and began piling a bewildering array of styles on the wooden countertop.

Miriam hesitated; she had two perfectly nice swimming costumes and really did not need to buy anything but a little voice in her head was urging her to do something frivolous for once. What had got into her? This trip to Italy was bringing out a side of her she did not even know existed. As Emilia proffered various swimwear options she found herself drawn to the gaily patterned bikinis. She hadn't worn one like these since the 1970s. She decided to try on a purple set printed with green palm leaves. It came with a matching cover-up, which she could keep on if courage failed her.

Miriam could tell that the dim light in the tiny changing area was much more flattering than daylight but to her surprise, instead of seeing a reflection full of flaws, she saw a happy, smiling person looking back at her. She would never be twenty-eight again but she had no desire to go back to those days. And wasn't seventy the new fifty or something like that? She did not know why she felt so

163

optimistic. It must be something to do with the sunshine. She would buy this bikini – to hell with what anyone else would think. Bluebell wasn't going to be the only one on this trip getting a swimwear upgrade.

'*Brava!* You have chosen well. So many customers I see, all their life they wear the sensible navy-blue and black swimsuits. They are a little scared to try something else. Then they try something new and look in the mirror. They are happy. And I am happy.' Emilia was beaming. She handed Miriam her receipt.

Miriam smiled back. Emilia was right. There was nothing like a fancy, frivolous and totally unnecessary purchase to lift the spirits.

Miriam walked quickly to the Hotel Sea Breeze. She needed to put on her new purchase before she had time to get cold feet. With the cover-up firmly in place and a substantial hotel towel on standby just in case, she headed for the pool. She stretched out on one of the loungers and picked up her book. She tried to concentrate on the story but every few minutes she checked her watch. Four o'clock seemed a lifetime away.

Chapter Twenty-Three

Bluebell held her breath as David knocked once more on the old green door. The orange poppy-print curtain was still fluttering in the upstairs window. She was right: it had definitely been sewn from the same material as the dress that she had been wearing the night they had met so briefly in Bar Gino.

A few minutes passed and still no one came to the door.

'Let's go round the side of the house,' said Bluebell. 'Look through this window. See, under the sink – that's the same material as one of the other dresses I found in the suitcase.'

David peered in the window and looked at the old dresser laden with ancient photos and china knick-knacks. An embroidered eiderdown was draped over a slightly saggy green armchair in the corner. Old wooden-handled saucepans and a traditional set of cast-iron scales were set upon the counter but there was no sign of any modern labour-saving devices. 'It looks like an old person lives here. Or maybe there's no one living here at the moment. There's a lot of stuff lying around but the place seems quite deserted,' he said.

'No, there's someone around. I can see one of those old hand-operated sewing machines on the kitchen table. It wasn't here when we looked the other day,' Bluebell replied.

'I can't imagine the girl I was looking for living in this house. They probably sell those fabrics in the local market and it's just a coincidence that whoever lives here likes the same patterns as she does.'

'You're right. I shouldn't have dragged you up here and got your hopes up. They must sell those flowery-patterned fabrics all over Italy.' She felt her heart sink to her feet. She was such an idiot. It was obvious now that this quirky old house full of bric-a-brac wouldn't have any connection with the girl David described – a stunningly beautiful girl with long dark hair wearing an exquisite dress that conjured up an image of an old Hollywood star. The girl probably didn't even live in Minori or Maiori at all. She probably lived in a flat in some chic Italian city and had been down here visiting old friends or just spending a day at the seaside.

As they descended the steps back to the main part of town Bluebell's legs felt heavy. There was a speck of grit in her eye and she could feel the beginnings of a blister forming on her little toe. She had dragged David on a wild goose chase and now he was going back to Maiori to teach his eleven o'clock class. He had only agreed to meet her this morning because he'd thought she might lead him to the girl he believed he was in love with. But now her crazy theory about the pink house had come to nothing she didn't expect she would see him again. She knew he had accepted Josie's invitation to join the ladies on their trip to Capri the next day, but she was sure he was just being polite. What man of nearly thirty would want to spend his day off on an outing with a bunch of over-sixties?

As she waved him off on the bus bound for Maiori her heart sank. He was due to meet them on board the boat to Capri the next day, but she knew he would make an excuse and cancel. He wouldn't be spending the day with them. She wouldn't ever see him again.

Bluebell trudged slowly back to the Hotel Sea Breeze. She knew Josie would be in Amalfi all day but there was a chance that Miriam would still be about. She looked around the reception area and the library but there was no one there. She took the lift up and knocked on Miriam's door but there was no answer. She let herself into her own room. The sight of the newly made bed and pile of clean, fluffy towels raised her spirits a little. She didn't know why the thought of not seeing David again bothered her. He was only ever going to be a friend and she already had plenty of those. It must be the thought of going home soon that was getting her down. Perhaps she should take advantage of the hotel's facilities whilst she was still here and go down to the pool for a read and a swim.

She changed into the polka-dot bikini she had purchased in Casa Emilia and threw on a shirt she found in the case. There was nothing that cheered you up like a new outfit. Now she felt ready for anything – as long as *anything* meant lounging by the pool with a cappuccino and a book.

She took the lift down to the pool, found a sunny spot and ordered a coffee from the pool bar. She spread out her towel and enjoyed the feeling of the warm June sunshine on her body. After a while she slipped into the pool. There were a couple of other holidaymakers sitting around reading chunky paperbacks, but she was the only one to brave a swim. It was a little cold, but the sun warmed her face as she moved smoothly through the water. Soon the chilliness diminished. It was blissful to have the pool to herself, to be able to navigate the waters without worrying about colliding with children splashing around or someone floating backwards.

As she powered along in a rather inelegant breaststroke she felt as though her hands weren't just pushing the water but pushing her disappointment over her failed relationship with Jamie further and further away. Pleasing him had been such a big part of her life for so long but swimming here alone she felt stronger with every stroke. And to think that she had been so reluctant to take Granny Blue's place on this trip.

After swimming until her fingers were grey and wrinkled, she climbed up the ladder and wrapped herself in a towel. Would it be greedy to order another cappuccino from the pool bar? Just then, Evie appeared, giving her a good excuse to call the barman over. Having another coffee was just being sociable, wasn't it?

Evie was clutching a couple of pamphlets on Capri in preparation for the next day's visit. 'By the time I've read all these I'll be an expert,' she said.

'I'll have to start calling you Brenda,' joked Bluebell. 'I can't believe how many guidebooks she manages to squeeze into that green shoulder bag of hers.'

'Did you have a nice swim, dear?' said Evie.

'Yes, lovely. I had the pool all to myself.'

'I thought I might find Miriam down here,' said Evie. 'Maybe she went out for a walk.'

Right on cue Miriam walked in. She was looking rather flushed. She must have caught the sun that morning. She had a hotel towel wrapped tightly around her but when she sat down, she shrugged it off to reveal a new bikini and cover-up. Its vibrant Italian style gave her a certain glow. Bluebell immediately recognised the Casa Emilia design and was thrilled that Miriam had found the confidence to go back to the small boutique.

Bluebell knew that Miriam was itching to find out how she and David had got on that morning, but they could not talk until they were alone. Luckily, after a light lunch of tuna salad from the pool bar, Evie decided to go back to her room for a lie-down, so Bluebell was able to fill Miriam in on their adventure.

'So, it was all a waste of time in the end,' Bluebell concluded.

'Oh, I wouldn't say that,' said Miriam. 'You managed to go back to the pink house and now you know the girl in the poppy-print dress doesn't live there, you and David can move on and look for her somewhere else.'

'If I ever see him again,' Bluebell muttered quietly.

'Of course you will!' Miriam's voice was high and bright. 'You'll be seeing him tomorrow when we go to Capri, won't you.'

'Maybe . . .' Bluebell was not convinced.

'He said he was going to meet us on the boat. Why ever do you think he won't turn up? He looks to me like a young man who's true to his word.'

'Mmm. So, what've you been up to today?' Bluebell did not want to spend any more time dwelling on her own morning with David.

'Oh, I just wandered around the town,' Miriam said. Her cheeks went a little pink.

Bluebell suppressed a smile. She would put money on Miriam having dropped into Tommaso's restaurant. 'Did you stop off anywhere for coffee?' she asked.

'Nowhere interesting. Just a drink in Trattoria di Napoli,' Miriam replied.

'Did you happen to have a chat with the owner?' Bluebell tried to assume an expression of innocence.

'We did have a little chat. In fact, he showed me some old photographs of Minori. They were rather interesting. Did you know the town was a famous centre for pasta production?'

Bluebell shook her head. She was pretty sure that Miriam and Tommaso had been talking about more than Minori's industrial heritage. She waited for Miriam to go on but instead of telling her more about her conversation with Tommaso, she started talking about the weather and their forthcoming trip to Capri. Before Bluebell had chance to press her any further Miriam scuttled off to her room, looking rather evasive.

Chapter Twenty-Four

Miriam felt a bit guilty. She had not actually lied about wanting to go back to her room, but she had omitted to mention it was only in order to fix her hair and get changed. She needed to meet Tommaso in something rather more demure than Casa Emilia's finest.

She put on one of her favourite summer dresses and crept out of the hotel. She seemed to be spending a lot of time sneaking around. First the fake ankle injury and trip to Maiori with Bluebell and now she was sliding off to meet Tommaso. She couldn't put her finger on why, but the prospect of Bluebell joining them on the outing to see Tommaso's elderly friend made her heart sink. Luckily the younger woman seemed happy to lounge by the pool and read for the rest of the afternoon. She was pleased that none of the others were in the reception area. She had nothing to hide, so why did she feel the need to conceal where she was going? There was no reason for her to touch up her make-up either. Glancing over her shoulder she made her way down the road towards Piazza Umberto.

Tommaso Amati was sitting at his usual table reading a letter. His forehead was creased with concentration. For a moment she hesitated. Perhaps she should turn around; she might be interrupting something important. At that moment he looked up and his face changed. A smile crossed his countenance like the sun emerging from behind a cloud.

He stood up as she approached and put the folded letter into his inside pocket.

'Shall we go, or would you like a drink first? A cup of tea, perhaps?'

'Shall we head straight off? I'm so looking forward to meeting your friend. It would be amazing if she really did know my father-in-law.'

'I'm quite intrigued myself,' said Tommaso.

'I thought I'd be reading a detective story by the pool this afternoon. Now I feel I'm starring in my own investigation.' Miriam laughed.

'And I am delighted to be a part of it,' said Tommaso. He smiled at her. She smiled back. His brown eyes were soft. She couldn't help noticing, again, how handsome he was.

They walked slowly as the sun was quite strong. Tommaso pointed out one or two places of interest, stopping for a brief word here and there, always politely introducing her, but after a while he stopped talking and they lapsed into a very comfortable silence.

As he led her towards the steps at the back of the Basilica of Saint Trofimena, Miriam realised that she was walking along the route that Bluebell had described taking with Josie on their early evening walk. She wondered if she would catch a glimpse of the pink house that Bluebell and David had tried to visit that morning. It now seemed quite unlikely that it had anything to do with the mystery girl or her suitcase; the curtains at the upstairs window and under the sink that Bluebell had described were probably a red herring. But if they passed by she would make sure that she asked Tommaso if he knew who lived there.

They paused to catch their breath at a conveniently placed bench, then, to her surprise Tommaso pointed out some steep stairs that led up to an old marshmallow-pink house. She looked up to see an orange poppy-print curtain catching in the light breeze.

'That is the house where Carmela Gentili lives.'

Miriam tried to keep a neutral expression. She could hardly confess that two of the *Loving and Knitting* party had been peering through the window. At least she now knew for sure that the occupant of the property was someone of nearly ninety, not the attractive young woman who had caught David's eye that day on the boat.

'Is she expecting us?' she asked.

'No, she is not expecting us, but she is always happy to have visitors. Her old friends find it difficult to climb the steps and her daughter is so busy that she cannot come as often as she would like. I know she and her husband have urged her to consider a flat in the lower part of the town but she is adamant that this is her home and she has no intention of moving. She has been here since she married even though her husband passed away some twenty years ago. She feels it is her destiny to stay here in this old house. Now, come, we will visit Carmela. It is rather steep; please hold the railing. I take it in turns with a friend to bring her a bag of groceries each week and sometimes it is treacherous. Hold tight, I do not want anything to happen to you.' Then he took her other hand in his to make quite sure.

When they reached the green door at the top of the stairs Miriam expected Tommaso to bang on the iron knocker. Instead he reached down and picked up a white pottery toadstool decorated with large red dots. He held it upside down and removed a key that was concealed in its base.

'Mrs Gentili is very deaf these days, and like a lot of elderly folk she doesn't like to wear a hearing aid. She cannot hear a knock at the door, but all her friends know her back-gate key is hidden in this toadstool and she is happy for us to let ourselves in.'

'Does she lip-read?' Miriam asked. It was beginning to sound like this might be a rather one-sided conversation.

'When people she likes arrive she will put in her hearing aid, but if she can't be bothered to talk she just leaves it out and pretends she cannot understand anything. I believe she can lip-read but it is more useful to her to pretend that she doesn't.'

Miriam fervently hoped that Carmela Gentili would take a liking to her or this would be a very short and unproductive visit. It was a fantastic coincidence that Colin's story about his father Jim had led her to the very same house that Bluebell and David had tried to visit that morning. No wonder no one had answered the door; the old lady would not have heard a thing. And providing she was happy to talk, there was an outside chance that she might somehow be linked to the identity of the girl in the poppy-print dress. Then a thought popped into her head: would Carmela speak a word of English or would Tommaso have to translate?

Tommaso led Miriam around the side of the house. Although it wasn't immediately obvious, one of the fence panels acted as a gate. A keyhole was barely visible beneath a sweep of sweet-scented, trailing jasmine.

Tommaso unlocked the gate, opened the unlocked back door and rang an old brass bell, dull with age, that was lying on an oak chest. The bell was loud enough to wake the dead but probably sounded like a gentle tinkle in the ear of Mrs Gentili. A few moments later a small, plump lady entered the room. She was dressed in an A-line patterned smock worn under a floral cotton pinny, and thick black stockings. She threw her arms around Tommaso and then

174

looked at Miriam for a second before enveloping her in an equally enthusiastic hug. It appeared that any friend of Tommaso was a friend of hers. She gestured towards a drawer in the bureau and pointed in the direction of the kitchen.

'She is going to put her hearing aid in whilst we put on the coffee pot,' said Tommaso.

The kitchen was just as Bluebell had described it. A long wooden work surface ran along the back wall, which was broken up only by a free-standing oven range and an old, slightly chipped butler sink. Beneath the sink was what looked like a piece of bamboo holding a row of metal curtain clips attached to which was a piece of gathered material that looked suspiciously like the bodice of the sunflower-print dress that Bluebell had worn on their trip to Ravello. Above the work surface a motley collection of pots, pans and utensils was attached to the wall by a variety of hooks. A traditional wooden clothes airer hung from the ceiling and a black-and-gold sewing machine with a wind-up handle sat on one end of the kitchen table, whose surface was pitted and worn. There were no signs of any modern appliances. Bluebell was right: it certainly did not look like the sort of house where David's fantasy girl might live.

Tommaso spooned some coffee into the stovetop pot and took three mismatched cups from the mug tree on the counter. As he switched on the gas the old lady entered right on cue, her hearing aid switched on in honour of her unexpected visitors. She reached into a cupboard under the counter and brought out a rather battered tin with kittens on the lid that contained half a cake. Miriam thought it looked as though the offering had been there for quite some time, but it was packed full of fruit and those sorts of cakes lasted forever, didn't they? Carmela accepted Tommaso's offer to pour the coffee and took them into a small sitting room. It was time for Miriam to be formally introduced.

'*Questa è Miriam; è inglese*. This is Miriam; she is English.'

The old lady spoke slowly. 'I am pleased to meet you. I surprise you, Mr Amati. You do not know I speak such good English.' She turned to Miriam. 'When I was a young girl, about twelve or thirteen, I met an American boy, a young man, about nineteen. I taught him some Italian; he taught me some English. We spoke every day for a few months. He stayed in our house, with my mother. It was during the war, a long time ago. When he left I did not want to forget, so I practised again and again. When it was Christmas I asked my mother for just one gift – an English dictionary – and after the war I found some English books. For many years I read a little bit when I had the time.'

'That boy was a soldier, wasn't he?' said Tommaso.

'You have a good memory. I did not think you always listened to my old stories.'

'Nonsense! I am always interested,' he replied with mock indignation.

'Tommaso, you are a good man, always such nice manners.' She chuckled. 'Shall I tell you more about him?'

Miriam nodded; she was not sure if Carmela was referring to the young soldier or the man who had brought her to the house. She wanted to find out more about both of them.

'It was a long time ago. Some days memories seem so far away, then a little bit of the past comes to you and disappears again like a bird that you glimpse up in the sky. Other days the memories seem so vivid it is a shock to catch sight of myself in the mirror and see that the young girl vanished decades ago. I am now nearly ninety years old and have seen so much but I have never forgotten that young soldier all that time ago.

'The war was hard on us all. I was sheltered from a lot of it, of course, being so young. It was just me and my mother living in Maiori, the seaside town just along the coast. A lot of my friends had fathers who were away fighting and had to deal with a lot more upheaval than I did. We didn't have a television in those days, of course; nobody did. In fact, I have never had one myself. We listened to the news on the radio, but my mother rarely believed what they said; she preferred to listen to the gossip in the street.

'I remember it was summertime, yes, July 1943 it was, when Mussolini fell from power. We were scared, even the people who did not support him. He had led us into this war, which was causing such poverty and hardship, but he had seemed such a powerful leader we did not know what would become of us. Then towards the end of that summer Italy surrendered to the Allies and joined forces to defeat the Germans, though of course it was a long time after that before the war finally ended.

'The day after the Italian surrender was announced we heard that thousands of American and British troops had landed along the Salerno coast in order to destroy the German positions in the south of the country. There was fighting on the plain between the beaches and the mountains all along here but by a quirk of fate there was no real German presence where we lived in Maiori so the American soldiers that landed in our little area did not meet any resistance until later on when they fought in the Chiunzi Pass high above the town.

'I remember being frightened and excited at the same time seeing all these soldiers marching up the high street. I was only young, maybe twelve years old. Can you imagine how I felt to see this happening right in front of my eyes? My mother had gone out to see what was going on. I was under strict instructions to stay at home out of the way and look at my schoolbooks, but the temptation was too much. I crept out of the house and went down into the town to where my friend lived. As soon as her mother's back was turned we ran out of the house and we went and stood in one of the side roads off Corso Reginna to watch the men go by.

'We could see where my mother was standing but she could not see us. She had a faded red dress she had sewn herself and held her old wicker shopping basket in the crook of her arm. She must have been to the bakery as I remember seeing a big loaf of bread sticking out and wondering what treat I might have for tea. Then suddenly we heard a commotion. We could not see what was happening; it looked like one of the soldiers had fallen. We were scared. I thought he might have been shot and we knew we were supposed to be safe at home. But we hadn't heard any gunfire and none of the adults seemed frightened.

'My friend was tugging at my sleeve and saying we should go but then we saw my mother stepping forward; we could pick her out of the crowd so easily in that old red dress she wore. She was bending over where the young soldier had fallen. Then another soldier came over. He was shouting in English. We didn't know what he was saying so we panicked and ran home. My mother never knew I was there that day.' Carmela chuckled.

'Later Mamma arrived back at home with three soldiers. Two older ones had carried this young lad to our house. Fortunately for them it wasn't up a steep flight of stairs like this one. He had fallen in the street and broken his ankle badly. My mother had qualified as a nurse before she became a teacher and she volunteered to take care of him until the injury healed. She told me later on that it was her way of contributing to the war effort as she had no husband or son to go and fight.'

'Weren't you scared to have this strange soldier staying with you?' said Miriam.

'No. I could tell at once he was a good person.'

'Yes, he was,' said Miriam. Carmela frowned and looked quizzically at Tommaso.

'We think the boy your mother took in was Miriam's father-in-law. We were looking at some old photographs in the back of my restaurant when she told me how her late husband's father had broken his ankle in the street during the war and been taken in by a lady in Maiori. I thought at once that the woman could have been your mother, so I thought the two of you should meet and find out more.'

'Did he have sandy hair and a fair few freckles?' Carmela said.

'Yes, that was Jim.'

'And now?' Carmela leant forward.

'I'm so sorry. Jim passed away some years ago, but I know he always remembered you and your mother's kindness to him,' Miriam said softly. She saw a flash of pain flicker across the old lady's eyes as she sank back in her chair.

'My mother kept him with us as long as she could. His ankle healed but it was never going to be strong again. She was so relieved when the army kept him behind in Maiori to help run the makeshift hospital they had set up at the Convent of San Domenico. I would ask Tommaso to take you to Maiori and show you inside, but it was closed after the earthquake we had in the town many years ago. Jim stayed with us for a few months whilst he worked there, but then he was transferred away from here to other duties and I never saw him again. For the rest of the war I hoped that he might come back. I thought I was in love with him, you see. A schoolgirl crush, I suppose. Then after the war my friend introduced me to her cousin from Minori. We married when I was nineteen and I moved to the house where you are sitting now.

'I had a good, long marriage and I was happy, though sometimes I did wonder what had happened to that boy, whether he had survived the rest of the war. And I hoped that he went on to experience the same good fortune that I did.'

'Yes, he did. But I know he never forgot his time here.'

'It is nice to be remembered,' Carmela said. She fell silent. Her dark eyes focused on a spot in the far distance.

After a minute or two Miriam said, 'My late husband told me that his father didn't like to talk about the war. I think he was embarrassed to have been felled by an injury caused by his own inattentiveness and he thought other people would judge him.'

'He must have been a modest man not to let you know that he was a hero to many people.'

'But I thought he only did clerical work at the hospital.'

'It was nothing to do with his work. It was early one morning when he was walking to the hospital. A scooter came racing out of a side street and the rider wasn't looking, causing a delivery truck to swerve at the last minute just as a little girl and her mother were crossing the street. Your father-in-law leapt in front of the truck and pushed the little one out of harm's way. The truck clipped his leg and knocked him down. He got up fine, but he had knocked his weak ankle and his walking was never quite right again. The mother of that girl was absolutely convinced that Jim had saved her daughter's life and made sure everybody in the town knew it. So, you see, he had nothing to be ashamed of. There is more than one way to be a hero.'

Miriam was truly touched by Carmela's tale. It was typical of her father-in-law to have kept quiet about risking serious injury to help the little girl. Colin had always looked up to his father, but it was a shame that he had never known about his bravery.

'Did Jim have any grandchildren?' Carmela asked. Miriam reached into her handbag and pulled out her mobile phone. She was sure she had a recent email from one of her nieces with some photos attached to it. 'I'm afraid there's no signal up here. My grandchildren always complain about that when they visit.'

'I'm sorry I don't have any photos of them in my purse, only a picture of Colin, my late husband. Do you have many grandchildren?'

'Just the two. My daughter Maria has a girl and a boy. Paolo is the elder, nearly thirty now. He's always been very bright. He was the first in the family to go to university and now he is a lawyer in Naples, doing very well. His sister Michela is twenty-five. She works at Il Gattino with my daughter and her husband Mario. She is a bright girl too. She has just come back from a year in London working at some fancy restaurant. The Golden Wolf they call it.'

'I've heard of it. They say a lot of celebrities eat there,' Miriam commented casually. But celebrities were the last thing on her mind right now.

'Michela will be finding it a bit different back in Minori.' The old lady chortled. 'Film stars and suchlike are a bit thin on the ground around here, though of course the famous director Roberto Rossellini made some of his great films up the road in Maiori.'

'Michela came back to work in her cousins' restaurant, The Old Fishermen, on the harbour in Positano, but she has had to change her plans as her father isn't too well,' Tommaso said.

'My good friend is too modest. My son-in-law had a heart attack very recently and is having to rest, but without Tommaso's help he wouldn't be here now.'

'You exaggerate, Carmela. It was the doctors who saved Mario.'

'Nonsense. Do not listen to him, Miriam. Tommaso saved his life. He came to the rescue and performed CPR until the ambulance arrived. My daughter and her family will always be grateful to him.'

'Do you have any photographs of your grandchildren?' asked Miriam. She was aware of Tommaso's discomfort at being described in such glowing terms. He would be glad of the change of subject and with any luck the old lady would have more to tell.

'Would you please fetch the black leather album from the top drawer in the bureau, Tommaso?'

He handed Carmela the photograph album and she motioned for Miriam to change seats and sit next to her so that she could look at the photographs more easily. 'My hearing is not too good these days but luckily my eyesight is still strong. I would hate not to be able to see these photographs clearly or to do my sewing and knitting. Here we are; this first picture is of Paolo as a baby. Look how cute he is!' Miriam looked carefully as Carmela took her through the photos of Paolo and Michela as babies and toddlers, trying not to let her impatience show as the old lady took her time over each picture, adding a little description or amusing story to each one.

'Here is Michela on her sixth birthday. Doesn't she look sweet in that dress I made for her?'

Miriam admired the pretty girl posing in a cotton dress printed with oranges and lemons. 'Did you make a lot of her clothes?' she asked.

'Yes, I have lost count of the outfits I have sewn for her. It is a great pleasure of mine.'

'Did you make the curtains and cushions in the house as well?' she asked.

'Yes, I have sewn many things like that over the years.'

'I saw an orange poppy-print curtain hanging in the upstairs window when we arrived. Did you make that?' Miriam tried to keep the excitement out of her voice. She was sure Tommaso must think her most peculiar to take such an interest in the old lady's soft furnishings.

'Such a lovely pattern. I found a roll of it in the market a couple of years ago. I couldn't resist those happy poppies. I had plenty left over so I made a sundress for Michela too. Wait a minute, I'm sure there is a picture in here of her wearing it at Mario's sixty-fifth birthday.'

Miriam took the photograph album from Carmela, her hand trembling with excitement. In the middle of the photograph, standing either side of Carmela, were her two grandchildren: on one side a handsome young man and on the other a younger girl with long dark hair. She recognised the girl immediately as the waitress who had been working in Il Gattino, though she had lost a little weight since the photograph had been taken and she no longer wore her long dark hair tumbling loose down her back. But it wasn't the girl's hair that made Miriam's hand tremble. It was the dress she was wearing: an orange dress covered in large white poppies.

'Are you okay, Miriam? You've gone very quiet,' said Tommaso.

'Of course. I was just thinking what a lovely photograph this is,' she said quickly.

'Let me show you some more,' said Carmela. She turned over the pages of the leather-bound album. 'Here is Michela again, with Maria, my daughter.'

Miriam looked at the next photograph. This time the girl was wearing the same daisy-print dress that Bluebell had worn the day they had gone to Maiori to look for David. 'I recognise your granddaughter from Il Gattino. We usually eat in the hotel where we're staying but we ate at Il Gattino the other night. The food was ever so good.'

'As good as mine?' said Tommaso. 'Don't worry, I'm only joking. Maria's cooking is legendary. I can close my eyes and smell her *ragù* right now. Mmm . . .'

'She is thinner than in these pictures,' tutted Carmela. 'She was working so hard in London, but I am hoping her mother's cooking will fatten her up again. At this rate I will have to sew her some more dresses. I think all she wore in London were those strange trousers – skinny jeans, I think they call them.' She turned a few more pages of the old album to show Miriam more family photos then asked her some questions about her trip and how she was enjoying her time in Minori.

Miriam answered her questions with enthusiasm. She would have happily chatted away for much longer, but after a while she sensed that the old lady was getting a little tired. Tommaso caught her eye, so they got up and made their farewells. As Miriam turned to go Carmela whispered in her ear, 'Take care of him. He's a good man.' Her face reddened at the old lady's assumption but fortunately it appeared that Tommaso had not heard her.

They made their way carefully down the steps, Tommaso taking Miriam's hand to make sure that she did not trip. As they turned to walk down the main road back into the centre of Minori she noticed a man with a clipboard standing in the neglected farmland that ran from the edge of the road on the far side of Carmela's house. He seemed to be measuring the land with some sort of hand-held measuring device. She hoped it wasn't someone planning to build on the plot and shatter the old lady's tranquil environment.

They were soon back down in the main part of the town. Miriam would have liked nothing better than to return to Trattoria di Napoli to spend some more time talking to Tommaso, but she knew he would soon be busy preparing for the evening's customers. Her natural reticence prevented her from risking overstaying her welcome, so when they reached Piazza Umberto she merely thanked him for taking her to the house of Carmela Gentili so that she could find out more about her father-in-law's time in Maiori.

'It was my pleasure. And I hope you all have a marvellous trip to Capri tomorrow.'

'I am sure we will, though I can't imagine I will enjoy it more than today.'

'There aren't many days I have enjoyed as much as today,' he said simply. Then he stepped forward. For a split second she thought he was going to take her in his arms and kiss her, but he just smiled and pecked her on each cheek. 'Please come and say goodbye before you go back to England,' he said.

'I will.'

Miriam walked quickly towards the Hotel Sea Breeze, knowing she was blushing. *Take her in his arms and kiss her* – was she quite mad? Carmela Gentili had mistakenly assumed that there was something between the two of them, but she knew better. He was just a nice, friendly man who had thought her story about Jim would interest an elderly lady. Today would have been a pleasant distraction from his busy duties at Trattoria di Napoli. By the time he was serving his first customers of the evening he would probably have forgotten all about their outing. Tomorrow he would be busy in his restaurant and she would be on a boat trip to Capri with Josie and Bluebell and the other prizewinners. The day after that she would be on a flight back to England.

Yes, she would go and say goodbye to him on that last morning, then she would be on a plane heading back to her life hundreds of miles away. The thought made her unaccountably sad.

Chapter Twenty-Five

Miriam hoped that the other women would not quiz her about her day. It was as though there had been something magical about the afternoon and talking about it would break the spell. She did not want to tell anyone about her conversation with Carmela Gentili, least of all Bluebell. She was bound to tell David as soon as they saw him the next day on the boat to Capri. And if David knew that his dream girl was living in the town, that would scupper any plans Miriam had to play Cupid. Tomorrow's trip to Capri was the perfect opportunity for Bluebell and David to spend more time together and she wasn't going to let the girl from Il Gattino wreck things. He and Bluebell might think they were just becoming good friends, but she could see there was more to it. As Josie said, you can't be a *Loving and Knitting* reader and not know a bit about romance.

Of course, she would have to tell them the truth eventually. It was only right that the two girls were reunited with their correct cases before the competition winners flew back to England, and it was only fair that David knew the whereabouts of the girl he had his heart set on. But they didn't need to know right now, need they?

Miriam arrived back at the Hotel Sea Breeze to find the others perched on stools around the pool bar. The heat had gone out of the day. To her surprise and embarrassment no one asked her about her day; they were too busy talking about her new bikini and cover-up from Casa Emilia. Bluebell and Evie had described her transformation in such glowing terms that she was urged to pop to her room and bring the garments down for the ladies' inspection. Although the women had previously admired Bluebell's yellow-and-white, pom-pom-trimmed, polka-dot bikini, they had assumed that there was nothing to be had for their own age group.

She rather reluctantly fetched the leaf-print bikini and matching kaftan, which was examined amidst a chorus of *oohs* and *aahs*. To her amusement she had finally become a trendsetter at the age of seventy-two.

The ladies decided to form a shopping party and quickly finished the remains of their cold drinks, which were now watery with melted ice. They trooped out of the hotel accompanied by Josie, who promised to give her true and honest opinion on everyone's purchases.

'You are back already!' Emilia came out from behind the counter and, much to Miriam's surprise, planted two kisses on her cheeks.

'Nothing more for me, but my friends wanted to see your shop.'

'Your new swimwear is a success. *Fantastico!*'

'I think everyone is hoping that you will help them choose something,' Miriam said.

'*Certo!* But I am afraid we do not have much space. No room to swing a cat, I believe you say. And there is only the one little changing room behind that curtain.'

'Oh, that's no problem, dear. I'm sure we can take it in turns, though I would like to sit down if I may,' said Evie.

'Please do.' Emilia gestured to a rickety ladder-back chair squeezed into the corner of the shop.

'Now, who is to be first?'

'What about you, Brenda?' Josie said.

Brenda leant her green cotton shoulder bag against the counter. A large fold-out street plan of Amalfi was now wedged in amongst her other guidebooks.

Miriam watched Emilia assessing Brenda's rather staid outfit: the baggy pink T-shirt, the elasticated-waist floral skirt and the sensible-looking grey leather sandals with wide Velcro straps.

'I don't want a swimsuit. I want something a bit different,' Brenda said.

Emilia frowned. Miriam guessed she had Brenda marked down for one of her more substantial creations. Emilia rummaged behind the counter then placed a tankini-style two-piece in a light and pretty print on the countertop.

'It comes with an optional sarong and beach bag,' she said.

'It's very pretty,' Miriam said. She could see Brenda hesitating. Maybe even this most modest of creations was out of her comfort zone.

'It looks very you, Brenda,' said Josie.

'It's just the sort of thing I would choose, but maybe for once I should choose something I wouldn't choose, if you know what I mean.'

Emilia looked puzzled by the woman's comment. She showed her a couple of other safe options, but Brenda shook her head and pointed to a bikini on one of the glossy white mannequins in the corner. A snake slid around the dummy's hips, its forked tongue pointing dangerously towards – oh goodness me! Miriam was utterly stupefied. Brenda was pointing at Emilia's *serpenti* design, her *serpenti* design in red, white and gold, no less.

'Does it come in my size?' she asked.

'*Certo!*' Emilia quickly ushered Brenda behind the curtain as if fearing she might change her mind.

'Ta dah!' Brenda leapt out from behind the curtain, striking a pose.

'*Brava!*' cried Emilia. Following a spontaneous round of applause she was besieged by requests for her brightest, wildest swimwear. Everyone left the shop with a little something wrapped in tissue paper in a *Casa Emilia* bag except for Evie who declared herself inspired to crochet some itsy-bitsy bikinis for the next church bazaar.

It was a busy evening at Trattoria di Napoli. Normally the sight of his restaurant full of happy customers was enough to make Tommaso Amati contented but tonight he felt restless and although he was as charming and courteous as always, he had one eye on the clock, looking forward to the time that he could pull down the shutters and close up for the night. He was desperate to be alone, to sit quietly behind his counter at the back of the shop and think. At last the final customers left, the two boys who worked for him went home and all was quiet.

Putting Trattoria di Napoli up for sale was a spontaneous decision driven by his old friend Mario's heart attack and his fear of suffering the same fate. But after this afternoon's visit to Carmela Gentili's little pink house he knew there was something else behind it or rather someone else. Someone he hadn't even met a week ago: a woman whose charm and gentle ways endeared her to him more and more each time he saw her: Miriam.

He could no longer deny that there was a certain emptiness in his life, no matter how busy he kept himself. He had barely had a social life these last ten years. Meeting Miriam had reminded him how important friendship was. But soon their short acquaintance would be over. It was a shame she would be going home the day after tomorrow, but she had done him a favour in the short time they'd spent together. She had made him realise there was more to life than his beloved Trattoria di Napoli.

He reached into his jacket and pulled out a letter from the inside pocket. It was the formal offer from Stefano Bassani and his business partner, Alberto, for the purchase of Trattoria di Napoli. Stefano was expecting his answer the next day, but there was no need to keep him in suspense any longer. The day with Miriam had helped him make his mind up. He took out his mobile phone and sent a message: *I wish to accept your offer. Come as soon as you like tomorrow. We open at seven for breakfast if that suits you.*

It was late now, but if Stefano did not read his text tonight he would see it as soon as he woke up. It would be the start of a new era for both of them.

He had one more thing to do. He went over to the window, removed the FOR SALE sign and turned it over. He wrote the word SOLD and put it back in the window.

Chapter Twenty-Six

The first hour of the day was always a busy one at Il Gattino. A steady stream of regulars came in to stand at the counter and enjoy their first coffee of the day before hurrying off to their jobs in the shops, banks and hairdresser's in the little town. Michela and Paolo worked non-stop: pulling the levers on the large chrome-and-black coffee machine; frothing up milk in a metal jug; serving pastries; washing up and, most importantly, exchanging gossip with the local townsfolk and updating them on their father's progress.

Just as Michela had finished wiping down the counter a woman walked in. It was the unmistakeable figure of Valentina Frandini. She was dressed in a skin-tight fuchsia dress better suited to a hen night in Malaga than her job at the local post office. She ordered a cappuccino and leant on the counter expectantly. *There's no chance of a few minutes' peace,* Michela thought wryly, knowing that Valentina loved nothing more than a good old gossip. Paolo conveniently vanished into the kitchen, declaring he had some urgent stocktaking to attend to, so she made the woman her coffee and resolved to look interested in whatever trivial news she was about to hear.

'How's your dear father? Such a shame.'

Michela was certain that Valentina already knew more about her father's heart attack and future prognosis than she knew herself, but she answered politely, 'Getting better all the time, thank you.'

'He must be getting impatient; he never was one for taking it easy.'

'My mother is making sure he follows the doctor's orders. Luckily she has persuaded him that we are able to keep Il Gattino going in his absence now that I am back from London.'

'How was your time in London? Such a big place. Lots of single men! You haven't brought one back with you then?' Valentina took a sip of her cappuccino leaving a smear of sticky, fuchsia lipstick on the white china.

'I was working long hours at the restaurant,' Michela said. She was not going to be drawn into her love life or lack of it with Valentina; she might as well chalk it up on the *Specials* board.

'The restaurant business is very long hours and a lot of hard work. No wonder Tommaso Amati has sold Trattoria di Napoli.'

'I don't think he's sold it yet; he's only just put it up for sale,' Michela said.

'Well, when I walked past a few minutes ago he had put a "SOLD" sign in the window,' said Valentina, smugly. She loved nothing better than being first with the news.

Michela felt a little sick; Valentina must be mistaken. She had only been talking to Mr Amati two days before about the possibility of her family purchasing the restaurant. He hadn't seemed enthusiastic, but he hadn't ruled it out, had he? Maybe he had been talking to her brother Paolo and realised he wasn't willing to commit to her plan. She didn't want to give Valentina the pleasure of seeing how shocked she was, so she just said, 'He found a buyer very quickly then.'

'Well, it's certainly going to be all change in Minori.' Valentina leant forward over the counter in a conspiratorial manner. Michela averted her eyes from the substantial breasts that were now resting on the counter top, nodded and waited for her to continue. 'We could do with somewhere trendy for the young people to hang out and eat.'

'Trendy? What do you mean?'

'Those burger places are ever so popular. I can't see the appeal myself, all multi-coloured plastic seats and bright lighting. Then there's the food. I don't know what they make those things out of but I'm sure it's not cows.'

'Trattoria di Napoli is turning into a burger bar? I can't imagine Mr Amati would want that to happen.'

'Well, I heard in the market that Stefano Bassani made him a very good offer.'

'Stefano Bassani is buying Trattoria di Napoli?' Michela gripped the counter top; she could not trust her legs to keep her upright.

'My friend told me she'd seen him going into the restaurant with her own eyes. And rumour has it he's had his eye on that place ever since he used to help your mother in the kitchen. Lucky for him he's got a wealthy father to help fund his plans,' Valentina added a little bitterly.

'Stefano Bassani opening a burger bar? I can't believe it,' Michela said, trying to keep the quiver out of her voice. He must have plans for one of those gourmet places where juicy patties made from the finest grass-reared beef were sandwiched between freshly baked buns and a variety of tasty salads made up the remainder of the menu.

'You can make a good living with one of those Chucky Joe's franchises.' Valentina smirked.

'He's opening a branch of Chucky Joe's on Piazza Umberto?'

'It's obvious that's what he's going to do, isn't it. He won't let those three years in Rome go to waste. They say head office has got plans to spread their restaurants all over the Amalfi Coast.' Valentina drained the last of her cappuccino. 'I must be off. I'm not one to stand around gossiping.'

Michela sat down with her head in her hands. This could not be happening. She thought of the hours Stefano had spent in their kitchen learning the traditional recipes that Maria and Mario had lovingly prepared for so many years. A picture of Mario teaching Stefano to identify the scent of the different herbs whilst blindfolded came back to her. Then her feelings of sadness turned to something darker.

Stefano must have known there was a chance that her family might want to buy Tommaso's restaurant. Papa had always spoken so highly about Trattoria di Napoli's professional kitchen and its prime position on Piazza Umberto. Sure, there was the small matter of raising the money they needed and, she had to admit, the chance that Mario would not be up for the challenge after his heart attack, not to mention persuading her brother, Paolo, to get on board with her plans. But right now that didn't matter. All she knew was that Stefano and his girlfriend had swooped in like a pair of rich, selfish vultures, taking advantage of her father's illness to snatch the Trattoria di Napoli from under her family's noses.

Stefano's fast-food joint was bound to take custom away from the traditional restaurants on the square, not to mention the families who came to Il Gattino for a plate of *spaghetti al pomodoro*. She had to tell Paolo straight away.

'Paolo, you can come out now!'

He emerged from the kitchen. 'Thank goodness that woman has gone. Hey, what's the matter? She hasn't upset you, has she?'

'Tommaso Amati has found a buyer for Trattoria di Napoli already,' Michela said with a sob.

'Don't cry, Michela. I know you wanted to find a way for us to buy it, but I honestly don't think it would be the right thing to do.'

'You don't understand, Paolo, it's not just that. Valentina said that Stefano is buying it.'

'Stefano? That's interesting. When I met up with some guys from school the other night they said they thought he was looking to open his own restaurant, but I didn't think it would be here, in Minori. That's amazing! I can't believe he's coming back. I thought when he moved to Rome he had gone for good.'

'I wish he had.'

'But why? I understand you're disappointed, but I thought you always liked Stefano, and would be glad he's moving back home. In fact, I reckon you had a bit of a crush on him. I remember the time I caught you two having a sneaky kiss.' Paolo laughed.

'Whatever I felt for him was a long time ago, especially now I've heard about his plans,' she said stiffly.

'He's always had vision, so whatever he does with the restaurant it's bound to be something interesting.'

'If you call frozen pizzas and cheap burgers interesting.'

'Burgers? No, you must have got it wrong.'

'Valentina said Stefano is opening a *Chucky Joe*'s franchise and he's planning to run a chain of them all along the coast.'

'You've got to be joking!'

'I wish I was. It's going to kill Papa to see Stefano come back here and open some place with plastic-flavoured food right near the seafront in place of the best restaurant in town.'

'Without Mamma and Papa he wouldn't have even thought of going into the restaurant business. Everything he knows about cooking he learnt at Il Gattino,' said Paolo fiercely, his dark eyes blazing. 'No wonder he hasn't shown his face in here yet.'

The noise of Maria's footsteps coming down the stairs halted their conversation. 'Is everything all right?' she said.

'Yes, Mamma, everything is fine,' said Michela. There was no point telling her mother about Stefano's plans. She had enough on her plate right now.

'Your father has asked for a little bread and jam. It's a good sign. I normally have to nag him to eat anything.' Maria went through to the kitchen in the back of the café and started bustling about.

'I think we are nearly out of peach jam,' Michela called out.

'We have just enough for his breakfast but could you get some more from the store for me? And what are you still doing here, Paolo? I thought you were visiting your cousins in Positano today. It will be your last chance before you return to Naples tomorrow morning.'

'He was hiding in the kitchen. Valentina came in for a gossip,' Michela replied. She was glad to be able to make a joke out of the distressing visit.

'Well, off you go, the pair of you. I'll see you this afternoon, Paolo. Don't be too long, Michela; there's lots to do.'

Michela was glad to go out and make the short walk up to the mini market. She needed to clear her head. As she left Il Gattino two of her father's friends came in, but she knew Maria would be more than happy to serve them and give them an update on Mario's progress.

She carried on up the road, her mood darkening as she thought about what Valentina had told her. As she glanced in one of the shop windows she saw that her brow was furrowed and she was glaring like an axe murderer. She tried to think of something nice, otherwise she would give the woman in the mini market quite a fright. She thought of her father sitting up in bed, enjoying eating his bread and peach jam.

She quickly located the jam on one of the lower shelves and added a packet of Mario's favourite apple biscuits to her basket. After exchanging a few pleasantries with the sales assistant and assuring her of her father's continuing recovery, she headed back to Il Gattino. As she rounded the corner, she heard someone call out her name.

She looked up, but she did not need to look to see who was calling her. She would know that voice anywhere. It was the voice that had been dear to her heart for as long as she could remember: the voice she had dreamt of hearing again for three long years. Now it was the last voice she wanted to hear. There was nowhere to run; she had to face him. She looked up into the smiling face of Stefano Bassani.

Chapter Twenty-Seven

Miriam stood on the pier, looking out to sea. She could see the white boat approaching from the direction of Maiori and watched it getting bigger and bigger and closer and closer until the little smudges above the railings turned into human faces.

She had always wanted to see Capri; it was one of the places she and Colin had once planned to visit together. Now she had the chance, she couldn't help wishing she was spending the day mooching around Minori. She had fallen in love with the little place. She knew it wasn't just the town that had captured her heart; when she returned to England, a little piece of her would always belong to Tommaso Amati.

If she told the other women how she felt they would think she was crazy. She had known Tommaso for less than a week, but there was something special about him. Something she hadn't found since those first few days with Colin. She didn't expect she would ever find it again.

The boat pulled up at the bottom of the pier. The gangplank was lowered and one of the workers caught hold of the thick rope to secure the vessel as a small number of people disembarked.

As people began to board, Miriam was aware that Josie was scanning the pier.

'Has anyone seen Evie?' Josie said.

Brenda closed her enormous guidebook and stuffed it back into her green shoulder bag. 'Sorry, I was so absorbed in my book I haven't been paying much attention, but now you mention it, I haven't seen her since we crossed Piazza Umberto.'

'Are you ladies getting on this boat or not? I need to see your tickets.' A dark-suntanned man in too-tight pink shorts and a striped linen shirt, opened to expose a wiry explosion of greying chest hair, was ushering them forward.

'Please wait! Please don't leave yet. One of our ladies is missing,' Josie said.

The man was suddenly all smiles and gestured for his mate to delay untying the rope. Oh, what it was to be young and pretty! Miriam was quite sure she wouldn't have the slightest chance of success if she was the one who wanted to hold up the boat.

At last, Evie came hurrying along the pier. In her bright turquoise dress she looked like a little kingfisher. She was clutching a cloth bag into which she was stuffing a ball of vivid yellow wool. A large Italian lady was running after her with another ball of the same wool.

The man in the pink shorts helped Evie onto the gang-plank with exaggerated courtesy, clearly trying to curry favour with Josie, who was young enough to be his daughter. Miriam was thrilled to see that David was already on the boat, as promised, waving to them from the top deck.

Miriam did not know what made her turn around, but she was so glad that she did. There, standing on the pier was Tommaso. She hesitated at the top of the gangplank. Tommaso took a step towards her. Miriam raised a hand in greeting. She felt her heart lift with joy.

Tommaso did not wave back; he was no longer looking in her direction. His eyes were focused on a woman who was tottering towards him on her high heels calling out his name. A woman whose skin-tight, flesh-coloured dress did nothing to conceal her stupendous figure.

Miriam could no longer see Tommaso's face. It was obscured by the curtain of thick glossy hair that cascaded down the woman's back as she swept Tommaso into her arms and smothered him in kisses.

One of the boat hands began to untie the rope.

'Move along, please.' The man in the pink shorts put a hand on Miriam's elbow, propelling her forwards. The rope was cast off. Miriam started to climb the stairs to the upper deck. The boat moved away from the shore. She could not bear to look back.

Chapter Twenty-Eight

Stefano crossed the street to where Michela was standing, her hand tightly gripping a carrier bag from the mini market. She had spent so long dreaming of seeing him again but now that he was standing in front of her he was the last person in the world she wanted to see. How would she bear his polite enquiries about her family now he had shown his true colours? To sneak in and buy Trattoria di Napoli whilst her father was still recuperating from his heart attack and in no place to make a counter-offer was the lowest thing she could think of.

If it hadn't been for Mamma and Papa, he would never have gone into the restaurant business at all. He would probably be working for his father's empire as a manager of one of his two hotels in Maiori. What had happened to the boy who had learnt his trade by sitting in the kitchen of Il Gattino stirring Maria's *ragù*?

Now he was walking straight towards her, smiling broadly – the nerve of the man! She tried to stop her stomach flipping over as she took in his dark eyes and handsome face. Her foolish schoolgirl fantasies were threatening to undermine her righteous anger. At least he hadn't got his stunning new girlfriend in tow. She would be able to give him a piece of her mind without being distracted by the sinking feeling in her heart.

'Michela, I've been looking for you all over!' He stepped

towards her, arms flung wide open. She stiffened away from him. He stepped back, confusion written all over his handsome face.

'Why were you looking for me? To tell me about your plans?'

'Yes, I'm coming back to Minori.'

'So I heard when I was in the market, and I have been speaking to Valentina too.'

'Then you know a bit already. My partner and I are buying Trattoria di Napoli. I can't wait to tell you all about it.'

His partner – so their relationship was serious. This golden girl from Rome was going to move to Minori with him and they were going to run their pile-it-up-and-sell-it-cheap restaurant together. Well, she was welcome to him. Michela remained silent; she did not trust herself to speak.

'Michela?' Stefano's golden brow wrinkled. 'Don't you want to hear about my plans?'

'Valentina told me everything. I don't need to know any more,' she said shortly. How could he think she could possibly want to hear about it? A restaurant by the sea – had he really forgotten the plans the two of them had once shared? Now he was going to live his dream. With someone else.

'I thought you might be pleased.'

'Pleased? Are you joking? Pleased that you and your partner are taking over Trattoria di Napoli? Pleased about your great, wonderful, modern plans?' She pronounced the words *partner* and *modern* with particular emphasis. 'I can never be angry with Mr Amati – he saved Papa's life – but you . . . you . . . how could you be so disloyal?'

'Michela . . . let me explain.' He stepped towards her.

Michela could feel tears gathering in her eyes; she couldn't let Stefano see them. He was so near that she could breathe in the woody scent of his cologne. It brought back so many old memories. Why couldn't he smell of the bins in the alleyway like the rat he was? She turned away so that he could not see her face.

'I don't want to hear it. Save your explanations for Papa and your so-called friend Paolo.' Her voice was breaking up like a bad mobile signal and a sob threatened to escape after the word *Papa*. If she hesitated she would not be able to contain her tears. She might even end up in his arms. Her head told her she despised him; she could not let her heart betray her. She spun around and marched off down the road with as much dignity as she could muster.

She headed in the direction of Piazza Cantilena and began to climb the steps behind the basilica. There was only one person she wanted to see right now – the one person who had a way of making everything right. Ever since Michela was a little girl, Nonna Carmela had found a way to put her broken world back together again. She remembered one time when she and Sofia had been playing hairdressers, plaiting and styling their dollies' hair. Before she could stop her, Sofia had picked up some scissors and chopped off Margarita's beautiful nylon hair. Sofia's mother had tried in vain to soothe her, but she had run off crying to the one person with the power to put things right.

Nonna had sat her down with a plate of *biscotti*, pulled out some old movie magazines and leafed through them until she had found some short-haired starlets. She then used a pair of nail scissors to fashion the remains of Margarita's hair into a neat bob worthy of Vidal Sassoon himself. By the time Michela had helped Nonna sew a new outfit for Margarita, she had forgotten why she was so upset in the first place and was looking forward to showing off her dolly's whole new look.

Not everything was as easily fixed as Dolly Margarita's hair, but everything felt better after a visit to Nonna.

She paused on the doorstep to send her mother a quick text to let her know where she had gone. She took the key from inside the pottery toadstool, let herself in and rang the bell as loud as she could, knowing that her grandmother would eventually become aware of a faint metallic sound.

Carmela embraced her and set to putting the coffee pot on the stove. Whilst her grandmother was putting her hearing aid back in, Michela carried some mugs and cake in the kitten-patterned tin through to the small sitting room. The tray she was using was one she'd painted in primary school and it was lined with a cloth embroidered by Maria. The familiarity of it all tugged at her heart. So much of her life was bound up with Nonna and her childhood in Minori. She wasn't going to let anything or anyone spoil her life here.

As she looked around the old-fashioned sitting room her eyes alighted on a pretty vase of flowers sitting on the bureau next to the framed photograph of her grandfather. 'Those roses are lovely,' she remarked.

'I was given them this morning. You're my second visitor today. You'll never guess who came to see me earlier this morning. I'm dying to tell you.'

'Paolo?'

'No, but he did come past yesterday.'

'Emilia Bellucci?'

'No, not Emilia. It was someone I have not seen for a long time, though he hasn't changed very much at all. It was Stefano Bassani.'

It was the last name Michela wanted to hear right now but she was glad he had shown some decency by visiting the old lady and taking her some flowers. It was the least he could do after the way he had treated her family.

'How was he?' she forced herself to ask politely.

'Very well and full of plans. You may have heard he and his partner are buying Trattoria di Napoli from Mr Amati.'

'Yes, I had heard,' she said flatly.

'He came to tell me he is also buying the old piece of farmland next to this house.'

'What on earth is he going to do with that? Surely he isn't going to try to get permission to build a house on it?' Michela couldn't imagine that lovely-looking girl with Stefano wanting to live on the far side of the town with only an elderly lady as her neighbour. In fact she couldn't imagine a glamorous girl like that wanting to move from Rome to Minori. Unless she loved Stefano very much indeed.

'Heavens, no! He wants to use the plot to grow vegetables for the restaurant.'

'To grow vegetables,' Michela repeated dumbly. The only green thing a restaurant like Chucky Joe's needed was the limp lettuce that went in the hamburger buns.

'He will be able to grow much better quality vegetables if he can oversee the whole process.'

'I can't imagine that's his main priority,' Michela replied.

Nonna Carmela looked at her curiously. Her lips moved as though they were about to form a question. Instead she said, 'Stefano's not the only interesting visitor I have had this week. One of my old friends dropped by. She was desperate to pass on the news she heard in the market about your old boyfriend Fabio.'

'Oh, what is it?' Michela no longer had any feelings for Fabio, but she hoped it was good news.

'Such a lovely surprise. Fabio is to become a father. Imagine that! His wife Daniela is pregnant and expecting a boy. Daniela will inherit the whole of their farm one day and now his parents know that the farm will continue on after that with their first grandchild.'

'And Fabio is pleased?'

'He's thrilled. He says he has everything he ever wanted.'

'I'm glad,' said Michela. She no longer needed to feel guilty about leaving Fabio. He clearly hadn't been heart-broken for long. It was strange to think that the boyish young man with his soft, round face and shy smile was now a married man with a child on the way.

'I know you felt bad about leaving him but perhaps losing you has made him appreciate Daniela more than he would have done and that will do their marriage the world of good. Look, I have found a spare piece of blue material to sew the baby a romper suit for when the time comes.'

'That is a lovely shade. It will be quite perfect for a little boy. Though I don't know how you're going to find the time for sewing with all these people dropping in,' Michela teased.

'I don't think I have ever had so many visitors in a week. Tommaso Amati came by yesterday too.'

'Did he tell you about selling Trattoria di Napoli to Stefano?' It pained her to ask but she had to face the truth.

'No, he didn't mention the restaurant. He brought an English lady with him. It was such an enjoyable afternoon, talking about the old days.'

'Tommaso brought a woman to visit you? Who was she?'

'Believe me, I was as surprised as you are. I haven't seen Tommaso enjoying the company of another woman since that awful day.'

Michela was quiet for a moment remembering the tragic car accident ten years before that claimed the lives of Tommaso's wife and son. 'Where on earth did Tommaso meet this lady? Did you say she was English?'

'Apparently she is here on holiday.'

'A holiday romance. How extraordinary! So, he hardly knows her.'

'I don't think it matters how long you know someone to know if they are right for you,' said Carmela.

'And sometimes you can know them forever and still get it wrong,' Michela said. Hadn't she thought that Stefano was the one for her since the first time Paolo brought him home all those years ago? How could she have been so wrong?

'Tommaso says this lady, Miriam, is just a friend, but I can see by the way he looks at her that there's something more, even though he probably does not know it himself yet,' said Carmela.

'He doesn't usually bring his friends to see you, does he?'

'He thought I might like to meet her. She knew someone I knew a long, long time ago.'

'Someone from England?'

'Did I ever tell you the story of Jim, the American boy I met during the war when I was just a young girl?'

Michela smiled. She knew her grandmother's stories off by heart, but she did not get tired of hearing them. Besides, she always wondered what had become of the soldier who'd made such an impression on the young Carmela all those years ago. She suspected that despite her long and happy marriage to her grandfather the old lady kept a place in her heart for the American.

'Tommaso discovered that this lady was Jim's daughter-in-law. You can imagine my surprise to have a visit from her after all this time. Miriam seemed such a lovely lady. I think she is having quite an effect on Tommaso. He seems happier and more light-hearted than I have seen him in years. It's a real pity she is only in Minori on a short holiday. I believe she is flying back to England tomorrow. I would love to see Tommaso settled down with a nice woman. It isn't good for a man to be alone.'

'Do you ever wish you had married again?'

'*Mamma mia!* Heavens, no! But women are different; we're the stronger sex whatever people say.'

Michela hoped she was right, but when it came to Stefano she wasn't feeling that strong right now.

She hugged the old lady and kissed her goodbye. Just a short time in the comforting surroundings of her grandmother's house had done her the world of good. She would have been happy to stay there all day, but she had to get back to Il Gattino. She must have been gone for nearly an hour and a half. Her mother would be wondering what had happened to her. She didn't hold out much hope that Maria had checked the mobile phone that Paolo had given her several Christmases before.

When she reached the bottom of the steps she turned and waved to Nonna Carmela who was still standing in the doorway. How wrong it was to think of persuading her to quit her little home and join forces to buy Trattoria di Napoli from Mr Amati. The old lady belonged here, no matter how much easier her life would be if she moved from this awkwardly sited spot.

The chance to buy Trattoria di Napoli had been and gone. Her plans had turned to dust, like the dreams she and Stefano had once shared.

Now she was determined to work as hard as possible for Mamma and Papa in order to make Il Gattino as successful as she could. It was funny: she was the one who'd left their small town to take her chances in the buzzing metropolis of London, but it was Fabio who had never travelled further than Naples whose life was transformed. She was back where she started, working at Il Gattino, with no man in her life and no one on the horizon. And now she didn't even have her foolish dreams of Stefano to keep her warm.

As she walked down the hill back into the town she looked behind her at the neglected farmland adjacent to her grandmother's house. 'Vegetables!' She snorted. If Maria hadn't brought her up so well she would tell Stefano exactly where he could stick his zucchini.

Chapter Twenty-Nine

Maria threw up her arms in delight when she recognised the tall figure standing in the doorway of Il Gattino. She had not seen Stefano Bassani since he had left the small town of Minori to make his own way in Rome. She was delighted that the hours he had spent in the kitchen of Il Gattino had inspired him to forge a successful career. He might not have much use for the family recipes that she had taught him, but she was proud to know that she and Mario had been the inspiration behind his success. She admired the boy for having the guts to strike out on his own, even if reheated frozen pizzas and factory-produced desserts were not to her liking.

Rome obviously suited Stefano. The baggy shorts and printed T-shirts of his youth were gone, replaced by well-cut trousers and a cool, short-sleeved shirt. She noticed that his cheeks had lost their boyish chubbiness and those newly prominent cheekbones combined with his dark eyebrows and rich brown eyes had turned him into someone more handsome than the pleasant-looking boy that she remembered.

'I am so pleased to see you, Stefano,' she said, hugging him.

'I am so sorry it has taken me so long to come. I just couldn't get here any earlier. I've had to attend to a few business matters since I arrived, though I know that's a pretty poor excuse.'

'You are here now — that's all that matters. And I am glad to see you looking so well.'

'But tell me, how is Mario? I was so shocked to hear what had happened. I bumped into one of Mamma's old friends just after I arrived, and she told me all about it.'

'Oh, he is so much better. We are all so relieved. He needs to rest for a while. Of course, he is itching to get up and around and start taking charge again, but he needs to take things easy. Thank goodness Michela has come back from London. I don't know what we would have done without her and Paolo being here.'

'Paolo. Is he here? I thought he was still in Naples. I would love to see him. It's been far too long.'

'He has gone out to visit his cousins in Positano today. I am so sorry that you've missed him. I know he would have been thrilled to see you; you were such good friends. It was so lucky he was nearby when Mario collapsed. He had come home for a couple of days so he could be here when Michela returned from England. We had arranged it as a surprise for her. He was out visiting a friend in town when it happened, but he was able to rush straight back and wait for Michela to arrive whilst I went to the hospital with Mario.'

'It must have been such a shock.'

'You can't imagine how awful it was. One minute I was busy in the kitchen, the next I heard a terrible crash. It happened just there, when he was clearing the two outside tables. I didn't know what to do. I rushed down the road and shouted for Tommaso Amati. He was outside Trattoria di Napoli sitting at his usual seat, thank goodness. He didn't hesitate — he was so calm and decisive — he ran straight here with me and gave Mario chest compressions . . .' Maria faltered, her voice cracking, the emotion of that day still raw.

'I understand if you don't want to talk about it. I did not mean to upset you,' said Stefano. His eyes were full of concern.

'I'm just being foolish.' Maria sniffed. 'Tommaso was a hero to me, to us. His actions saved Mario's life, I have no doubt about that. That and the workings of the good Lord.'

'And is he expected to make a full recovery?'

'Yes, he should be fine, but it has been a warning to him that he must slow down. He is not as young as he was, none of us are. At least now Michela is back perhaps he will feel he can start gradually handing over some of the work to her. We've always hoped that Michela might want to take over the business and perhaps that will happen sooner than we imagined. Michela has developed so much from her time working in London. It's a shame she is out at the moment but of course now she is back you can call on her anytime.'

Stefano frowned. He did not seem at all interested in asking after Michela; in fact anyone would think he had no feelings for the girl at all.

'How is Paolo?' he said.

'Paolo is very happy, though worried about his father, of course. But I don't think he will ever move back here permanently. He is so settled in Naples and doing so well at his law firm.'

'He seems to have found his niche.'

'Yes, we are so proud of him. And you? I hear you were doing very well in Rome at Chubby Joe's.'

'Chucky Joe's,' Stefano corrected her, laughing. 'Though Chubby Joe's is a pretty good name, but perhaps a little too accurate a description of some of the customers. I learnt a lot there but now I'm ready to move on. I'm planning to open my own restaurant with my business partner,

Alberto, who I met in Rome. He's from Ravello so he knows this area well.'

'Are you planning on opening a restaurant nearby?' Maria said.

'Not just near here. We're planning to open our own restaurant right here in Minori.'

'How wonderful! I am sure Mario will be so excited to hear what you are up to.'

'Is he well enough for me to pop upstairs to see him?'

'Oh, I should think so, but I will come upstairs with you to check he is not sleeping. I am so glad you came by. Hearing all about your plans will be just the tonic he needs.'

Maria led Stefano through the back of the café bar and up the stairs into the bedroom that she and Mario shared. Stefano thought back to the last time he had been in that room, playing hide-and-seek with Paolo and Michela whilst Maria and Mario were busy downstairs. The walls were still the same faded primrose yellow; it was almost certainly the same paint on the walls as all those years ago. The room was dwarfed by the large wooden bedstead with a carved headboard, above which hung a small picture of the Virgin Mary, her hair an improbable shade of blonde, just as he remembered it. Mario was sitting up in bed, a greying vest visible under his striped pyjama top. His face had lost some of its colour like the faded candlewick bedspread.

Stefano was careful not to let his face betray his shock at Mario's frailty, but he was sure that once Mario was back downstairs in his beloved Il Gattino, chatting to his regulars and sitting at one of the outside tables in the sun the colour would begin to come back into his cheeks.

Once Maria was satisfied that Mario was feeling up to receiving the unexpected visitor, she bustled off to get a couple of cold drinks for the two men to enjoy then she left them to their conversation whilst she busied herself downstairs in the kitchen.

As Maria had predicted, Stefano's arrival provided a welcome boost to Mario's spirits. It was good for him to catch up with the boy who for so many years had been like another son to him. He chuckled at Stefano's tales from Chucky Joe's but he did not conceal his distaste for their business methods.

He listened with interest but what he really wanted to hear was Stefano's plans for the future. He had heard a rumour from one of his visitors that Stefano was planning to operate a Chucky Joe's franchise here in Minori and when he had heard that his good friend Tommaso had put Trattoria di Napoli up for sale it had not taken him long to put two and two together. As a young man, Mario had dreamt of having a big restaurant on Piazza Umberto just like his friend Tommaso, but this heart attack had shown him the futility of such a dream. But it had also taught him that however much business success he achieved it was nothing compared to the love and support of his family.

'So, tell me about these plans you have to open a restaurant back here in Minori,' he said.

Stefano told Mario all about his dreams for his own restaurant, the dreams that had begun to slowly form in his mind from the very beginning when he was sitting on a stool carefully stirring Maria's *ragù*. He told him how he'd met his business partner Alberto, the loan his father was kindly making to them and the meeting he'd had with Tommaso and Nicoletta. As he outlined his vision for the transformation of Trattoria di Napoli, Mario's eyes began to shine and Stefano could swear that a pink flush began to form on the old man's cheeks.

When Stefano got up to leave, Mario shook his hand as firmly as he could manage. He was determined to get well as soon as possible. He would eat up every morsel that Maria brought him, and he would start to do some light exercise even though he hated the very sound of the word. He would be up and around as soon as possible. Finding out about Stefano's exciting plans was all the motivation he needed.

Maria looked up as Michela slunk back through the door.

'Michela, where on earth have you been? I have been worried about you. You were gone nearly two hours. Whatever happened? I thought you had only popped out for the jam. Did you get caught by that dreadful gossip Valentina again?'

'I sent you a text, Mamma, to say I had gone to visit Nonna Carmela. I didn't want to ring in case Papa was sleeping.'

'I didn't hear anything go *ping*. Anyway, you know I'm no good with these newfangled devices. What's more, I haven't had a moment to look at a phone. I've been busy non-stop since you left. There's a huge pile of washing-up building up in the kitchen.'

Maria settled down at one of the tables to check over the week's bookings. She decided against mentioning Stefano's visit. She was certain that Michela was sweet on him, and she could have sworn he was keen on her too, but it was now quite clear that he wasn't interested in her. Now Stefano was no longer an option, if he ever had been, she just hoped that Michela had done the right thing by ending her relationship with Fabio. He was now happily married to Daniela and all set to take over his wife's family farm one day. His parents no longer had any worries about his future. Maria was looking forward to the day she could say the same.

Michela went through to the back of Il Gattino, turned on the tap and added a slug of washing-up liquid. She pulled on a pair of rubber gloves and sunk her hands into the froth of bubbles spread over the cups and plates. The task was dull but at least she didn't have to talk to anyone or listen to anyone talking about Stefano and his girlfriend's exciting new plans. Eventually a sparkling pile of crockery was stacked on the draining board. She watched the last of the water drain away down the plughole. If only her troubles would wash away as easily.

Chapter Thirty

The other women were busy chatting and taking photos, but Miriam was miles away. The thought of seeing Tommaso again had been at the forefront of her mind ever since she had left him in Piazza Umberto. After their visit to Carmela Gentili she couldn't fool herself any longer. She knew she was falling in love with him and she had stupidly believed that he might feel the same way.

She hadn't dared pluck up the courage to approach him when he appeared so unexpectedly that morning. But as the boathand was helping Evie aboard, she had believed – for a sweet, fleeting moment – that he was about to walk towards her. Then that voluptuous, glamorous Italian woman appeared and took him in her arms. She had been knocked off cloud nine by a sucker punch to the jaw. She had to face facts: she was an ordinary-looking, grey-haired woman leading a quiet existence in a tiny cottage in a sleepy English village. How had she ever thought that a man like Tommaso would fall for her when there were so many gorgeous Italian women to choose from?

Now that her foolish imaginings had come to nothing, she was more determined than ever that Bluebell would be lucky in love. She was so relieved that David hadn't changed his mind about joining them. Her new young friend might have no designs on David but that certainly wasn't going to stop her from trying to bring the two young people together. And what could be more romantic than falling in love on the island of Capri?

Bluebell needed to realise she needed a proper partner, not a daft fling with a cheeky, philandering waiter like Andrea, however good-looking he might be. As for David, he was looking for a fantasy woman in a poppy-print dress he had glimpsed on a boat. He seemed to believe he was in love with a girl he had never even spoken to. But maybe it was no more ridiculous than a quiet seventy-two-year-old widow in sensible shoes deluding herself that a kind, handsome Italian restaurant owner might be falling in love with her.

Miriam was pleased to see that Bluebell and David were chatting happily together as they walked through the Marina Grande. Miriam couldn't help chuckling at the way Evie's short legs were working overtime to keep up, her eyes darting here and there, taking in the big white yachts and the crowds. Josie was leading the way whilst Brenda brought up the rear of their group.

'Our first stop is Piazza Umberto, known as the Piazzetta. It's the main square in Capri where all the rich and famous go,' said Josie.

'Suits us then,' quipped Evie, flicking back her short hair as if it was a cascade of glossy, glamorous locks. 'Ooh, look, do you think that woman's a film star?' she whispered.

Miriam looked over at the woman Evie had spotted. She was wearing a giant pair of tortoiseshell-rimmed sunglasses, a long cream linen dress and a wide-brimmed straw hat. Her dark wavy hair reached nearly to her waist; her toned limbs were tanned and golden. She walked past them leaving a cloud of expensive scent hanging in the air.

Miriam sighed. If only she looked as good as that then things might have worked out differently. She fell into step beside Brenda who was bound to have amassed an encyclopaedic knowledge of today's destination. She hoped that listening to Brenda's stories would take her mind off the scene on the seafront. Sure enough, Brenda was delighted to share her knowledge of the island's history as they made their way through the marina, happily telling Miriam stories about the glamorous figures from Gracie Fields and Jackie Onassis to Mariah Carey who had lived on or visited the island.

Miriam tried to take it all in, but her thoughts kept drifting back to Tommaso. How would he be spending his day? Perhaps he was catching a boat to Ischia; he'd said his sister lived there. Would he tell her about his visit to Carmela Gentili? Was there a small chance he might mention her? More to the point, why was she still thinking about him? She was going home tomorrow. And Tommaso had somebody else.

'Capri is pretty hilly, so we're going to take the funicular railway up to the Piazzetta,' Josie said.

Miriam felt her mood lifting a little as the small train began its upward climb. Soon she would be walking in the footsteps of those who had once made Capri the playground of the jet set. She was determined to put aside her nonsensical daydreaming about Tommaso and enjoy their final outing. She had been looking forward to today for a long time.

Bluebell looked out of the window of the railcar as it left Piazza Vittoria and began its steady climb. She tried not to think about the mechanism that held their carriage in place. Logically, she knew that the steel cable was not going to snap but she would feel happier when her feet were back on a nice, solid pavement. She was so glad that David had been true to his word and met them on the ferry that morning. There was something about his presence in the compartment that made her feel safe.

She looked around at the other women, none of whom seemed at all perturbed by their unusual mode of transport. They were all chatting away, and little Evie was taking the opportunity to knit a few rows of a striped waistcoat. Her mysterious secret knitting project was out of sight in her hotel room.

Bluebell was pleased to see that Miriam was now talking to David. She sensed that something wasn't quite right with her friend and hoped that whatever was on her mind would be forgotten in the excitement of exploring the island. She could not hear what Miriam and David were talking about, but Miriam was looking quite surreptitious, as if she was plotting something.

David's head was turned away from her, so Bluebell was able to watch him unobserved. He was dressed in a plain white T-shirt and steel-grey shorts. She could not help noticing how his legs were muscular and tanned with just the right level of hairiness. She couldn't help comparing them to Jamie's rather skinny legs, which had protruded from his many-pocketed red shorts. His legs had looked so white against the bright material; he never seemed to tan even after a fortnight abroad. To be fair, Jamie looked much better in formal clothes than he did in his holiday garb. She began to wonder how David would look in a suit, perhaps a single-breasted, navy-blue number paired with a crisp white shirt.

'Are you okay?' David said, interrupting her musings. She blushed furiously, conscious of the silly grin on her face. Heaven knows why she was picturing him in a nice piece of tailoring. She would be imagining him in a morning suit next.

'Just thinking about my next cappuccino.' Bluebell spoke rather louder than she had intended.

'Not long now, Bluebell; we all know you've become quite the caffeine addict,' Josie joked.

The *Loving and Knitting* group soon found some shady seats outside one of the cafés in the famous Piazzetta. 'Don't even look at the prices. The magazine is picking up the bill for the coffees,' said Josie, as she sat down next to Bluebell.

'That is a misprint, isn't it?' said Bluebell. She dropped the menu as though it was red hot.

'It will probably cost us more than dinner at Il Gattino but it's a once-in-a-lifetime treat,' said Josie.

'And Leonardo di Caprio never visited Il Gattino.' Evie giggled.

After coffee they tore themselves away from people-watching in the Piazzetta and made their way through narrow lanes flanked by whitewashed buildings bedecked with window boxes and terracotta urns from which tumbling flowers fell like vivid waterfalls. Jewel-like boutiques as irresistible as boxes of truffles beckoned to them but they walked on. There was no time for shopping; there was too much to see.

As they walked through the flower-lined paths of the Gardens of Augustus, their party split into small groups as one thing or another attracted their attention and soon Bluebell and David found themselves separated from the others. It seemed to have happened naturally, but Bluebell suspected that Miriam and the others were conspiring to leave them alone together as much as possible. If the ladies were matchmaking they were barking up the wrong tree, but it was nice to have a bit of male company for a change. In fact, she could not think of anyone she would rather be with right now. She only hoped that Miriam had not used the funicular ride to the Piazzetta to sing her praises; that really would be embarrassing.

They climbed up a few steps to the viewing terrace of the garden overlooking the small marina on the south side of the island. Below, the sparkling sea was an intense shade of blue. There was a perfect view of small white boats sailing between the *faraglioni,* the three large rocks synonymous with the island. David took a selfie of the two of them and showed it to her. To her surprise she actually looked half decent. She wasn't sure if it was her tan or wide smile that made the difference.

They left the gardens to walk to the nearby Carthusian monastery of San Giacomo where the old monks' cells and frescoed walls imparted a cool tranquillity.

'What a beautiful place,' Bluebell said.

'I've been thinking about becoming a monk,' David said.

Bluebell almost tripped over a paving stone. 'What?'

'Your face! I was only kidding.'

'That wasn't funny,' Bluebell scolded him, but she couldn't help laughing.

David kept making her laugh as they took the bus up the steep, zigzagging route to the island's second largest town: Anacapri.

After a welcome stop for lunch, in a shady square, they climbed a few stairs to the clifftop Villa San Michele. Bluebell was gladder than ever that she was wearing her trusty trainers.

Whilst the others explored the garden, Bluebell and David loitered in the villa's cool rooms, full of old furniture. Storyboards explained how a Swedish doctor had restored the property in order to create a home *'open to the sun and the wind and the voice of the sea'.*

'It must have been really strange to move from chilly Scandinavia to live in a place like this,' Bluebell said.

'An Italian island in the sun? I think I could get used to that,' David joked.

'It might be nice to stay here for a while . . .' Bluebell couldn't imagine living anywhere but England. She would miss her friends and Granny Blue, not to mention her mum's roast dinners.

'I've loved living in Maiori, but I don't really see myself moving out to Italy forever. I think I'd miss the rain after a while, and my mum's cooking,' David said.

'That's just what I was thinking.'

They wandered out to join the others in the garden. Miriam was standing a little way apart from the group, looking out over the sea towards the island of Ischia.

David took out his phone and persuaded Bluebell to put one hand on her hip and blow a kiss to the camera. He grinned broadly when she took his picture. How different he was to Jamie who had fussed around for ages making sure his hair looked just right and insisted Bluebell only took pictures of his 'best side'.

'Let's take a group selfie,' said Josie.

Bluebell put her arm around Miriam.

'Say cheese!' said Miriam. Her voice sounded overly bright but no one apart from Bluebell seemed to notice. They were too busy talking about where to go next. Brenda's suggestion won the day: a nearby church that she deemed a *must see* on account of its striking, majolica-tiled floor depicting the Garden of Eden.

Josie duly led them past a curious red fort-like building to the church of Saint Michael. Once inside, they had to squeeze onto a narrow wooden platform in order to edge slowly around the perimeter of the floor upon which wild and domesticated beasts roamed over tiles coloured in greens, yellows and blues.

'Look, at that cute porcupine,' said Josie. 'And there's Adam and Eve.'

'Eve's looking rather coy,' remarked Brenda.

'The first of a long line of temptresses,' said David. Bluebell felt her cheeks burning even though she was pretty sure that a curvy, five-foot-four assistant bank manager with a touch of sunburn wasn't many people's idea of a seductress.

The sun felt particularly hot as they emerged from the cool of the church, so Bluebell was rather glad when everyone agreed it was time to head in the direction of the port. They did not have to wait long for a bus, which was soon wending its way along the winding road on the way back to the harbour.

'My poor feet!' exclaimed Evie. 'I'm glad I wore my comfy shoes.'

'We've got plenty of time to get a cold drink by the marina before we catch the boat back. But I wouldn't advise anything more to eat. We've got our farewell gala dinner at the hotel tonight,' said Josie.

'Not even an ice-cream for me,' said Bluebell, determined to keep to her word for once.

'It's so sad that this is our last trip,' said Brenda.

'I expect my grandson will have left a huge pile of washing for me to come home to,' said Evie. 'He's been housesitting for me. I told him he could have a couple of friends round so there'll be a whole week's worth of empty takeaway boxes in the kitchen. I don't think he's worked out where the oven or the bin are.'

Miriam said nothing, but Bluebell noticed the faraway look in her eyes. She wrinkled her brow with concern. She suspected her friend's sadness at returning to England was nothing to do with going back to an empty house devoid even of unwashed socks and the discarded packaging of ready meals. She was pretty sure it had a lot more to do with leaving behind a certain charming, bearded restaurant owner.

The bus lurched violently as they turned another corner. 'I was such a nervous traveller when we first arrived, but now I've finally got used to dicing with death on the roads,' joked Josie. Bluebell was about to reply when she caught sight of a large white van hurtling towards them at speed. The bus driver veered away from the oncoming vehicle. Instinctively the women ducked down.

The front of the bus mounted the narrow strip of pavement, knocking over a metal ice-cream sign with an almighty clatter. Children clutching ice-cream cones scattered, crying out in terror. Letting rip a string of swear-words, the bus driver jumped out of his cab as the rogue van hurtled away in the opposite direction. He shouted at the passengers to stay seated, but David had already leapt off the bus.

'Everyone else stay here,' said Josie. The passengers were crowding at the windows to see what had happened.

'Shouldn't we go and see if we can help?' said Brenda.

'Bluebell, go and ask if they need anyone else. If they don't, we'll be better off out of the way.'

The bus driver was on his phone talking rapidly and gesticulating dramatically with his free hand at a stout woman who was kneeling on the pavement wailing over the prostrate form of a large black-and-white dog with shaggy hair. The dog was quietly whimpering, and its face, which looked up at Bluebell, was tense with pain and shock. By its side lay a partially eaten ice-cream that was spreading a sticky pink-and-white stain across the paving slab. Kneeling on the other side of the dog and talking to him calmly was David. He was using his T-shirt to staunch the flow of blood from the dog's side.

Bluebell could not help her eyes travelling over David's bare torso. His shoulders and chest were strong, and the tops of his arms were surprisingly well muscled. His tanned chest was sprinkled with fine hair and a narrow strip of darker hair ran from his taut stomach to the waistband of his shorts.

She struggled to put her finger on the strange sensation she was feeling. It was something she had not felt for a long time. Then it dawned on her that her admiration for David's quick response to the dog's plight was tinged with something far baser – lust. Realising how inappropriate it was to feel this way in the midst of a traffic accident she looked away from him and focused on the pitiful creature. One of its legs was bent at an odd angle. A piece of bone was poking through the flesh.

Bluebell was conscious of someone bending over her. She could hear her name being called. It sounded far away as if it was coming from down a long tunnel. A face was hovering a few inches from her own. She looked up into a pair of blue eyes. They were as bright as the sky above her. 'Are you okay?' David said. He was looking a little self-conscious in a rip-off replica Napoli football shirt, which must have been pressed on him by one of the nearby shop owners. She was aware that underneath it he smelt of something pleasantly citrusy.

'What happened?'

'You fainted, but you'll be fine. See if you can get up, but do it slowly.'

She got to her feet steadily, feeling a bit dazed. She could see the black-and-white dog being lifted into the back of a van and a policeman talking to the bus driver.

'I tried to talk to the policeman, but he waved us all away and told us to get on the next bus. I guess he has enough witnesses without the need to try and translate convoluted statements from a bunch of Englishwomen,' said Josie. 'The lady who runs the ice-cream stall has insisted that we all have a cup of tea on the house whilst we wait for the bus.'

Bluebell and David pulled out a couple of metal chairs and joined the rest of the group who were huddled on the narrow strip of pavement. A middle-aged lady wearing a pinny printed with lime-green owls came over with another two cups of tea and a brandy 'for the little one,' which wasn't how anyone had described Bluebell in the last twenty years. 'You have a lovely boyfriend,' the lady whispered as she put down the drinks.

'He's not . . .' Bluebell began. *But suddenly I wish he was.*

'And handsome.' The woman gave her a broad wink. He had a pretty fit body too. That girl David was searching for was going to be one lucky woman.

Bluebell couldn't help watching David out of the corner of her eye as Josie made sure everyone was safely seated on the next bus. The journey was over all too quickly, but they arrived at the port with just minutes to spare before the ferry docked.

David stood up and hugged and kissed all the *Loving and Knitting* ladies as the boat pulled into the harbour at Minori. Although he promised to keep in touch, Bluebell knew he was just being polite. He would probably forget all about their little group by the time he returned from Italy. A few days ago she probably wouldn't have given him much thought either, but now everything had changed. Their casual friendship had turned into much, much more. She had fallen for him big time even though she knew he wanted someone else. What a fool she was.

As they walked up the pier, she turned to give David a last wave as the boat continued on its way to Maiori, but he had his back to the shore and was looking out to sea. She walked towards the Hotel Sea Breeze, feeling close to tears.

Chapter Thirty-One

The glossy, toffee-coloured lips of Donatella Frandini were moving but Tommaso was not listening.

'Don't you agree?' she said.

He hesitated, realising he hadn't a clue what she was talking about. Donatella hadn't stopped talking since they had boarded the boat to Ischia, but he had barely taken in a single word. He settled for a non-committal grunt. He dared not risk a *yes*. Donatella had a habit of getting men into trouble if they said yes too quickly to one of her suggestions.

'I hoped you'd agree with me; you're always so wise.' She beamed.

He immediately felt rather guilty. He wasn't an unkind man and although Donatella was a shameless gossip, she did not share her sister Valentina's malicious delight in unsettling and upsetting people with her stories. Donatella just loved hearing about other people's lives. Since she had moved from her home town of Minori after her divorce to work as a hairdresser on the island of Ischia she was keener than ever to find out about the lives of her old friends and neighbours.

Tommaso passed on a few small pieces of news about mutual acquaintances, but he was careful not to reveal anything he knew to be private. If you shared a confidence with Donatella or her sister Valentina you might as well hang a banner across the front of the Basilica of Saint Trofimena.

Donatella had plenty to talk about for the rest of the voyage so Tommaso only needed to nod or shake his head at the appropriate moment. At least the effort involved in trying to follow the thread of some of her convoluted tales distracted him from thinking about Miriam and the day they might have spent together if only he had plucked up the courage to approach her before she and her friends sailed away.

If only he hadn't taken that telephone call from his supplier just as he was leaving; if only he hadn't stopped and spoken to a neighbour on the way; if only he had walked straight up to Miriam instead of dithering, he would have spoken to her before Donatella appeared. So many *if onlys*. Instead, when he finally managed to pull away from Donatella's grasp, he could only stand and watch as the *Loving and Knitting* women sailed away. Soon Miriam was lost in the crowd of holidaymakers on board. But he could just make out the back of her young friend's bright auburn hair glowing in the sun before she too disappeared out of sight. It was at that moment he knew for sure. What he had found with Miriam wasn't simple friendship. It was much, much more.

The boat arrived at the port of Ischia not a moment too soon. As they prepared to disembark Donatella squeezed his arm in a conspiratorial manner. 'She looked nice,' she said.

'What do you mean?' he asked.

'The one in blue getting on the boat to Capri. You couldn't keep your eyes off her, you naughty boy.'

'Oh, she's just a holidaymaker who ate at my restaurant the other day,' he said quickly.

'If you say so. But I saw the way you looked at her and it's not the way you usually look at your customers.'

Tommaso was stunned into silence. If Donatella had seen him looking at Miriam the way she'd described, why in heaven's name had she flung her arms around him and smothered him in kisses?

'I thought I'd do you a favour,' Donatella continued. 'There's nothing like a bit of competition to spark a woman's interest.'

They made their way down the gangplank, Donatella holding on to the guide rope with one hand. Tommaso clamped his hands firmly to his sides. Right now he did not trust himself not to push her overboard. Competition – as if! Donatella had all the appeal of a bunch of gaudy plastic flowers. Miriam was like a fragrant bloom in an English summer meadow.

'So lovely to see you again,' Donatella trilled and she waved enthusiastically at her latest beau, who was waiting for her in the port, leaning against his motorbike.

'You too,' he managed through gritted teeth.

'I saw the way she looked at you too,' she added over her shoulder as she headed towards her boyfriend's open arms.

Tommaso gave his sister a huge hug. It was good to see her again. Silvia was overjoyed to hear that he had found a buyer for Trattoria di Napoli and that he was planning, at last, to move to the island of Ischia where she and her family lived. She immediately started preparing a delicious lunch, chopping vegetables at an alarming speed and insisting that there was absolutely nothing he could do to help.

Afterwards, having been given no opportunity to decline dessert, he indulged in a short snooze before they made their way into the centre of the town to visit the local estate agent, where they were pleasantly surprised by the number of available properties within his budget. Silvia was adamant that she and her husband would welcome a helping hand in their fish restaurant down in the harbour at Forio. Tommaso should have been over the moon but as he walked back towards the port he could not shake off the feeling of melancholy that hung over him like a dark cloud on a sunny day.

He checked his watch; there was a good half-hour until the early ferry was due. He decided to stop for a quick coffee and gather his thoughts. He took a seat at one of the outside cafés on the main square, which were all busy with locals and tourists enjoying their *bruschette* and carafes of wine. He picked up a newspaper lying on a nearby chair and waited for a waiter to approach.

A trio of musicians was busking in the square: one with a squashed straw hat was plucking a double bass; a round chap with too-short trousers held up with braces played the violin; whilst a cadaverous-looking fellow with a withered leg added his own improvisation with a battered mouth organ. The three men were making a jolly sound, giving every impression they were happy with life despite the meagre amount of money they were collecting in the empty violin case at their feet. Everywhere he looked, couples were chatting or sitting in companionable silence. Even those distracted by their mobile phones would look up occasionally to comment on something they saw on their screens or to take a selfie together.

He ordered an espresso and tried to imagine himself living on the island, coming to this square for his morning coffee, helping out in his sister and brother-in-law's restaurant and then walking up through the town to an evening alone in a small house, perhaps with a garden or patio to sit on as the sun went down. Usually he was glad of the peace and silence he found when he sat alone outside a café reading a paper, but now he felt restless.

He paid for his coffee, made his way to the port and found a seat at the back of the boat next to a young Japanese couple. Over the years Tommaso had picked up a smattering of all the languages spoken by his customers but visitors from the Far East were rare so his Japanese was limited to the words for *good morning* and *good evening*. He greeted them in his customary polite manner, but it was quickly established that they spoke little more Italian than he spoke Japanese. Even with this language barrier, the young couple conveyed by their gestures and body language that they were on their honeymoon.

As they exchanged smiles, holding hands and laughing, Tommaso opened his newspaper; he did not want to intrude any longer. He could not help envying these two people embarking on a new life together. He lived in one of the most beautiful places in the world but what did that matter if he had no one to share it with?

His thoughts were interrupted by the man asking if he might take a photo of him and his new wife and Tommaso was happy to oblige. As he looked through the viewfinder the woman pressed closer against her husband. Their smiles spoke of great happiness. For the last ten years Tommaso had convinced himself that he was content to be alone, that his work at Trattoria di Napoli was enough. The long hours kept him too busy to contemplate his future and at the end of the day he was exhausted and fell asleep immediately. But soon he would no longer be able to rely on the routine of his restaurant to fill his days. He would be stepping into the unknown. He looked up; a gull was flying overhead, the single bird the only speck of white in the wide expanse of blue sky. It seemed to symbolise both freedom and loneliness. He felt himself shiver despite the heat.

His mind kept drifting back to the moment he saw Miriam on the pier. How was it possible that her face had become so dear to him in such a short period of time? And how lovely she had looked this morning in that fresh linen blouse with embroidery on the collar and that cornflower-blue skirt. Around her elegant neck a string of blue beads interspersed with small silver beans had sparkled in the morning sun. It was a simple outfit, but she could not have looked better if she had been dressed in the finest fashions from Milan. If only he had plucked up the courage to speak to her before Donatella's unwanted intervention.

Perhaps it was for the best. Miriam might have been horrified if he had suggested she abandon her outing to Capri to accompany him on his trip to Ischia. After all, she hardly knew him. What sort of crazy fellow would try and drag a woman away from a boat trip with her friends? Miriam had probably not given him a moment's thought since they had parted. The visit to the pink house on the hillside would have been nothing more than a pleasant interlude on an interesting holiday. She would remember exchanging stories about her father-in-law with the old lady. The restaurateur who had introduced them would soon be forgotten.

Even if Miriam did have some sort of feelings for him how could he possibly consider bringing her to live with him in a tiny house in the back streets of Forio, with its treacherously narrow pavements, washing hanging from balconies, scooters leaning up against old doors, shutters with peeling paint and scraggy cats skulking in doorways.

He pictured her living in a rambling old stone vicarage with roses around the door, or in a smart stucco-fronted house flanked by pillars. In his imagination she walked down a sweeping carriage drive to reach her front door, behind which lay a substantial property with at least four bedrooms, a large kitchen, a library stacked with books from floor to ceiling, a comfortable sitting room with doors leading out to a long, well-kept garden, perhaps with a stream running across the bottom. She almost certainly lived in a large city like Cambridge with every convenience on her doorstep; perhaps she made regular trips to London to visit the theatre and art galleries.

What on earth would persuade someone like Miriam to move to a small island like Ischia? *Love,* a tiny voice in his head said. But he had no reason to think that Miriam was falling in love with him; it was only a silly remark made by that daft Donatella. He didn't have a shred of any other evidence, did he?

Tommaso turned the *CLOSED* sign on the door of Trattoria di Napoli over so that it read *OPEN* once more. He had several bookings for the evening but none of them were due yet. He longed for some customers to arrive so that he could throw himself into his work. He took out his phone, hoping that flicking through his emails would take his mind off Miriam. There was a new text from his sister: *Wonderful to see you today. So excited you are moving to Ischia. Don't let her go before you tell her.* She had added a heart emoji.

Fantastic to see you too. Tell what to whom? He added a puzzled-face emoji. He was sure he hadn't said a word to his sister about Miriam. His sister replied quick as a flash: *Your new friend Miriam. The one you kept mentioning.*

Had he really made it that obvious? *She's just a friend,* he texted back.

How he wished there could be something more between them, but there was no chance of that. It was all too late. Tomorrow Miriam would be gone.

He knew he would never forget her. In the short time they had known each other she had changed his life. His heart had been sealed shut for so long, but Miriam had prised it open. Work was no longer his priority. He was ready to find someone to love.

He looked up. An elderly couple whom he recognised were approaching the restaurant. He put a big smile on his face, stood up to greet them and ushered them to one of his nicest tables. He switched off his phone and put it down by the till. Then he took two glasses of white wine and a basket of bread to his waiting customers.

Chapter Thirty-Two

Miriam checked her watch. She had a good hour before she needed to freshen up for the farewell dinner. That was plenty of time for what she planned to do. She walked down the road and made her way to the small church of Santa Lucia. The cool of the interior was a treat after the heat of the day. There were only two other people inside. One a wild-haired man with sunken cheekbones who was kneeling in front of the gilded wooden altar muttering repeated entreaties to the saints. The other was the proprietor of Casa Emilia who was arranging some white flowers by the pulpit and gave her a nod and a smile of recognition.

Miriam approached the display of small candles and dropped a fifty-cent piece through the slot in the collection box. A candle flickered then gave off a steady light. Then she said quietly, 'Rest in peace, Jim. You didn't have to die on the battlefield to make a difference. I wish Colin had known that you had saved that little girl's life. But it wouldn't have changed how he felt about you. You were always a hero to your son.' She closed her eyes for a minute then she smiled and nodded farewell to Emilia Bellucci. She walked back to the Hotel Sea Breeze feeling calmer and more contented, and as though some small thing that had been missing had at last been found.

★

Bluebell could hardly believe that they would soon be eating their farewell dinner. Exhausted by the day's events she could think of nothing better than flopping on the small balcony of her hotel room and reading a few pages of the book she had barely touched since their arrival. She grabbed a can of orange soda from the minibar, made her way out onto the balcony and picked up her book. After five minutes she realised she was reading the same paragraph for the third time.

It was no use; concentrating was hopeless task. Her mind was running over and over the day's events. The trip to Capri was one she would never forget. She tried to tell herself it was because of the beauty of the scenery, the sensation of being bathed in sunshine, people-watching on the Piazzetta whilst sipping the most expensive cappuccino she had ever drunk and the white buildings dressed with tumbling flowers. When she got back to England she would tell Granny Blue it was all these things and more. Then she would describe the drama of the bus accident on the road back to the port. But she wouldn't mention the most memorable part of the day to anyone. The moment when she looked up into David's eyes as she lay flat out on the pavement, and she knew, just knew, that she had fallen for him.

She put down the book, the leaflet on Sorrento still marking the same page where she had opened it. There was just over an hour before the farewell dinner. It wouldn't take her more than five minutes to get ready – okay, maybe ten. She might as well make good use of the time. She picked up her bag and made her way down to the town to investigate the ceramic shop.

As she entered Piazza Cantilena she noticed the doors of the yellow basilica were open. The memory of meeting

David on the steps outside, before their fruitless trip to the pink house, came flooding back. As she paused at the bottom of the stairs, she saw a male figure appear in the doorway. He appeared to be talking to someone inside.

It was difficult to make him out clearly, but he looked ever so like David. But it couldn't be David. He had stayed on the boat and gone back to his rented room in Maiori. The light in the doorway was dim but she could make out that lightweight jacket she had borrowed on the boat, that unmistakeable dark hair. Her heart was racing. It was him. She didn't know how or why he had come back, but if he was here there must be a chance he felt what she had felt that day. She began to run up the steps.

She felt herself falling as if in slow motion. As she instinctively put out an arm to break her fall it was grabbed by a slim, white hand. 'Josie?'

'Bluebell, are you okay? I came out for a quick stroll before dinner and I was just taking some photos of the basilica when I saw you standing there staring into space. You were miles away; you didn't even see me. I was just about to speak to you when you started to run up the stairs. Are you sure you're all right?'

'Yes, umm, thanks. I don't know what I was doing really. I only came out to have a look round the ceramic shop.' Bluebell looked up towards the door of the basilica. She grabbed hold of Josie's arm again, feeling quite faint as she saw David coming towards them.

'Look, doesn't that boy look like David!' Josie exclaimed.

'Really, where?' She tried to sound surprised.

'Coming out of the doorway. Ahh, is that why you were standing there staring like that?'

The boy took a couple more steps towards them. Of course, it wasn't David. How could it be? She must be

240

going crazy. Thank goodness Josie was here to distract her, not to mention preventing her from landing in an undignified heap. She needed to get on with looking for a present for Granny Blue not indulge in foolish fantasies about someone who would only ever see her as a friend.

'Come on, let's have a look together. I might get something for my mum,' said Josie.

The heavy wooden doors of the ceramic shop were covered in plates painted with scenes depicting the many attractions of the Amalfi Coast. Inside, large plates and platters big enough for a wedding feast were mounted on the walls. Bluebell recognised a couple of large platters in the same design as those on the wall of Il Gattino. Leaves and vines, flora and fauna, cherubs and mermaids in pinks and greens, oranges and yellows ran riot over jugs and pasta bowls. Spoon rests and olive dishes were piled up next to pasta jars of every size imaginable.

'Good evening, ladies.' A man in his fifties with a pleasant, round face looked up from behind his desk where he was painting a simple scroll border on a plain white platter.

'*Buonasera*,' Bluebell replied. She would miss exchanging friendly greetings with every shopkeeper when she got back to England.

'Please take a look around,' the man said. 'We can arrange shipping for you in case you would like a whole set; our larger pieces are rather heavy. We have plenty of smaller pieces too, a little jug or decorative tile, perhaps, if you are looking for a small souvenir.'

Bluebell hesitated over a decorative dish depicting the Villa Cimbrone in Ravello. So much had happened since that first outing. When she'd stood on the Terrace of Infinity looking past the white statues out into the blue yonder it was Andrea she'd been fantasising about. A couple of days later she'd been in his arms on the beach at Maiori, her inhibitions dulled by the drinks at Bar Gino, her passionate fantasy rudely interrupted by Ludo, the furry white dog, and his fuming owner. Now she was looking for a souvenir, her holiday nearly over and her evening with the handsome Andrea was just an amusing story to entertain her friends.

The dish was very pretty but she decided on a small rectangular box with a simple sketch of the seafront of Minori on its lid. She picked it up carefully, clutching her bag closer with her other hand. The way her mind was jumping around right now a split second's inattention might send a teetering pile of dishes flying. She was happy to part with a few euros for Granny Blue's present but the thought of picking up the bill for toppling two dozen dishes did not bear thinking about.

Josie was already paying for her purchases, which the shopkeeper was wrapping in several layers of soft blue tissue paper. Bluebell joined her at the counter, noticing that he had been busy working on the scroll-edged platter whilst they'd been browsing. A side plate in a similar design sat half-finished near the till.

'A present?' The man took the lidded box from Bluebell.

'Yes, for my grandmother.'

'Very good,' he replied, selecting some tissue paper and a patterned paper bag.

The man moved the scroll-edged platter out of the way to wrap her purchase. 'I like that design,' Bluebell commented.

'I think the border works quite well. It is just a sample piece I am working on. We have a commission for a new restaurant in the town.'

'Really? Whereabouts?' said Bluebell.

'Trattoria di Napoli is changing hands.' The man handed Bluebell the patterned bag and took the ten-euro note she was holding.

'Oh, that's a shame. We ate there the other evening; it was really nice,' Bluebell said.

'The owner was lovely too,' said Josie.

'The owner is retiring. I believe he will be moving to the island of Ischia where he has relatives. A young man and his partner are buying him out. It's the end of an era, no doubt about it, but the new owners have wonderful plans.' He picked up a dinner plate from beneath the counter. 'A classic but modern look, at least I think so. I hope they will like the way I have interpreted their ideas.'

Bluebell and Josie admired the white dinner plate with its simple bottle-green scrolled edge. Three small lemons were grouped together in the centre of the plate. Below the lemons, painted in the same bottle-green as the scrollwork, was the name of the new restaurant: *Trattoria da Mario*.

Chapter Thirty-Three

'It's been so lovely to see you!' Michela hugged and kissed her brother.

'I wish I didn't have to go back so soon but I really can't take any more time off. I've kept on top of my emails but there's only so much I can do from here.' Paolo shrugged. He was trying to cram a huge plastic tub of Maria's home-made tiramisu into his already overstuffed holdall.

'Don't worry, Paolo. Mamma and I will take good care of Papa.'

'Oh, I'm quite all right now. No need to make a fuss,' Mario said. He wore an old, grey knitted cardigan belted over his striped pyjamas. A couple of days' stubble dark-ened his jaw.

'You will ring as soon as you get to Naples, won't you?' said Maria. 'It's a good thing you're making such an early start; you will avoid the worst of the rush hour. *Mamma mia* – the traffic in that city – I can't bear to think of it.'

'Yes, Mamma. I'll phone just as soon as I get to the office. But don't forget I'm making a detour to the airport, first, to see if they have Michela's case.'

'Don't worry too much if they don't have it, Paolo. All the really important things I need were in my hand luggage. It's been too hot for a lot of my London clothes and the dresses Nonna Carmela made for me will still be a bit big, though of course I'd love to have them back for sentimental reasons.'

'I'll see what I can do. I just hope if they've got your case they'll let me have it without too much fuss. I've got the copy of your ID, but you know how bureaucratic they can be at the airport.'

He hugged his parents again. 'I'll come home again in a couple of weeks. Have fun, Michela, when Mamma lets you out of the kitchen! Look after yourself, Papa. Don't work too hard, Mamma. Oh, and when you next see Stefano please say *hi* from me. It would be great to meet him for a beer next time I'm back.'

Paolo set off in the direction of the car park on the seafront, the holdall over one shoulder, the pink-and-purple suitcase bumping along behind him. The three of them stood at the top of the road watching and pointlessly waving until all they could see was a dark blob followed by the bright blur of the paisley-patterned suitcase with its mysterious contents.

'It's been so lovely having him here,' said Maria, failing to stifle a little sob.

'It's okay, Mamma, he'll be back before you know it.' Michela put a comforting arm around her mother.

'Thank goodness he was here when your father . . .' Maria's words tailed off into a sob as she reached into the pocket of her apron for an embroidered handkerchief.

'Come now, Maria, I am perfectly fine now. I'm quite capable of getting back to work soon. Now no more tears and nonsense from either of you.' Mario walked behind the counter, his hand on the lever of the coffee machine. 'Perhaps I will sit and have another coffee before I do anything else. I don't suppose I'm allowed a pastry. Michela, would you fetch a bread roll and some of that peach jam? That will do instead.'

Michela made herself a cappuccino and joined her father in eating one of the bread rolls though she was longing for one of the delicious pastries that had only just come out of the oven. She was pretty sure that her father wasn't ready to come back to work but there was a definite colour in his face that had been sadly lacking in recent days. In fact he looked almost animated. She just hoped he wasn't going to try to run before he could walk. She munched on a roll. It had been years since she last ate peach jam. She had forgotten how nice it was.

Mario ate slowly but clearly relished every mouthful. 'That was delicious. I'm going to go upstairs for a shave, now. I caught sight of myself in the glass behind the bar. I can't be seeing my customers in this state. I don't want them gossiping down in the market.'

Maria and Michela tidied away the breakfast things and attended to their usual chores in silence. Michela knew that her mother was thinking about her brother's visit and how much she would miss him in the coming days. She had something else on her mind. Why had Paolo sounded so cheerful at the prospect of meeting up with Stefano again? Yesterday he had been as indignant as she was at his plans to transform Trattoria di Napoli into the Amalfi Coast's first branch of Chucky Joe's.

Bluebell double-checked her hand luggage. She mentally ticked off her passport, paperback and washbag along with the underwear bought in Ravello, the pink-and-turquoise dress from Positano and her new pom-pom-trimmed polka-dot bikini. Everything that was legitimately hers was safely packed away in her large shoulder bag. The hotel launderette had done a fantastic job with the clothes she had borrowed. The stripy top and trousers, daisy- and sunflower-patterned dresses were washed, ironed and neatly folded. On the very top of the pile was the fit-and-flare orange dress with the large white poppies.

She opened the pink-and-purple case with a sigh and placed the pile of clean clothes on top of the dark jumpers and skinny jeans that would have been too hot to wear even if she could have fitted into them. Although they had a whole morning left in Minori before Massimo drove them back to the airport, she felt as though all the fun and laughter of the past few days was being packed away too. She would drop the case into the lost luggage office at Naples Airport and hope that hers had turned up there. She didn't hold out any hope of a sympathetic response from the travel insurer after failing to report her mislaid case for over a week.

It felt strange to catch sight of herself back in the loose cotton trousers and unflattering T-shirt she had travelled out in but at least she now saw a girl with a healthy glow rather than a pasty complexion looking back at her in the mirror. It was time to go down to the hotel dining room and enjoy her last breakfast. A couple of those delicious pastries were calling to her. She had never quite got round to the fruit-only breakfast but, then again, she had been doing an awful lot of walking.

Brenda and Miriam were already in the dining room when Bluebell walked in, swiftly followed by Evie who was carrying a cotton bag containing her secret knitting project. As they took their seats Andrea came over with a small teapot for Brenda and a latte for Evie. He turned to Evie with a wide smile as he put down her drink. A delicate, pink rosebud was sitting in the saucer. The women looked at each other in amazement.

'Has he been chatting you up?' said Bluebell.

'Yesterday he asked if I would like to go for a walk on the seafront with him when we got back from Capri, but I said I would be too tired.'

'He must think you're just playing hard to get.' Bluebell laughed.

'When she came into the dining room he asked if she was feeling more energetic this morning,' said Brenda. She was pretending to sound shocked but was clearly trying not to laugh.

'I think he was hoping for a big tip at the farewell dinner. But can you imagine his face if I actually said *yes*,' said Evie. She gave a mischievous little giggle.

Andrea returned with Bluebell's cappuccino whilst the other women tried to keep a straight face. Josie arrived in time to see her prizewinners desperately trying to suppress their laughter. 'What's so funny?' she asked.

'Just talking about Evie's admirer,' Bluebell explained. She just about managed to conceal a fit of giggles as Andrea brought over her drink and gave Evie a cheeky wink.

'He must be devastated that you're leaving for the airport at lunchtime,' Josie joked.

'That probably makes you his ideal woman,' said Brenda.

'Talking of departures . . .' Josie said. She quickly ran through the day's arrangements. All rooms had to be vacated by ten o'clock and their suitcases stored in the hotel's luggage room. Everyone would be free to use the hotel pool if they did not mind taking soggy swimwear in their hand luggage, or else they could while away the time pottering around the town until Massimo met them at twelve o'clock for the drive back to the airport.

Miriam raised her coffee cup and proposed a toast to Josie for all her good work organising the holiday. Then Evie announced that she had a small gift for them all to remember the holiday by.

'This hasn't got anything to do with your secret knitting project, has it?' joked Bluebell. She had spotted Evie finishing off something that looked suspiciously like a pile of giant yellow egg cosies and couldn't for the life of her work out what on earth they could be.

'I thought it would be nice to knit everyone a little souvenir; after all we are all on a *Loving and Knitting* holiday.' Evie opened up her cotton bag and produced six curious knobbly knitted objects in a virulent shade of yellow. Everyone was looking a little puzzled, but they were too polite to ask what the heck they were. 'Amalfi lemons!' she announced.

'Knitted lemons? How amazing!' exclaimed Brenda.

Bluebell wondered what on earth you were supposed to do with a knitted lemon. Did you put it in your fruit bowl?

'Thank you so much. Whenever I look at it I will think of our holiday,' Josie said diplomatically. Everyone gave Evie a spontaneous round of applause.

Miriam was doing her best to look cheerful, raising a chuckle at Andrea's cheeky behaviour and Evie's mad presents, but a glum feeling was settling over her like a fog. The last thing she had expected from this holiday was to fall for another man, and now she had finally admitted to herself how attracted she was to Tommaso Amati she had nothing to look forward to but a friendly farewell coffee and perhaps exchanging Christmas cards.

She kept replaying the moment when she spotted him on the pier and for a perfect, golden instant believed that he might ask her to spend the day with him. That foolish moment before she saw that glamorous Italian woman throw her arms around him and smother him in kisses. At that moment she had felt as pale (despite her subtle tan), dumpy (despite her modest dress size) and uninteresting as a woman of seventy-two could ever be. At least she had been able to hide her disappointment during their time on Capri and had tried her best to encourage Bluebell and David to spend as much time together as possible.

She had hoped that there was still a small chance that love would blossom for the two young people. If only it would distract her from her own daft fantasies. But sadly, despite her best endeavours, it seemed that Bluebell and David were destined to remain nothing more than friends. And now she had run out of time. In less than an hour she would tell the pair of them what she had uncovered about the identity of the owner of the poppy-print dress and David would discover that the girl of his dreams was right here in Minori, working in Il Gattino.

To make matters worse, she knew from her conversation with Carmela Gentili that Michela was single, having split up with her long-term boyfriend, Fabio, before leaving for England. David was due to spend at least another week on the Amalfi Coast – plenty of time for him to pursue his fantasy girl and forget all about Bluebell.

Miriam sighed. It had been foolish to think that anyone would find Love on the *Loving and Knitting* trip. All they had found was Knitting courtesy of Evie's quirky hand-made lemons.

Miriam looked across the breakfast table at Bluebell who was staring down at her plate, picking at her crois-sant. She was tempted not to tell her about the arrange-ment she had made to meet David later that morning, but her conscience would not allow her to let Bluebell take Michela's case all the way back to the airport. And if David and Michela were destined to be together how could she stand in their way? Besides, meeting David at Trattoria di Napoli would give her the chance to say goodbye to Tommaso in a casual, friendly way without making a fool of herself.

Breakfast was over. Miriam and Bluebell were waiting for the small lift to come back down, having let the others go in first. 'I've got a bit of a surprise for you this morning. I hope it's a nice one,' Miriam said.

'Not more knitted fruit? It's going to be a bit of a puzzle working out what to do with one knitted lemon,' Bluebell joked.

'I've arranged for David to meet us at Trattoria di Napoli at ten o'clock. We're meeting up for a farewell coffee and to give me some moral support when I say goodbye to Tommaso.'

Bluebell smiled; it was the nearest Miriam had come to admitting her feelings for the restaurant owner. But she was not one to talk; she was keeping her feelings for David very close to her chest. 'Are you sure David's going to come?' She tried to sound casual.

'We exchanged mobile numbers on the boat and he texted to confirm this morning.'

'Talk about a dark horse.'

Bluebell's hand shook as she cleaned her teeth. She could not believe how nervous she was. She wished she was still wearing one of the dresses from the suitcase, not her old cotton trousers and unflattering T-shirt. But the dresses were all washed and packed away in the case, ready to be left at the lost property room at the airport.

When she and David had said goodbye on the boat back from Capri she'd thought she would not see him again for a long time. He had mentioned meeting up with her in London for a friendly drink sometime when his teaching job in Maiori finished. But she was careful not to raise her hopes. She knew that David had no romantic feelings towards her, and that would never change, even if Granny Blue always insisted that sometimes these things developed over time. She couldn't help feeling glad that the marshmallow-pink house had turned out to be a red herring. David might forget all about his fantasy girl once he was back in England. There was next to no chance he would track the girl down now before he left. That gave her half a chance, didn't it?

But whoever this girl was, she was indebted to her. Without the orange poppy-print dress she would never have met David at all, and even though she knew that it was unlikely that they would ever get together at least she would have a new friend to meet up with now and then. She had once been good friends with a boy she had met on one of the bank's training courses, but Jamie's suspicious nature had turned their occasional meetings into a hassle instead of a pleasure. It would be nice to enjoy some male company again. She could hardly bear to wait until ten o'clock; she would be counting down the minutes.

Chapter Thirty-Four

'Would you take this fresh jug of water up and put it on
the side table for Papa? Just in case he decides he wants
to go back to bed.'

'Of course, Mamma.' Michela walked up the narrow
staircase to her parents' bedroom. She could hear her
father humming to himself in the bathroom as he shaved.
Something had certainly cheered him up. She placed the
pitcher of water down rather clumsily, knocking the alarm
clock onto the floor. It bounced off the tapestry rug and
landed under the bedside table. She bent down to pick it
up, at the same time retrieving a lightly crumpled paper
napkin from the floor. She recognised the distinctive blue-
and-yellow design immediately. Wondering how one of
the napkins from Trattoria di Napoli had ended up on her
parents' bedroom floor, she was about to throw it into the
wicker waste-paper basket when she noticed something
written on it in a hand she would know anywhere. It was
the handwriting of Stefano Bassani.

She carefully smoothed out the paper. Written in ball-
point pen across the middle of the napkin were the words
Trattoria da then something beginning with an *N* or maybe
an *M* which she could not make out. Below that was a
doodle, which looked like a scroll design with three small
lemons. Puzzled, she folded it up and put it in the pocket
of her apron and went back downstairs. She knew for a

fact that Mario had not left Il Gattino and its upstairs flat since his return from hospital. There were only two possible ways that napkin had turned up on the floor under her father's side of the bed: either someone who had been in the presence of Stefano had picked it up and dropped it there or Stefano himself had been upstairs in her parents' bedroom. The brass cheek of the man beggared belief. But whether it was Stefano or someone else who had dropped the napkin, what did it all mean?

She hesitated at the top of the stairs; she could hear voices drifting up. A group of local men had arrived for their first coffees of the day; she would need to go and help Maria. When there was a quiet moment she would ask her mother if Stefano had been around. She decided against asking her father directly; she did not want to risk upsetting him. Imagine if Stefano had told him of his plans to sell frozen pizzas and burgers right here in Minori. The shock could have killed him.

'Two more espressos and one cappuccino for these gentlemen, please, Michela, then could you take a couple of pastries outside?' Maria was carrying a coffee through to one of the outside tables where a large man with a shiny domed head sat reading the paper. A small fluffy ginger dog perched on one of his thighs.

'Yes, Mamma.' She busied herself with the pastries and hot drinks, hoping for a quiet time when she could talk to her mother. Maria had other plans. She made it clear she was far too busy right now to be chatting. She wanted everything running smoothly in case Mario appeared downstairs at any moment.

'Would you run down to Trattoria di Napoli and give this note to Mr Amati. It's his evening off today and I believe your father has arranged for him to come over.'

'Certainly, Mamma.' She took the envelope her mother was holding out. It was addressed to Tommaso Amati in her father's spindly handwriting; it was even worse than Stefano's. She was tempted to peek inside, but the envelope was sealed. It was unusual for her father to write a note to his old friend but perhaps he did not feel up to speaking on the telephone.

It would be her first encounter with Tommaso since hearing about the sale of his restaurant. She was angry with him for selling it to Stefano, but she would keep her feelings to herself. She knew Tommaso's quick actions had saved her father's life. She and her family would be forever grateful to him, whatever happened to Trattoria di Napoli.

Tommaso was sitting on his usual chair and stood up when Michela appeared. He hugged and kissed her, insisting on bringing her a cool drink even though she told him she did not have time to linger. She handed over the note from her father, which he opened, quickly read and put into his top pocket. 'Such a shame you were not here a few minutes ago. You have just missed Stefano,' he said.

Michela coloured angrily. 'What would I want to see him for?'

Tommaso frowned. 'I thought you would be excited to see him. You have heard that I have sold the restaurant to him, haven't you? I know that you were wanting to raise the money yourself to buy it for your family, but I truly believe it would be too much for your father to cope with. This way everybody will be happy, don't you agree?'

Michela had promised herself not to mention Stefano's plans to Mr Amati but the way he spoke to her in such reasonable tones was too much to take. Happy! How could he think for a moment that such a plan would make her or her family happy? 'I don't think watching the restaurant my father always admired turn into a burger bar is going to make any of my family happy,' she replied icily.

'Burger bar? Where on earth did you get that idea? You can't think Stefano Bassani would name a burger bar after your father, do you?'

'What do you mean?' A sick feeling gripped Michela's stomach like a clammy hand. She reached into the pocket of her apron and pulled out the napkin with Stefano's handwriting on it.

Tommaso took the napkin and smiled. '*Trattoria da Mario*, it has a certain ring to it, doesn't it? Stefano told me how thrilled your father was when he visited yesterday and told him of his plans. Are you okay? You've gone very pale.'

Michela's head began to spin. She felt as though she was wading through a treacle-filled lake. Everything she had believed about Stefano's plans was slipping from her grasp like a handful of jelly. 'I'm, I'm fine,' she eventually stuttered. Then she pulled herself together just enough to ask, 'What are Stefano's plans? My father hasn't mentioned anything to me yet.'

'Nothing to do with burgers.' Tommaso laughed. 'It was supposed to be a wonderful surprise for you. Your father has invited me over this evening so that we could all get together and share our plans for the new restaurant. Stefano and his partner will be there as well. It's a shame Paolo left for Naples this morning, but I think Stefano met him on the pier last night to tell him before he left.'

'But Valentina said . . .' Michela began then fell silent. Why on earth had she listened to Valentina Frandini's gossip? She and her sister Donatella were notorious for spreading nonsense and stirring up trouble.

As Tommaso explained Stefano's plans Michela felt sicker and sicker. Trattoria di Napoli would have a subtle facelift.

It would be a smart but welcoming trattoria updating and popularising the traditional dishes of the area. Stefano had offered his old mentor Mario a role as a consultant in exchange for a share in the new business that would be named in his honour.

'So that's why he is buying the fields next to Nonna Carmela to grow vegetables,' she said.

'Yes, he wants the restaurant to grow as much of its own produce as it can. He is planning to run a path through the fields down to the main road. It will make it easier to transport his vegetables and he is planning to add a gate leading into your grandmother's little garden. She will be able to use the path to get to the bus stop. It will save her going up and down those treacherous steps.'

'Oh.' It was all she could say. How could she have shouted at Stefano in the street and accused him of betraying her family? His plans would bring great happiness to her father. He would have the fun and enjoyment of being involved in a large restaurant on Piazza Umberto without the stress of being the proprietor. And he would be chuffed to bits to have the place named after him. The path leading from Nonna Carmela's garden through Stefano's field to the bus stop on the main road would save the whole family a great deal of anxiety. No wonder Paolo was going to buy Stefano a drink next time he was in town.

She had behaved terribly towards Stefano, the one man who she had always loved, yet he was willing to come and eat with her and her parents that night. He would probably treat her with feigned politeness. She could hardly bear the thought of it. And he would be bringing his partner as well: the gorgeous girl from Rome with the cascading corkscrew curls. She would have to sit and watch him with his new love. She would be the only person not looking

257

forward to tonight's dinner. It would be the meal from hell but for her family's sake she would have to get through it.

She said goodbye to Tommaso, thanked him for the lemon soda and promised to tell her parents that he was looking forward to coming over that night. As she walked back to Il Gattino she knew she had never felt so miserable. She slunk back into the kitchen hoping in vain that her mother would not comment on the length of time it had taken her to simply drop an envelope off with Tommaso.

'Really, Michela, what took you so long?' Maria scolded and without waiting for an answer handed her a dishcloth. 'And you've missed Stefano. He wanted to introduce us to his friends before they all come around for dinner tonight. That boy has such good manners. It's such a shame you weren't here; they only left a couple of minutes ago. His business partner Alberto seemed such a lovely chap and his fiancée from Rome, Nicoletta, is charming. They were just on their way to call in to Alberto's parents in Ravello whilst Stefano has some business to attend to in town. That Nicoletta is a lovely girl, so well dressed and attractive and she was most complimentary about Minori. Apparently Stefano has been showing her around because Alberto couldn't get away from Rome until yesterday evening.'

Michela's hand clenched the dishcloth tightly as Maria chattered on. 'Michela, there is no need to stop wiping up just because I'm talking to you.'

'Where did he go? Where did Stefano go?' She shouted so loudly that her mother jumped in fright.

'In the direction of the seafront. Michela, wait! Where on earth are you going?'

'It's an emergency, Mamma!'

She flung the dishcloth into the sink and ran out through the café almost knocking over a couple of tourists who had just sat down at one of the two outside tables. She ran blindly down the street, dodging tourists with cases, locals with shopping bags, pushchairs and mopeds, then across Piazza Umberto and down to the seafront. *Please, please, let me find him.*

She didn't know what she was going to say when she found Stefano. All she knew was that she had made the biggest mistake of her life listening to Valentina's foolish gossip and then jumping to conclusions when she had seen him on the pier talking to the girl with the corkscrew curls. Stefano, the boy she had always been in love with, was moving back to Minori. He had wanted her to share in the excitement of his new venture and she had rejected him. She hadn't even bothered to hear him out. He might not want anything to do with her after the way she had spoken to him yesterday and she wouldn't blame him. It was all her own stupid fault.

She stopped at the top of the pier, head swivelling from side to side. Then she saw him. He was sitting on a white bench just a few metres away from where she had seen him with the beautiful girl from Rome. He was staring down, fiddling with his phone. She walked towards him as calmly as she could. Her heart, which had already been pounding with the exertion of running in the heat, now felt as though it was about to burst through her chest.

Chapter Thirty-Five

Bluebell waved as David approached Trattoria di Napoli. His ready smile did little to dispel her nervousness. She felt as unprepared and vulnerable as a newborn kitten. He greeted her and Miriam enthusiastically and ordered himself a cappuccino. 'Now what's all this mystery, Miriam? I can tell you've been up to something,' he said.

Bluebell and David listened attentively as Miriam told them how Tommaso had taken her to the pink house on the hillside. As she described meeting Carmela Gentili and seeing the photo of her granddaughter Michela wearing the poppy-print dress, Bluebell's heart sank. The owner of the suitcase had been in Minori all along, working at the little café bar where they had eaten on the evening of their boat trip to Positano. It would be extremely fortuitous if she managed to swap suitcases with this girl before returning to England, although she would be sad to say goodbye to her new vibrant summer clothes. She knew that now they had been washed, ironed and folded by the hotel laundry she must return them to their rightful owner and she would need the contents of her own suitcase back before she returned home.

But when they took the case round to Il Gattino she would be leaving David with the girl he had been searching for and her fate would be sealed. Worst of all she would have to pretend to be pleased for him. He deserved to be happy, but it was going to be one of the hardest things she had ever done.

David was silent. He seemed to be in a state of shock.

'To think that she was serving us in Il Gattino the other evening!' Bluebell said. 'If I hadn't got soaked on that ferry to Positano and bought that new dress I would have been sitting in that café wearing one of her dresses.'

'That would have been more than a bit awkward,' Miriam said.

'You must be so thrilled you're finally going to meet her,' Bluebell said bravely. David muttered a quiet *yes*. He took a sip of his coffee. The cup rattled on the saucer as he replaced it.

Bluebell put on her very brightest voice. 'I guess I'd better go back to the hotel to fetch my case when we've finished these drinks. Then we can take it round to the café.' There was no point putting it off any longer.

'I'll stay here,' said Miriam.

Bluebell nodded. Leaving Miriam sitting outside Trattoria di Napoli might give her some time alone with Tommaso. It was obvious that there was something brewing between them. At least things might work out for one of them. She swallowed hard. 'Come on, David, let's go.'

'Good luck. I'll save you the seat next to me on the minibus so you can tell me all about it whilst Massimo is driving us back to the airport,' said Miriam.

Just as they stood up to leave a dishevelled young woman wearing an apron rushed past almost knocking their table over. 'Watch out, Michela!' called Tommaso from his seat by the door.

'Oh my giddy aunt, that's her!' said Miriam.

'Yes, you're right. That's the girl from Il Gattino. There can't be many apron-wearing Michelas around.'

'Well, follow her!' Miriam said.

'We'll just jog though; we don't want a high-speed chase like we're a pair of crazy stalkers,' said David firmly. He and Bluebell jumped up.

'Are you excited?' she said.

'More intrigued than excited,' he replied. They set off in the same direction as the girl from Il Gattino. She was heading towards the seafront at quite a speed but when she got to the top of the pier she slowed down, glancing this way and that. She was clearly looking for someone.

'Pretty, isn't she?' Bluebell said.

'Yes,' he replied distractedly. Well, what had she expected him to say?

They stood and watched from a discreet distance as Michela turned and ran down the pier towards a well-dressed, dark-haired man of around thirty sitting on one of the white benches fiddling with his mobile phone. He leapt to his feet when he saw her. It was too far away to hear what they were saying but they could tell from their gestures, which were particularly animated even by Italian standards, that this was no ordinary conversation.

Bluebell felt awkward watching them. It was obvious that these two people were having an important private conversation. They could hardly go up and interrupt them to talk about missing suitcases. She didn't want to disturb them but at the same time she couldn't tear her eyes away. But just as she was about to suggest that they leave, the boy flung his arms around the girl from Il Gattino and pulled her close.

'Let's go,' David said. He turned and walked in silence in the direction of Trattoria di Napoli where they could see Miriam deep in conversation with the owner.

'Let's not interrupt; let's go and sit at the café near the basilica,' Bluebell said. Though David seemed remarkably calm she was sure that he needed a stiff drink.

They walked quickly into Piazza Cantilena to a small café with a handful of metal chairs set out on the pavement. She pulled up two chairs whilst David popped inside. That was strange; he knew someone would come out and serve them in a few minutes. Not long afterwards a waiter emerged carrying a small silver tray with two glasses of prosecco.

'To Miriam and Tommaso,' David said. He clinked his glass against hers. 'Wouldn't it be great if those two got together?'

'It would be fantastic,' she said. She was glad that he did not want to talk about the girl from Il Gattino. She felt ever so guilty that the sight of Michela in another man's arms had cheered her up no end. What a dreadful person she was to be glad that the girl he had been looking for was so clearly mad about somebody else. It just showed what a great guy he was to be able to find joy in other people's happiness whilst putting a brave face on his own disappointment. But she thought she ought to say something. 'I'm sorry about that girl,' she said. She hoped she did not sound too insincere.

'At least I won't have the embarrassment of admitting I've been searching for her for the past year,' he said easily. 'Now I guess we can just wheel your suitcase round to Il Gattino. We could leave it there with a note.'

'Yes, I'll just write something now, and then I can leave it with my contact details,' Bluebell said. She rummaged in her bag for something to write on. She pulled out a leaflet on the Gardens of Augustus and wrote on the other side: *I picked up your suitcase at the airport by mistake. Please accept my apologies for borrowing some of your clothes. They have all been washed and ironed by the hotel. I found out who you were because the owner of Trattoria di Napoli introduced my friend, Miriam, to your grandmother, Carmela. She showed her a photo of you in your orange poppy-print dress that I borrowed. All your dresses are so beautiful, that one especially.*

Then she added her name, address, email and mobile number. 'That's all bases covered. I think something brief is best, don't you? If I start trying to explain anything else I think I'll just confuse her even further.'

'If you start telling her you were trying to track her down via a set of curtains in a house on the hillside she'll think you're crazy,' David said.

'And she'd be right.'

'Come on, let's go and collect your case.'

Miriam toyed with her empty coffee cup. She had finished her drink and Bluebell and David had gone. Why was she still sitting there? Any sensible person would have paid the bill and left instead of hanging around feeling more self-conscious by the minute.

She looked across the piazza to the beach where the light danced on the sea. She rubbed her thumb across the silver links of her bracelet. She was going to miss this place, but she would always have her memories. During her long, happy marriage to Colin she'd already had more than her fair share of love. Perhaps it had been greedy to expect something more.

Tommaso was busy serving other customers. She would slip away quietly. That was the best thing to do. She tucked some money under the saucer and stood up. She pushed back her chair. The metal legs scraped against the pavement.

Tommaso looked up. Miriam raised her hand to wave goodbye. Tommaso took a step towards her. 'Please, stay . . . for a moment.'

She sat back down feeling more awkward than ever. It had been wrong of her to sneak away. Their friendship – for that was all it was – deserved a proper goodbye. Yet a tiny part of her dared to hope that she had seen something in his eyes. Something more. She had to be brave, to stay and take a chance, however slim that was. She sat and waited.

Tommaso walked over to Miriam's table and put down two glasses of sparkling water.

'I thought for a moment you were going to get up and go.' He pulled out a chair. 'May I . . .'

He sat down opposite her. She could not stop her heart pounding in her chest, her stomach was lurching, and her mouth felt dry. She took a sip of water gratefully and surreptitiously wiped her clammy hands on the fabric of her skirt. 'I saw you on the pier yesterday morning,' she said. She might as well hear about his lady friend straight away; there was no point prolonging her agony.

'I've been hoping I would see you again from the moment you got on that boat to Capri. I wanted to speak to you on the pier but I was waylaid.'

'By your glamorous friend,' she said.

'Glamorous!' He laughed, but not unkindly.

'It looked as though you knew each other very well,' she said. She was trying to sound matter-of-fact although she was sure that her voice betrayed her feelings.

'That was Donatella Frandini. We grew up together. She lived around the corner when I was young. I spent most of my spare time playing football with the boys but she and her sister Valentina used to hang around with us quite a bit. In fact, Donatella was the first girl I ever kissed.'

Miriam's heart sank. She remembered the family photos Tommaso had shown her. He had been a nice-enough-looking teenager though not one who would stand out in a crowd. She could just imagine his delight at smooching with a teenage Donatella – all big hair and long legs.

'We were both five years old. She caught me in a game of kiss chase. I was petrified.'

Miriam laughed with relief, the image of a seductive teenager in a too-short skirt replaced by a picture of a little girl with a pinafore dress and pigtails.

'I've been quite frightened of her ever since,' he said with a laugh. 'She and her sister scared the pants off most of the boys in Minori when they were growing up. I was more than a bit relieved when my late wife agreed to go on a date with me. The other girls left me alone after that; there were plenty of unattached lads to pursue. Donatella always had good morals; mind you, Valentina might be inclined to pinch someone else's man if she thought she could get away with it.'

'So, she's not an old girlfriend.'

'Definitely not. And she's certainly not going to be a new one, if I was looking for one, which I'm not.'

Miriam's heart sank again. Donatella might not be a threat, but he was spelling out his intentions, or lack of them, quite clearly. He had no interest in seeing her as anything other than a friend. Then as she tried desperately to hold back the tears she felt sure were about to come, he reached across the table and took hold of her hand. He was about to speak again, to let her down gently, she supposed. If she was bolder and tougher she would take the initiative and get up and leave right now. Instead she stayed rooted to the spot, looking down at the tiled table top as if she was fascinated by its blue-and-yellow pattern.

'I have lived alone for ten years. Of course I have missed my wife, I still do, but I thought I was destined to be alone. I've been burying myself in my work. In a way you could say I've been married to Trattoria di Napoli. I wasn't looking for someone new. But now everything has changed.'

266

Miriam stopped examining the tiles and looked up. He was smiling at her. She held her breath as he continued. 'You remember Carmela mentioning that my old friend Mario suffered a heart attack? Seeing how his family rallied round made me take a good look at my life and realise what was missing from it. Then by a wonderful coincidence your group of ladies came for dinner at my restaurant. I've served thousands of tourists over the years but somehow that evening was different. Seeing you all enjoying your holiday made me realise how unhealthily focused I was on my work. I knew then that I should put the restaurant up for sale and move to Ischia. You remember me telling you that my sister lives on the island, in a town called Forio?'

'Were you on your way to visit her yesterday? Was that why you were at the pier?'

'Yes, that's right. We went to one of the estate agents in Forio together. But when I walked around that town I realised that I couldn't imagine living there by myself anymore. I'm not looking for a new partner to share my life with because I believe, I mean I hope, that I might have found one. We've known each other for such a short time, Miriam, but I can't imagine a future for myself that doesn't somehow have you in it.'

Miriam was silent. She could feel a huge lump in her throat. She did not think she could speak.

'You look so shocked. I probably sound crazy. I'm not asking you to make any rash decisions. I'll be staying in Minori for another couple of months; it will take a while before the sale of the restaurant is all sorted out. Perhaps you could come and visit again, just for a few days?'

'I'd like that very much,' she replied. She didn't trust herself to say anything else right now that would not sound ridiculously soppy.

'I almost didn't have the courage to say anything but when I saw you this morning I knew that I couldn't just say goodbye and let you go back to England without telling you how I feel.'

'But now we can say goodbye knowing I'll be back soon, for a few days,' Miriam said, though she wanted to say *for as long as you want.*

'For a few days,' he repeated, smiling.

'Perhaps we could visit the island of Ischia together.'

'Perhaps we can,' he said. His wide smile and sparkling eyes told her there was no *perhaps* about it.

Miriam walked back across the piazza and up the road towards the Hotel Sea Breeze. At least she supposed she must have done. It felt as though she had floated all the way there without her feet touching the ground.

'Stefano . . . I'm so sorry. I don't know what to say.' Michela could hardly get the words out; she was panting after running so fast.

Stefano's brown eyes locked on to hers as if he was seeing her for the first time. Michela held her breath, afraid to say anything that might break the spell.

'Oh, Michela,' he murmured.

'I thought . . .' Her voice trembled. She could not say anything more, even if she could think of the right words; Stefano was holding her so tight she could hardly breathe.

'I shouldn't have left you wondering why I came back home. I wanted to surprise you, but I should have told you my plans straight away. I just heard that crazy rumour that I was setting up a branch of Chucky Joe's. No wonder you were mad at me.'

'I should have known it wasn't true.'

He touched her cheek. 'My beautiful Michela. Why did I stay away so long? I've wasted so much time. How could any girl in Rome compare to you?'

He tilted her head towards his. Their chaste, teenage kisses were sweet, perfect memories seared on her heart forever. This kiss was different. She kissed him with the fervour of a woman whose lover had come home unscathed from a battlefield. And he kissed her back as though the thought of her had kept him alive.

Eventually, they pulled apart.

'So, what do you think of my real plans for Trattoria di Napoli? Or, should I say, Trattoria da Mario?' Stefano's eyes were shining.

'Wonderful. No wonder Papa was looking so thrilled. He must be so excited about getting involved. It will be far less stressful for him than worrying about Il Gattino.'

'And you? I'd love you to be part of it. Do you remember those days when we sat on that dusty step in the alley talking about running our own restaurant by the sea?'

She smiled up at him. 'Of course I do. But what about your partner Alberto and his fiancée?'

'They've fallen in love with Minori but Alberto's a wealthy guy. He's got all sorts of investments. He's already looking at a nightclub in Ravello where his parents live. I think he and Nicoletta will make their home there. Either way, he's not interested in being hands-on. Alberto's more than happy to leave the day-to-day running of Trattoria da Mario to people who'll love working there . . . and who love each other . . . I love you, Michela. I don't know why I ever denied it.'

Michela swallowed the lump in her throat. 'You were young.'

'Young and foolish. Come on, let's go to Il Gattino and see your parents.'

Mamma looked set to give Michela an almighty ticking off, but when she saw the two of them enter Il Gattino arm in arm her face lost its cross expression in a trice. Soon she was opening a bottle of prosecco – who cared if it was only halfway through the morning – and pouring them all a glass.

Michela's happiness was complete when Papa appeared downstairs. Although he declined a glass of fizz and settled for a sparkling water, he was equally delighted to hear that she had, at last, got together with his old kitchen protégé.

In the midst of all the excitement Maria remembered the English couple who had brought Michela's suitcase. Maria understood a fair bit of English, but she hadn't made head or tail of their strange story. Michela quickly sent a text to the number on the note to inform the mysterious Bluebell that Paolo had taken her suitcase to the lost luggage room at the airport that very morning. Then they all started talking at once about the new restaurant and their plans for the future.

Seven pairs of eyes looked out of the minibus windows as Massimo began the winding route back to the airport. Miriam and Bluebell sat together at the back of the bus so they could quietly exchange stories. Miriam was already planning her return visit to Minori and Bluebell was thrilled to see her looking so happy. She tried her best to concentrate on her friend's good fortune rather than dwell on what might have been.

Any joy she'd felt at finding David's fantasy girl wrapped in the arms of another man had evaporated as soon as he'd told her his plans. When the Italian school term finished he and his friend Oliver were going to spend a few weeks travelling around the south of the country before they returned to England. That was more than enough time for them both to meet a whole bunch of attractive Italian girls, let alone the inevitable English girls with inhibitions lowered by the heady combination of sun and alcohol. Not that she could talk, after her escapade with Andrea that night on the beach. She felt relieved that Ludo the dog had interrupted them.

Massimo got them to the airport in good time. Bluebell hoped they would zip through all the procedures so she would have time to mooch around the Duty Free and have one last real Italian cappuccino before they boarded the plane.

'Are you sure we're in the right queue?' Bluebell said. It felt like they had been standing there forever.

'Yep. I've checked twice. We are in the right place but there's still no one sitting behind the check-in desk,' Josie said.

'At least we're near the front of the queue,' Bluebell said, looking round at the increasingly long line of people and luggage building up behind them.

'According to the app, the flight's supposed to be on time,' Josie said. She slid her phone back into her shoulder bag. 'It's a shame to be going home. I think I'm going to miss Minori.'

'Same here. I loved the hotel, especially those amazing breakfasts.'

'And those cocktails we had in the hotel bar.'

'Mmm, they were amazing. I can't believe what a great holiday it's been,' said Bluebell. She always hated that end-of-holiday feeling and this time she didn't even have the compensation of knowing it was twelve months before she would have to share another villa with Jamie's friends from uni.

'I was a bit worried about all the things that could go wrong, but everything worked out well in the end,' said Josie.

'Better than okay. And everyone got on so well,' Bluebell said.

'I'm gutted this is the last one I'm going to organise,' said Josie.

'Really, why?'

'I'm going to be leaving *Loving and Knitting* at the end of next month. I've got a friend who runs a travel website for singles so I'm going to be working for her writing travel content. I hope I might be able to organise some trips too. Something for people in their twenties and thirties who want to see a bit more than the inside of nightclubs. I've really enjoyed working with the older ladies, but it will be fun to do something with people nearer my own age.'

'It must have been a bit of a surprise when I turned up at the airport,' said Bluebell.

'Well, it would have been if I hadn't had your date of birth on the form.'

'The form?' Bluebell chewed her bottom lip.

'Yes, the form you sent back with your confirmation. The one for the emergency contact numbers and details of any medication, all those sorts of things. That had your date of birth on it.'

'I gave my date of birth and my emergency contact details when I confirmed my place on the trip?' Bluebell realised she was in danger of sounding a bit simple.

'Yes, you put your mum down.' Josie was looking at her a bit quizzically.

'Oh, that's right,' she said quickly. It looked like Granny Blue was going to have one heck of a lot of explaining to do.

Chapter Thirty-Six

The smell of wet paint still lingered in the kitchen. Bluebell surveyed her handiwork and smiled. Her new, bright yellow walls would bring a bit of sunshine into her flat even on the gloomiest days, and the cheerful checked cushions run up on Granny Blue's trusty sewing machine were only a little bit wonky. Even the old venetian blind didn't look too bad after she had set about it with an old toothbrush and a bottle of bleach.

It was six weeks since her return from Minori but the holiday still loomed large in her mind. The postcard Miriam had sent two weeks earlier was pinned to the fridge. It seemed that she and Tommaso were having a wonderful time. They had even visited the island of Ischia to look at properties together. Josie had kept in touch too. Bluebell had even heard from Brenda. David had put her in touch with a teacher who ran the holiday clubs at his old school, and she had been invited to come and give some history talks. She was ever so excited about it.

A message buzzed on Bluebell's phone: a picture of a cat wearing sunglasses, a thumbs-up and a four-leafed clover. Bluebell laughed. Miriam must have just learnt to send emojis. *Thanks xx,* Bluebell sent back. She could hardly believe she had been shortlisted for the marketing job at head office after her first fuzzy interview over Zoom.

Her phone buzzed again: David. *Are you still okay for today?*

He had messaged her earlier in the week to tell her he was back in England: *Would you like to meet for a drink?* It wasn't her first text from him. That had arrived a couple of weeks earlier, forwarded from a number in Italy. Bluebell had clicked on a link to a video clip. A large, hairy, black-and-white dog with a heavily bandaged leg was barking excitedly. He was trying his best to chase after a ball.

She couldn't help feeling a rush of excitement at the thought of seeing David again, but she was wary of making a fool of herself. He was only interested in being her friend after all. Even so, she was determined to meet him feeling and looking confident. She rarely bothered to blow-dry her hair, instead usually letting it dry naturally, but today she stood in front of the mirror and picked up the round brush her hairdresser had persuaded her to buy some years back, which had lain unused in her bedside drawer ever since.

'A bit of make-up and I'll be half decent,' she said aloud. She pulled on her favourite jeans and a gypsy top, which showed the merest hint of cleavage. She was just fastening her old silver locket, a twenty-first birthday present from Granny Blue, when she was aware of a knocking sound coming from the hallway.

'Bell's broken again, is it?' said the postman. He held out a brown paper package. 'All this internet clothes shopping will be the death of me. It's nothing but parcels these days.'

'I've not ordered anything,' she replied truthfully. She had enough trouble choosing clothes when they were hanging on the rack in front of her without scrolling through hundreds of images of Meghan Markle lookalikes on a Californian beach and wondering how they'd translate into her own rather less glamorous life.

'Well, it's for you. Perhaps it's something from a secret admirer,' he said jovially.

It was probably some strange garment ordered by Granny Blue after a few sherries. Then she noticed the Italian postmark. She rummaged in the kitchen drawer for some scissors and carefully cut open the brown-paper wrapping. She gasped when she caught sight of the familiar orange-and-white pattern. Carefully folded between two sheets of blue tissue paper was the poppy-print dress. Tucked underneath it was a postcard showing a scene of old Minori. Turning it over she read: *Clearing out my wardrobe because I'm moving in with my fiancé. I hope it brings back happy memories. Michela from Il Gattino XXX.*

She hung the dress over the back of a kitchen chair. She could just about get away with not ironing it. According to the clock on the oven she would just have time to shave her legs. She yanked off her jeans and slipped on the dress. David would get such a surprise when he saw her in this.

She set off in the direction of the Tube station. They were meeting for lunch, but she had kept the whole day free just in case. There was a pub a few minutes' walk away that had a beer garden. It was not anything fancy, but the food was simple and tasty. The landlady had brightened up the decking with beer barrels sawn in half and filled with bright flowers and there was a small lawn with a few picnic benches. She hoped he would like it. They did not have trendy bars like Bar Gino in her unfashionable part of South London.

She got to the station a few minutes early. He was already waiting, holding two small bunches of flowers. She had not seen him in jeans before. He certainly had the bum for them.

'Wow, look at you! I thought you had given all the clothes back,' he said.

'It only arrived this morning. Michela sent it to me. She must have kept hold of my address. She put in a note saying she was having a clear-out.' She deliberately did not mention the girl's engagement. There was no point rubbing salt into old wounds.

'These are for you.' He handed her one of the bunches of flowers.

'Who else are you meeting?' she asked, half teasing.

'I thought we were having tea with your gran.'

Bluebell thought David was joking about wanting to meet Granny Blue, but it appeared he was serious. 'Sure, we can call in on Gran after lunch. I'll just send her a quick text.' An impromptu visit would cheer Gran up. She had been a bit down in the dumps since her hip replacement had been rescheduled again. 'There's a pub just up the road. It's quite old-fashioned but it's got a beer garden.'

'This is great.' He carried a pint and a bottle of strawberry cider over to one of the picnic benches on the scrubby grass at the back. 'Much more my style than that flashy Bar Gino where I saw you and your boyfriend.'

'My boyfriend?'

'That Italian chap you were with. I wasn't sure if you were just friends; then I saw you with him later, down on the beach.' Bluebell's face turned the colour of her strawberry cider. 'You were kissing and paddling in the sea holding hands.' He smiled, looking at her rather curiously. She was picking little pieces off the edge of a cork coaster and had assembled quite a pile.

'Did you see a big, furry, white dog on the beach?' She tried to keep her voice light.

'No, I was only there for a minute or two 'til Oliver decided to drag us off for another drink at a bar around the corner.'

Relief flooded through her. 'That guy, he isn't . . . wasn't my boyfriend. He was just a waiter from the hotel. I thought it would be fun to go for a drink with him.'

'And was it?'

'Yes, but not as fun as being with you.' Why on earth did she say that? She looked down and began picking at the drinks coaster again. David seemed keen to change the subject too and began telling her about his travels with Oliver. The conversation flowed so naturally that the tension in her body gradually evaporated and the beer mat escaped a complete mauling. They were so busy chatting that they had to jog up the road to Granny Blue's. She was delighted to see them and dug out a tin of her special shortbread biscuits from the back of the larder.

Watching David listening intently to her gran and showing a genuine interest in her stories, she thought again what a lovely guy he was. He would make someone a wonderful partner one day.

'He's a keeper,' Granny Blue whispered as Bluebell and David said their goodbyes.

'He's a friend,' Bluebell replied firmly.

'Well, he won't be for long.'

'Gran!' She prayed that David had not overheard them.

'You can't subscribe to *Loving and Knitting* magazine without being a bit of an expert on romance,' Granny Blue whispered.

'It was great to meet your gran. After all, if it hadn't been for her you would never have been on that tour of the Amalfi Coast,' said David, as they sat sharing a bottle of wine in Bluebell's kitchen.

'It's a shame she missed out, but I ended up having a fabulous time.'

'And so did your friend Miriam.' He picked up the postcard of Ischia pinned to the fridge.

277

'I can't believe she's thinking about moving in with Tommaso already. I'm just sorry things didn't work out for you as well.'

'I wouldn't say that. I think that everything's working out just perfectly.'

His words were like a punch in the stomach. David must have gone back to Il Gattino and somehow got it together with Michela after all. But that didn't make sense. The note Michela sent with the poppy-print dress said that she was engaged, presumably to the handsome fellow she was embracing that day on the pier.

'What do you mean?' she asked. She might as well hear the worst.

'I spent the best part of a year looking for my dream girl, a dark-haired girl in an orange poppy-print dress.' Bluebell said nothing, she could not have spoken even if she had wanted to. She just had to sit and wait for David to tell her that it was Michela, the girl from Il Gattino, he wanted and that no Italian fiancé was going to stand in his way. She looked down at the table.

'And I found her,' he said. He gently tilted her head up so that her eyes met his. They were even bluer than she remembered. He pulled her towards him and kissed her briefly and tentatively.

Her heart pounded against her chest as she struggled to make sense of the feelings of shock, confusion and oh, such joy. 'You mean you don't still want to go out with the girl who works in Il Gattino – Michela, the girl you were looking for?'

'Not since the moment when I tapped a girl on the shoulder in that bar in Maiori and it was you who turned around. I couldn't believe it when I went up on the deck on that ferry to Positano and found you again. I didn't think that Italian guy looked serious, but you were so keen for us to find my mystery girl I just assumed that you couldn't be interested in me. Then when we went to Capri I thought I might have a chance. Bluebell, you're the only girl in a poppy-print dress that I want.'

Then he kissed her again, this time in a way that left no room for doubt.

Acknowledgements

Firstly, thank you to the people, towns and villages of Italy which inspired this book. Secondly, I must mention the Romantic Novelists' Association's *New Writers Scheme* which showed me how I could turn my manuscript into something that might, one day, find a publisher. Thanks also go to the many wonderful members of the RNA I have met for your encouragement by word and example.

Thank you to my agent Camilla Shestopal of Shesto Literary for your faith in *The Italian Holiday*, your enthusiasm, persistence, and most of all your unflappable, calming aura.

Thank you to everyone at Orion, especially Charlotte Mursell, Victoria Oundjian and the editorial team for making this book the best it could be and to everyone in cover design, sales and marketing for all their hard work behind the scenes.

Finally, thanks to friends and family for reading various drafts and giving me their invaluable and honest feedback. Particular thanks are due to Tina Page, Nicola 'Sham' Geller and my husband, Robert Wasey.

Printed in Great Britain
by Amazon